Chaos in a Cake Basket

SALLY WOLFGANG

MYSTIC VALLEY PRESS

Contents

1. Chapter 1   1

2. Chapter 2   11

3. Chapter 3   19

4. Chapter 4   23

5. Chapter 5   27

6. Chapter 6   31

7. Chapter 7   35

8. Chapter 8   37

9. Chapter 9   41

10. Chapter 10   45

11. Chapter 11   49

12. Chapter 12   55

13. Chapter 13   59

14. Chapter 14   63

15.	Chapter 15	69
16.	Chapter 16	75
17.	Chapter 17	77
18.	Chapter 18	79
19.	Chapter 19	85
20.	Chapter 20	89
21.	Chapter 21	97
22.	Chapter 22	101
23.	Chapter 23	103
24.	Chapter 24	105
25.	Chapter 25	109
26.	Chapter 26	111
27.	Chapter 27	119
28.	Chapter 28	125
29.	Chapter 29	129
30.	Chapter 30	133
31.	Chapter 31	135
32.	Chapter 32	139
33.	Chapter 33	143
34.	Chapter 34	147
35.	Chapter 35	151
36.	Chapter 36	155
37.	Chapter 37	159
38.	Chapter 38	161

39.	Chapter 39	165
40.	Chapter 40	169
41.	Chapter 41	175
42.	Chapter 42	181
43.	Chapter 43	187
44.	Chapter 44	191
45.	Chapter 45	197
46.	Chapter 46	201
47.	Chapter 47	207
48.	Chapter 48	211
49.	Chapter 49	215
50.	Chapter 50	219
51.	Chapter 51	225
52.	Chapter 52	229
53.	Chapter 53	233
54.	Chapter 54	237
55.	Chapter 55	239
56.	Chapter 56	241
57.	Chapter 57	245
58.	Chapter 58	247
59.	Chapter 59	251
60.	Chapter 60	255
61.	Chapter 61	259
62.	Chapter 62	261

63. Chapter 63   265

64. Chapter 64   281

Epilogue   287

Acknowledgments   291

About the Author   293

Lake Pend Oreille   295

Tunnel 57   297

The Lake Isle of Innisfree

I will arise and go now, and go to Innisfree,
And a small cabin build there, of clay and wattles made:
Nine bean rows will I have there, a hive for the honey bee,
And live alone in the bee-loud glade.
And I shall have some peace there, for peace comes dropping slow,
Dropping from the veils of the morning to where the cricket sings;
There midnight's all a glimmer, and noon a purple glow,
And evening full of the linnet's wings.
I will arise and go now, for always night and day
I hear lake water lapping with low sounds by the shore;
While I stand on the roadway, or on the pavements gray,
I hear it in the deep heart's core.

- William Butler Yeats

Chapter 1

JUNE 4, 2015 THURSDAY

Afton Laurie felt all her fears and worries, past and present, drift away as they always seemed to do whenever she drove from her woodland cabin, down unpaved Littlecatch Road, and into the small town of Wildcreek, Idaho. The drive to Wildcreek took twenty minutes, but it never disappointed. She loved to look down upon the majestic vista of water extending from the southern shore of the town all the way to the skyline. Myriad species of birds, towering lodgepole pines, and even signs like "Turtle Crossing" made it hard to keep her eyes on the road.

Only the two-mile drive over the Long Bridge south of Sandpoint could match the exhilaration she felt. Today, the lake was blue, the sky was blue, and the rolling forested hills and mountains made her feel like she was entering a new world full of beauty and promise. She wished life could always look that way.

When Efrain McKinley called her earlier that afternoon, she was happy to drive into town for a visit. He was her only close friend for fifteen hundred square miles in any direction, and she was starved for human conversation. Her dog, Ralph, like most Old English Sheepdogs, enjoyed only a limited vocabulary. He liked to talk about food, wild rabbits, and taking rides in the minivan. Afton needed more... occasionally anyway.

By her own design, she hadn't made any other close friends since her move to the North Idaho Panhandle two years before. She had left her southwest home in Brewster County, Arizona, on Efrain's recommendation, and traveled north, nearly to Canada. She had hoped to disappear, to live in solitary peace, and possibly to heal. Efrain McKinley was one of the only two people now in Wildcreek who had known her in her earlier life, and the only one she actually liked.

For her first two years in Wildcreek, she enjoyed her isolated existence. Efrain called her from time to time to ask for her advice on legal or criminal issues... and to relay news or gossip about people in their shared past. She enjoyed his company, his discretion, and his seeming admiration for her ability to ferret out the truth of things and untangle impossible situations. But now, she was starting to think she might like to get to know a few more people. She had been feeling a bit lonely at times. Perhaps Efrain would be a good person to help her with that. So, a visit to Efrain's office seemed like a good idea.

Ralph thought it was a good idea, too, and immediately dropped his worked-over, stuffed lambie for a run to the door. He had seen Afton put on her outside shoes and that meant she wasn't going anywhere without him if he had a say in the matter. And most times, due to his size and boundless energy, Ralph *did* have a say. As soon as he was able, he jumped into the back of Afton's 2009 Honda Odyssey, and they set off on the twenty-minute drive to Wildcreek.

Afton turned from Littlecatch Road onto Wildcreek's Main Street, which closely tracked the north shore of Lake Pend Oreille. The street was teeming with brightly colored summer tourists. Many of them had traveled from the hot, dry parts of California and Arizona or the cold, short-summered provinces of northwestern Canada to enjoy the milder climate of the North Idaho Panhandle. Some of them, like her, had stayed.

She smiled when she noticed the clothing sale racks spilling out of retail shops with goods marked up to double their normal prices. Café tables, chairs, and benches were filling up a sizable share of the remaining sidewalk space. Locals and visitors were jostling to enjoy the refreshing lake breezes, locally roasted coffee, and artisanal pastries. Of course, parking places were nearly impossible to find, second only to finding any standing room in the small outdoor patio fronting Fu Hong's Burritos.

Afton slowed down when she got to the end of Main Street and began looking on both sides of the street for a parking place. As she approached Efrain's office, she noticed Mrs. Moser waving and smiling. Afton waved back, a little surprised. She barely knew the owner of the Wildcreek General Store and Café and always puzzled over the strange crossed out lettering on the sign above the door. Mrs. Moser's unexpected friendliness caught Afton off guard. To Afton, the wave was as cheering as the opening of an auspicious fortune cookie. Maybe her social life *might* improve.

Feeling lucky, Afton soon found a small parking space next to the Happy Cat Vintage Clothing Shop. She squeezed her aged Honda Odyssey between two new Outlanders and let Ralph out of his space in the back. He waited while she attached his harness, and then they both walked the half block to Efrain's office. As soon as she and Ralph walked through the door, Afton felt the warm blast of Davina Binns' greeting.

"My two favorite people in the whole world! Afton and Ralph!" Ralph loved being called a "person" and bounded forward to catch the treat he knew would be coming. He caught it neatly in his hairy jaws. Afton realized again how much she liked Davina.

Davina was Efrain's receptionist-secretary, and she lived with Afton's formidable Aunt Biddie, the other person in Wildcreek who knew Afton from her earlier life. Eleven months ago, Aunt Biddie's presence in Wildcreek had nearly destroyed Afton's healing cocoon. Only Efrain's idea to forge an improbable alliance had saved Afton's sanity.

Biddie Laurie, Afton's aunt on her father's side, had come to visit Afton in Wildcreek for a so-called "brief" visit. After a difficult three weeks, however, Biddie decided that she would stay. Having no resources of her own, she seemed inclined to remain with Afton permanently. Along with the pronouncement of her new residency, Biddie informed Afton that Ralph would have to go. Biddie, who could not abide dogs, gave Afton a one-month deadline to find Ralph a new home.

Instead, Afton began considering a new home for Biddie... one in the deepest part of Lake Pend Oreille, perhaps. Lake Pend Oreille, 1,158 feet at its deepest point, had been deep enough for the U.S. Navy to use for submarine training in WWII, so Afton thought that the bottom of the lake might do very well for Aunt Biddie's new forever home. Ralph was *not* going anywhere.

At this disastrous turn of events, Efrain realized he would need to intervene. In a masterful feat of linguistic engineering, he managed to convince both Davina and Biddie that they would be happy sharing Davina's large, otherwise empty, nineteenth century family home in town. Within a week, Biddie had moved into her new home with Davina, thereby unknowingly managing to avoid her certain disappearance into the watery depths of Idaho's deepest lake. Afton avoided the need to manufacture an alibi.

Even though Biddie and Davina were opposites in nearly every way, the new partnership seemed to work. Biddie found someone who could live with her dominating and difficult personality. Davina, who loved all things mysterious and unseen, found Morris, an otherworld spirit who came to her rescue and specialized in thinking up strong measures to deal with people like Biddie. Davina insisted that he really did talk to her. In any event, Morris provided the advice, and he also took the blame whenever Biddie, or someone else, complained about his counsel.

The greeting rituals completed, Davina got right down to telling Afton the latest news about Biddie. "Last night Biddie told me to stop stirring the gravy because I was making lumps. She grabbed the whisk right out of my hand! Morris was livid. He made me tell her that she was the one stirring the pot... and that if there were any lumps to be found, they would certainly be located somewhere near her right temple. Oh dear! I don't think Morris really meant it, but Biddie *did* let go of the whisk."

Before Afton could respond, Efrain stuck his head out of his office door and called out, "Afton! Good to see you. Come and talk to me." He gave Davina a look. Not a pleased one. Efrain was not a fan of Morris stories.

After Afton sat down in the lovely old leather armchair opposite Efrain's desk, and after Ralph lay down on Afton's feet between the chair and the desk, Afton and Efrain both shook their heads and said at the same time, "Morris!"

Davina believed that Morris was real and supernaturally wise, but most people, including Efrain, thought Davina imagined him. Real or not, Morris often got to say things that Davina claimed she would *never* say herself. An outside-the-body kind of coping strategy, but effective.

"You needed to see me?" Afton got straight to the point, as usual.

"Yes, about a couple of things. One concerns you. Russell T. Hatcher called me from Brewster County yesterday to ask for your address. I told him I didn't know it."

"Thank you." And Afton meant it. When she left Brewster County two years earlier, she intended to leave everything and everyone behind. Especially County Attorney Russell Theodore Hatcher. Efrain was well aware of her feelings on that issue. But Afton couldn't resist asking, "So why do you think Rusty Hatchet called?" She still hadn't forgiven him for all the suffering he had caused her and still called him by his popular nickname.

"He didn't say, and I didn't ask."

Afton wasn't sure that was the truth. But she changed the subject. "And your other concern is what?"

"Well... I just wanted your thoughts on something. Totally hypothetical, of course."

"Of course." Afton prepared herself for one of Efrain's mind-boggling tangles of human behavior.

"Say a thief steals money from a really bad person, like a terrorist or a human trafficker. And then another person comes along and takes the money from the thief and uses it for a good purpose."

Afton felt a headache coming on.

"And then, what if someone else finds out about the stolen money that was being used for a good purpose and demands a percentage of it from the person who now has it and is using it for good?"

Afton really did have a headache now.

"And, finally, what if the person demanding the percentage is a very, very bad person... even worse than the original really bad person? What should the person with the money do?"

"Kill the very, very bad person, obviously," Afton answered. "Anything else?" Afton wasn't sure where that answer came from, but her head felt a lot better.

Efrain asked, "Is that really your final answer?"

"It's the best I've got right now. Ask Morris if you want an expert opinion." Afton flashed an evil grin.

Just then, Davina popped her head around the door to announce Efrain's 4 p.m. appointment. Afton took this opportunity to wake Ralph and say goodbye to Efrain. Ralph gave a great "woof" and walked out after his mistress, leaving a fairly large drool mark on the carpet.

As Afton headed over to Davina's desk, she saw a tall man with wide cheek bones and short red hair jump up from a nearby club chair, swerve around the information table, and stride into Efrain's office without a glance toward Afton or Davina. The office door closed with a loud bang. Davina looked after him and whispered, "That was Joe Ivan. Morris says he's going to be trouble. Maybe I should put out the cookies. You know, just in case."

A few minutes later, the new client re-opened the office door and marched angrily out into the street. When he was out of sight, Afton looked at Efrain, who had followed his client to the door. She asked, "That didn't take long. What was that about? Davina tells me that Morris doesn't like him."

Afton didn't like him either and wasn't sure why. Was the red-haired man the blackmailer in Efrain's tangled question about stolen money? Efrain shot her a look that said, *Nice try!* and went back into his office. Afton's attempts to pry actual client information from Efrain never worked. Davina, on the other hand, was a goldmine.

Failing to get any details from Efrain, Afton turned to Davina, "So what do you think that guy wanted?"

Davina, looking toward Efrain's door, softly said, "Well dear, I think Joe Ivan is hunting somebody. But I don't know who."

"And why did you want to give him cookies?" Afton frowned at Ralph as she asked the question. Ralph had recently devoured eleven of a dozen sugar cookies that were cooling in a pan on Afton's kitchen counter. He ignored Afton's severe look and concentrated on Davina, a likely cookie source.

"Oh no! The cookies aren't for you *or* Ralph." Davina unsuccessfully tried to wave Ralph away. "Your aunt made them. I bring them to work and save them for the clients that we never want to see again."

Afton knew immediately what Davina meant. Biddie's cookies, because of an excessive use of vanilla, were only good for people in need of an emergency emetic.

After a few minutes more of talking with Davina, Afton knocked on Efrain's slightly open door to say goodbye again but saw that he was on the phone. She stepped back and began closing the door just as he was saying, "Don't worry, Myra. Don't do anything. Julien's just guessing about the money."

Afton closed the door quietly. Hearing the words "Myra" and "money" made her instincts for sensing trouble jump into high gear. Worried, she walked out through the street door with only a nod to Davina. Ralph seemed to nod, too, but it was probably just a hopeful beg for a parting treat.

Efrain looked up in time to see Afton closing the door. He hoped she hadn't heard his conversation with Myra. The situation with Myra and Katharine, the owners of Greengrocers, was getting serious. Julien

Pidgeon was hinting that he knew about "the money" and now this stranger, Joe Ivan, was asking about businesses in Wildcreek. Joe told Efrain that he wanted to invest in one, but Efrain suspected that this was just a pretense. Joe was too specific about wanting to find a business that was started approximately fifteen years ago, possibly by two women. Efrain told Joe that he couldn't help and told Joe to go check with the Chamber of Commerce. Efrain had decided not to tell Joe about Greengrocers. He had also decided not to tell Myra about Joe's questions. In retrospect, as it turned out, both decisions were poor ones.

As soon as he was sure Afton had left, Efrain continued his conversation with his Greengrocers client. "Myra, you'll only make things worse if you offer to pay Julien. Please promise me you won't. You know he'll never stay quiet. You'll never get rid of him." Efrain was using his most stern and formal lawyer's voice. He hoped it would work.

"Okay," Myra finally replied. Silence. More silence. Then, "I guess you're right. I'll let Katharine know. Bye." Myra abruptly hung up.

Chapter 2

June 4, 2015 Thursday

Almost immediately after Afton and Ralph left Efrain's law office, Afton saw Rascal and Sarah Woods walking into Mrs. Moser's store on the corner diagonally across the street. Their farm manager, Thor, followed them inside. Rascal and Sarah owned Bullhead Farm and had a booth at the Wildcreek Farmers' Market on Saturdays and Wednesday afternoons. It occurred to Afton that this might be a great opportunity to get to know them better. She'd really only discussed spicy mustard, spinach and the weather with them in the past. And... she wouldn't have to find a new parking place. So, turning to Ralph, she pleaded, "Okay, Ralph. We're going into a store that has breakable things. I want you to be extra good and stay right by me. If you do, maybe Mrs. Moser will give you sausages like last time." Ralph seemed to nod in agreement. He *really* liked sausages.

Afton and Ralph entered The Wildcreek General Store ~~and Cafe~~ just as Rascal was shouting, "Hey Mrs. Moser! When are you going to let me repaint your sign? Only a few of us still remember why you crossed out the 'and Café' part. Don't you think it's about time? It's been more than three years now since Johann died."

Mrs. Moser, who was knitting in the back, as usual, smiled, waved at Afton, and answered, "Never ever, Rascal. Johann *likes* it like that." No one missed Mrs. Moser's intentional use of the present tense.

Melina Moser's husband, Johann, had been dead for three and a half years, and she missed him deeply, utterly, and a bit unsoundly. It was Johann who ran the Café and provided all of the personality. On the day he died, Mrs. Moser closed the store, took a three-inch chip brush, and painted a dripping, tearful, black line through the words "and Café" on the sign outside. She then went to work turning the table space in the café into an expansion of the dry goods part of the store—all except for the old glass-enclosed cafe counter that Johann had built for display. On the days, months, and years afterward, when she felt like it, she used the refrigerated shelves under the counter to sell a few of Johann's favorite pastries from their native Austria. Johann especially loved her *Marillenknödel*, apricot dumplings, and her sour cherry *Weichselstrudel*. Melina had no doubt that Johann approved of the changes... because he often told her so.

The café display case on this Thursday was devoid of pastries, however, so Rascal immediately turned to a different display, the one with rows of recently stocked Messermeister chef's knives. Sarah followed Rascal over for a closer look and motioned for Afton, who had been admiring the knitted woolen hats in the window, to join them. Thor wandered off to the back of the store.

"Hi, Ralphie Boy!" Sarah's greeting was delivered in a sing-songy voice with ear-scratching included. Ralph preferred treats but this was okay.

Afton said, "It's so nice to see you all without vegetables for a change! How are you?"

"We're good. How are you? We're just doing a little stocking up. Things in town are getting a little crazy. So many people!" Sarah answered for Rascal as well. He seemed mesmerized by the knife display.

Mrs. Moser, noticing a group of customers now, arranged her silver curls, dropped her knitting, and targeted her guests for a little gossip, a little news, and perhaps a big sale. "I'm coming! Wait for me! I don't want to miss anything!" To Mrs. Moser's delight, the gossip was forthcoming and substantial from both Sarah and Rascal.

From Sarah, "You won't believe this! Helaine Pia may be seeing another man. Julien Pidgeon hinted that he was the one, but that *cannot* be true. Really, who*ever* listens to Julien anyway?"

Mrs. Moser frowned at this and shook her head. "Julien Pidgeon would say anything to make himself the center of attention."

Afton wondered if this Julien was the same Julien that Efrain was talking about during his phone call with Myra.

From Rascal, "Why would Helaine risk losing a husband who cooks like Umberto!"

At this, Rascal, Sarah, and Mrs. Moser closed their eyes in an appreciative and reverent moment of silence. Rascal looked over at Afton, "Umberto is Corsican and is an amazing chef. His lamb and chestnut stew is a path to enlightenment! He and his wife, Helaine, own The Magpie, the bar and restaurant across the street. You'll probably see their son, Ben, waiting tables and tending bar sometimes. Ben may look young, but everyone, even the sheriff, chooses to believe he's twenty-one."

From Sarah again, "Barbara Jones is telling everyone that Gloria Peabody's dogs got loose and ate five of her chickens."

Mrs. Moser commented, "Those dogs are always getting loose."

Sarah agreed, "True. But Barbara won't keep her chickens in any kind of enclosure. She says that they have a right to be free and that she can taste the freedom in their eggs." Four sets of eyes rolled in unison.

Afton added, "Ralph would never eat live chickens... or eggs, either, unless they're scrambled hard." Ralph looked dubious.

Rascal, tired of chicken talk, attempted to move on, "We had a record flower crop this year. Not sure why, but the bees were all over it. So... we're going to start a few hives next year."

Afton looked over at Sarah. Sarah frowned and looked up at the ceiling in conspicuous silence. No doubt about it now, Afton observed. Rascal was the idea man, and Sarah was the practical planner. And apparently, in this case, the bee idea had not reached the "planner" stage yet.

Afton chose a neutral response. "Thanks, Sarah! If you all have honey next year, I will *bee* your first customer. The thought of Sarah and Rascal wrangling bees—and each other—made her smile.

Sarah sighed and looked over at Thor, who was still at the back of the store. "Sometimes I think about giving up the farm. It's such hard work. But then I would have to give up skiing... And that's not going to happen!"

Rascal agreed and shook his head emphatically. "A lot of people in Wildcreek plan their lives around the winter ski season at Schweitzer Mountain Resort. We work in the summer, so we can ski in the winter!"

Mrs. Moser, who didn't ski any longer and who barely eked out a living in the summer or the winter season, had stopped listening and had turned her attention to Thor. He seemed to be admiring the silver cake basket in the locked antique cabinet. "What is Thor doing back there? What could he find so interesting about an eighteenth-century cake basket? Does he bake?"

Sarah and Rascal both shook their heads, and Sarah said, "Never! He only likes to buy baked goods from Katharine Holmeier at Greengrocers. I think he's smitten with her."

Rascal spoke softly, "We got lucky when Thor agreed to help us with the farm—he has a degree and years of experience in organic farming. And more importantly, he works hard, asks for less money than he could get anywhere else, and has a great truck. We can't figure out why he stays around. It's definitely not Sarah's cooking!" Sarah dealt Rascal a swift kick in the left ankle and changed the subject.

"We really love this store," Sarah gushed.

Mrs. Moser smiled at them—a rare sight. The couple reminded her of happier times with Johann. A moment of warmth and generosity overcame Mrs. Moser. "Just one minute. I'll be right back."

She dashed off through the door to her private rooms and reappeared almost immediately with a cracked blue mixing bowl. She handed it to Sarah. "I used to mix Austrian-style potato pancakes in that bowl for dinners in East Berlin. No eggs. We didn't have eggs. It was one of the things I brought with me when Johann and I escaped. You know, of course, that we crawled through Tunnel 57 in October 1964, right? You've heard of Tunnel 57, right?"

Sarah and Rascal both thought Tunnel 57 was a television series about time travel, but Sarah graciously accepted the bowl and nodded solemnly. What else could she do? Mrs. Moser had tears in her eyes.

"I love giving things from my past to young people like you who will enjoy them. I gave Helaine Pia a necklace with a piece of the Berlin Wall as a pendant. She wears it almost all the time. She really does care about other people."

Rascal, thinking about Mrs. Moser's generosity and in hopes of getting a knife to go along with the bowl, craned his neck around to look at the knife display. He cleared his throat a few times. Mrs. Moser did not seem to take the hint. Sarah, realizing what Rascal was trying to do, quickly turned to Afton.

"Afton, are you coming to the Magpie to celebrate the beginning of the St. John's Wort harvest this year? It starts at Happy Hour on Friday, the 26th. We'd love to see you there. We can introduce you to some of the people we've been talking about today. Gossip is everything in this town."

Afton laughed, "I hope there's none about me! I'm really not interesting at all."

"Well," Sarah smiled. "We'll have to do something about that!"

Thor had quietly returned to the group. He spoke up, "The harvest is looking good. You might want to stock up on tea infusers, Mrs. Moser." And then, to everyone's surprise, he asked her the price of the cake basket.

"Well," Mrs. Moser pitched, "it's very old silver and in excellent condition. I've only had it for a short while, and I had to pay a big price for it. I'm sorry, I must ask you for five thousand dollars." Rascal and Sarah looked down at their boots.

Thor didn't blink. "Fine. Will you take a credit card?" After a minute of embarrassed silence, Mrs. Moser took a key out of her dress pocket and walked to the antique cabinet. She brought the cake basket back to the sales desk and began to write out a receipt. Thor offered his card and, while waiting, examined the bottom of the basket carefully. Sarah and Rascal were barely breathing. Everyone, including Afton was thinking, *Five thousand dollars for an antique cake basket? What was he going to do with it?*

After the transaction was completed, they all left the store in silence. Mrs. Moser followed. As she watched Thor walking back to his truck with Rascal and Sarah, she looked at her copy of the receipt, then up at Thor again. She muttered to herself, "Oh dear, I wonder..." and "Could he be...?" But, Johann had no answers for her this time.

Chapter 3

JUNE 4, 2015 THURSDAY

Afton, meanwhile, had just placed her hand on the sliding side door of her Odyssey when she remembered that she had intended to buy one of Mrs. Moser's knitted hats. Should she go back? Yes! She turned to Ralph and said, "We didn't get this wonderful parking space for no reason. It's a sign that we should buy things. We're going back for hats!" And they did.

But just as she was crossing the street, she saw a tall, thin, sharply angled man enter Mrs. Moser's store. When she got to the door, she heard sounds of a not-so-friendly conversation.

"So, Mrs. Moser! How's that Nazi-Stalinist ghost of a husband? Still dead?"

Should she wait outside on the bench, or just go home? For a minute or two Afton struggled between parking space karma and good manners. Parking space karma, of course, won. She sat on the bench outside with Ralph and tried not to listen to the loud discussion inside. But to no avail.

Through the glass store window, Afton could see the man walking along the aisle farthest from Mrs. Moser's corner, picking up a few things as he moved along, reading the backs of a few boxes, and putting a few things in his pockets.

When he got to the end of the aisle, he stopped in front of the antique cabinet. Mrs. Moser, who had been watching him carefully while pretending to be absorbed in a difficult round of stitching, barked out, "Julien, you evil child, please put the shot glasses back on the shelf. Only you would think that petty theft is performance art. You are no artist. You're a thief!"

Ignoring her, Julien exclaimed, "Hey! The cake basket is gone. I bet you made enough money on that sale to keep you in support stockings for years. You owe me."

"I owe you nothing! No doubt you stole that beautiful basket from your own dear mother. I couldn't bear to see it in your hands another minute."

"Oh, not *my* mother. Somebody *else's* mother."

"Well, I just sold it moments ago to a nice young man... one with manners."

Through the store window Afton could see the man Mrs. Moser called Julien grin and savagely bare all his teeth. His spiked, highlighted hair completed his wolf-like appearance. To Mrs. Moser's and Afton's surprise, he tossed a couple of twenties onto the counter. "These are better than manners." Then, he stepped out onto the sidewalk, taking one of the hats from the window display with him.

For a split second, the man turned and looked malevolently into Afton's eyes while she was still sitting on the bench. Seeing that, Ralph immediately leapt up, harness and all, and nearly buried his large sharp teeth into the offending stranger's calf. Afton pulled Ralph back just in time but did not apologize. The man, Julien, laughed and continued down the street. Afton, who had encountered a few like him in the past, could recognize a dangerous personality disorder when she saw one.

"He's looking for his next victim—probably Myra or Katharine at Greengrocers," opined Mrs. Moser standing in the open doorway of her store. "I should call them and warn them. Maybe they should close for an hour or two."

"I don't know, Mrs. Moser. Has anyone called the sheriff? I just came back for a hat. I'm sorry you had to deal with that!"

"Hah! That sheriff—he is useless! Come in. I will give you a hat to match your beautiful eyes. Your eyes look all different colors!"

Afton went home with a lovely woolen hat, and Ralph got three sausages.

Chapter 4

JUNE 4, 2015 THURSDAY

That evening, back at the Big House on Bullhead Farm, Sarah, Rascal and Thor were eating dinner around one end of the enormous fourteen-foot-long kitchen table. At 8 p.m., the sun was just starting to set, and they were tired from their long day of shopping in town. Not very enthusiastically, Sarah asked, "So, Thor, are you sure we'll be ready for the St. John's Wort Celebration?"

"Well... We have about three weeks to worry about it. Why start now?" Thor realized his mistake as soon as he heard Sarah drop her spoon loudly on the table. He immediately tried to correct the flippant sound of his response. Bullhead Farm, after all, had been Sarah and Rascal's sole source of income and skiing funds for the last ten years.

"So far, the crop looks really good. We won't be harvesting right on the Solstice, and I realize there might be some grumbling about that, but my tests show that waiting until the 25th will increase the amount of hypericin this year. The buds should have lots of red in them by then. And we can deliver a more potent product closer to distribution that way, too." Thor was a strong proponent of science over what he considered to be folklore.

"We're all set to start cutting on June 25th. Then, bundle, pack, and store—cooled and hydrated—by midday on the 26th and distribute samples later that day at the Magpie Happy Hour. Then, we'll truck in full bundles to the Farmers' Market and Greengrocers on the 27th."

Mollified, Sarah moved on, "Helaine told me she's really looking forward to the Celebration this year. She's setting up more tables and chairs outside, and Umberto is supposed to be adding a surprise Corsican ingredient to the red sauce. Anyone who guesses the ingredient gets a free dinner for two." Sarah and Rascal both looked at Thor.

Sarah asked, "Thor, who would you invite if you won a free dinner?" At her question, Thor looked down at his plate and started making a pyramid with his Brussels sprouts. "I'm betting you would ask Katharine Holmeier. Am I right?"

Thor wisely decided to exercise his right to remain silent. But his reddening face was all the answer they needed.

After Rascal finished about half a portion of Sarah's latest lentil-based iteration of "chicken" pot pie, he took his plate to the sink, scraped it, and asked with a self-protective grin, "So, are lentils good for dogs?" Sarah didn't seem to view the question as humorous and picked up her spoon again. Rascal ignored the warning sign and continued, "I still don't think this tastes anything like Chicken Pot Pie. And... whatever happened to the mashed potatoes and gravy?"

"Rascal!" Sarah barked in her sternest spoon voice, "We've talked about this. The lentils have enough starch. I put bacon in it this time and drizzled it with honey just for you. You don't need potatoes. Don't you agree, Thor?"

Thor, again, wisely remained silent.

"Well," Rascal growled. "All these lentils are getting depressing. I don't want to eat another Doom Casserole for as long as I live!" And from then on, Sarah's lentil experiments were always called Doom Casseroles.

Rascal grunted and left the kitchen. Thor left, too, and headed for the safety of his cabin. Sarah got up without a word and began cleaning up. The kitchen was her territory, and she liked to work in it alone. Rascal and Thor had stopped offering to help long ago. That was just fine with her.

As soon as Thor stepped inside his small cedar-sided cabin, originally designed as guest quarters for the Big House, he locked the door and went over to the kitchen table. He never ate in his own kitchen, so the table looked more like a work-bench-slash-computer desk. It was covered with a laptop, various electronics, books, gloves, and debris from his work on the farm. He'd cleared one end of the table for the cake basket, and that evening it absorbed all his attention.

He picked up the finely crafted silver basket and examined every part of it. He looked for a long time at the markings on the bottom of the basket. He carried it over to the sink and placed it on the counter on its side. The nearly full moon, its bright light shining through the window over the sink, illuminated each delicate etching on the flat surface of the tray. Thor stared at it for another long period of time—almost ten minutes. He also took down a large spoon hanging on the wall. He turned the spoon over so that he could see the back of the handle and held it next to the markings on the bottom of the cake basket. They matched. He stared at the markings on both pieces until his eyes burned and blurred. Then, he lifted his head and gazed out the window, studying the rising Venus in the sky and the still waters of Bullhead Lake.

But the beautiful nightscape brought him no peace. As he watched, a large owl flew across the waning gibbous moon with a rabbit in its talons. The owl's haunting cry caused Thor to grip the sharp, worn silver spoon handle so hard that blood dripped onto the floor from a cut in his hand.

Chapter 5

JUNE 26, 2015 FRIDAY

T wenty days later, on June 26th at approximately 4 p.m., Helaine Pia froze in mid-pour right where she was standing. She happened to be standing behind the bar of the Magpie Café where she was brewing coffee and filling glasses for the many orders of Pica Pica, the Magpie's signature drink, that she and Umberto hoped to sell during the St. John's Wort Celebration scheduled to begin in an hour.

The drink name came about after Helaine learned that *Pica pica* was one of the names for the Eurasian Magpie, a favorite of both Helaine and Umberto. They discovered the delightful bird during their honeymoon tour across Europe before settling down in Wildcreek to open a restaurant and bar. Helaine was thrilled to learn that the clever *Pica pica* was considered one of the most intelligent animals on earth after human beings (although some avid birders disputed *any* placement of human beings in the list of intelligent species).

From then on, Helaine was determined to learn more about the feathered creatures who shared a planet with her. Umberto's interest in birds was more limited. He enjoyed watching their antics, but he mostly liked to cook them.

Suddenly, pulled from her avian thoughts, Helaine's worst fear materialized. Julien Pidgeon had arrived for the party, and even worse, he was early. Typical Julien, he completely ignored the "Closed until 5 p.m." sign on the door. Her paralysis continued as she watched him take a seat near the door to the kitchen. There was only one thing to do. Hide!

She found her son working in the kitchen. "Ben, Julien Pidgeon just walked into the restaurant. Go out and see what he wants. But don't stand too close to him. And, if he asks, tell him I'm not here!" Ben knew his mother harbored an intense dislike for Julien Pidgeon, but he was a little surprised about her order to keep his distance. Nevertheless, he trusted his mom, and he did as he was told.

Ever since Nurse Darling had let it slip that Julien had XDR tuberculosis and was recklessly, even arrogantly, refusing to wear his mask or show up for his checkups, Helaine had obsessed about his condition, and the danger she imagined it posed to her community. She alternately wanted him banned from all public places, including the Magpie, have him arrested, or kill him and make it look like an accident.

Helaine knew that Julien was arriving at the Magpie early to ask her to dinner at his house. He fancied himself a chef and wanted to make his self-described "green garlic pesto" for her, so that she would try to persuade Umberto to let him cook part-time at the Magpie. She didn't want to get Nurse Darling into trouble, but there was no way she would ever let Julien inside the Magpie kitchen.

Her cell phone rang. It was Ben. "Mom, he asked for you, and I told him you were out. Now what?"

"Ben, don't get too close to him and just keep giving him free beer. Hopefully he'll soon fall asleep like he did last week."

"Okay, Mom." Ben could not understand why someone like Julien Pidgeon got free beer, but he knew this was not the time to argue. Fortunately, Julien fell asleep after draft number seven.

When she heard Julien's snores, she moved out of the kitchen, silently grabbed Julien's glass, and tossed it into the trash. She looked at the heaving form and whispered, "Stay that way!" If only she had a magic potion to make him nap longer. Or maybe... permanently.

With the Julien problem temporarily solved, Helaine began putting small bouquets of St. John's Wort into beer glasses and placing one on each table. She stacked yellow-flowered wreath crowns on the bar for those who liked to wear them. Then, at 5 p.m. she opened the restaurant and waited outside the door to welcome her guests.

The first people to arrive were Rascal, Sarah, and Thor. Following right after them were several other Magpie regulars—Myra Briney and Katharine Holmeier from Greengrocers, Afton Laurie and her neighbor, Greg Alatza, and Mrs. Moser from across the street. For a fleeting moment, Helaine wondered if one or more of them could help her quickly wrap up Julien in the entry-way carpet and drop him off at Thompson Park about a mile north of the Magpie. Would he be terribly upset?

Soon the Magpie was filled with yellow-crowned customers eating, drinking, talking, and laughing. Only one guest seemed subdued. A strange young man with red hair sat in a far corner sipping his Pica Pica at a glacial rate. He appeared to be completely and utterly distracted. His conversation had been non-existent all evening long, and his Pica Pica was still three quarters full. He had spent the whole of the St. John's Wort Celebration staring at Katharine Holmeier as if he had never seen a beautiful woman before in his life.

Helaine was enjoying herself so much that she didn't notice the ominous absence of snoring. When she finally did look over to check on Julien, she saw to her horror that the chair under Julien's table was empty. Before she could recover from the shock, she heard loud cries and clanging pots coming from the kitchen.

"Andre! Ben! Try to use the mop and the baking sheets to herd him out the door into the bar. And get that spoon out of his hand! He's going for the red sauce!" Umberto sounded frantic. Mops and baking sheets were not his usual weapons—a stroke of luck for Julien.

Helaine watched as Julien retreated from the kitchen, backside first. He fell over and flailed around in a helpless fit of coughing. Instinctively, the celebrants backed away. Then, in front of Helaine and all the guests, he stood up in a sloppy drunken slant and shouted, "Helaine *Pee-ya*! I expect to see you at my house at six *pee-em* tomorrow night for green garlic pesto. You better be there, honey, or I'll be coming back here until you do!" Julien loved to say the word "pee" whenever he got a chance.

Helaine, frantic to get him to leave, shouted, "Fine! But you'd better go home now and start getting ready. I'm a tough critic, you know. That's it, now. Just go out that door behind you. Good, good. That's right..." And obediently, Julien stumbled out the door—with stolen breadsticks in every pocket.

Chapter 6

JUNE 27, 2015 SATURDAY

On the Saturday after the St. John's Wort Celebration, Myra Briney and Katharine Holmeier were having lunch at the Magpie as was their usual custom. Davina Binns was looking after the store until Myra and Katharine could return and close up at 5 p.m. Lunch was their time to talk business. And they had a lot of business to discuss.

Their morning had been doubly chaotic. Not only were the Community Supported Agriculture, CSA, bags being distributed, but Thor had delivered bags and bags of St. John's Wort flower bundles. More than they could ever sell. The entire south corner of floor space was covered indiscriminately with bags of green garlic, vegetables and St. John's Wort flower bundles.

"So, Katharine," Myra teased. "What's with all the blushing and soft toned 'my name is Katharine' thing? I saw you flirting with that red-haired stranger."

"His eyes are *so* blue, Myra. He seemed so interested in our store and in us. And maybe in me. I would love to get to know him better." Myra knew that there was no mistaking that wistful look in Katharine's eyes. The proverbial lightning bolt had struck Ms. Katharine Holmeier.

Myra continued to tease about the budding romance, but her stomach was in knots the whole time. There was something important she needed to tell Katharine. She managed to wait only until their drinks arrived. "Katharine, I've made a terrible mistake. I must tell you about it—now!"

"Myra, don't worry so much! Forgetting to cross parsley off the list of ingredients in the bags is no big deal. You did get the green garlic in, right? That was the most important item this week. We might get a few calls, but, oh well, nobody's perfect."

"Katharine, it's not about the parsley. And it's not about the one bag that didn't have a name tag. I don't know how that happened, by the way, but we have bigger problems!"

Katharine frowned. "Like what? Everything seems okay to me."

"Well, Kath, I probably should have talked to you sooner. I *know* I should have. Julien saw the money that I picked up a few weeks ago. He opened my backpack at the register while my back was turned. Now he wants some of it. He came into the store a few days ago and made veiled hints about loans and free groceries. In front of customers like Afton and Mrs. Moser! I am so sorry. I had hoped he would just forget about it."

Katharine studied her calloused, burned, and re-burned baker's hands and said, "Not Julien. He enjoys causing pain just as much and maybe more than extorting money. He'll never relent. What are we going to do, Myra?"

At that moment, young Ben Pia arrived to take their order. "The usual and the usual?" he asked.

"Yes and yes." They both smiled. Ben saluted and immediately headed back to the kitchen for two Fromage Burgers, an iced green tea, and a coke. No fries.

The second that Ben was out of earshot, Myra continued, "Do you think I should just offer to pay him something? I'm sure he only knows about the money in the backpack. I called Efrain the day it happened. He told me not to do anything. I'm *sooo* sorry I didn't tell you. I was in such a panic. What do you think we should do?"

Katharine shrugged. "I think we should talk to Efrain again before we say anything to Julien. You need to tell me everything from now on, Myra. And, just so you know, I'd rather give Julien all our money and leave Wildcreek with just the organic bacon-flavored tempeh in our pockets than spend five minutes trying to negotiate with him."

Their burgers arrived, and for five minutes they ate in silent contemplation of their mutual troubles. Myra spoke first, "Should we move it?"

Katharine finished chewing and said, "No, I don't think so. Like I said, let's call Efrain before we do anything like that. Don't go anywhere near it for now."

"Okay," Myra nodded. "You're probably right. We might still be safe. Julien doesn't seem to know that there is more or where it came from."

But someone did know. Myra had failed to notice the man tucked into the corner of the booth next to theirs. That was her biggest mistake of the day, but how could she have known? Efrain had decided not to tell her about Joe Ivan's visit to his office.

Joe Ivan, who was sitting on the other side of Myra and Katharine's booth and listening intently to their discussion, was extremely interested in "it" and where "it" came from. In fact, "it" was the reason he had come to Wildcreek.

Earlier that morning he had narrowed his search down to a few businesses. Now he was almost sure that Greengrocers was the right one. Moreover, its owners, Myra and Katharine, had to be the two bakery employees who were questioned by Seattle police detectives after someone stole his brother's money seventeen years ago. Joe Ivan had come to Wildcreek to get it back. Now, it seemed, his hunt was over.

Joe Ivan slowly sipped his third vodka while he watched Myra and Katharine pay at the counter and leave. He considered his options. Would this Julien person be another problem? If only he could be sure. A mistake would send him to prison—the same fate his brother suffered because of the same money.

Joe needed more time to think. Another vodka, he thought, or maybe two, might help the process. He saw Umberto walking over to his table and took that as a sign he was right. "May I have two more?"

"Sure, of course." Umberto was thinking that this customer was drinking so slowly that two vodkas would last until dinnertime.

"Hey, what do you know about that guy Julien? I saw him bothering your wife at the party last night. Is she really going to his house for dinner tonight?"

In a quiet voice, Umberto lowered his head and said, "That Julien is a snake, a demon, and a devil. He insults my wife and tries to force her to agree to come to his house. She just wants him to stay away from the Magpie and her family. So, for Julien's sake, I hope that she does not go. In the view of *some* Corsicans, vengeance is *not* best left to God."

Chapter 7

June 27, 2015 Saturday

After a day of packing, making deliveries, and unloading the remaining flower bundles, Thor finally got a chance to relax. Relaxing meant drinking at the Magpie. He arrived there right at the start of the 3 p.m. Happy Hour. The first thing he noticed was Helaine, hands on hips, talking loudly to Ben and Umberto behind the bar. He sat down at the end of the bar and, in that location, was able to hear quite well.

By then, Umberto was the one talking loudly, "Birdwatching! You are birdwatching all of the time now. This is too much birdwatching. What are you really doing?"

"I am going to look for Boreal Owls—like I told you! And it's birding... not birdwatching!" Helaine was using her best outraged victim voice. "Two owls were sighted a couple nights ago at Bongo Lake. Anyway, Julien called and canceled the dinner tonight, so I thought the best thing to do would be to stay unreachable in case he changed his mind.

"That's right, Dad. I talked to Julien. He was coughing so much it was hard to understand him." Ben often played the role of peacemaker.

"Bah! Helaine, you were never going to eat with that Julien person anyway. No one would be so crazy. Who are you really going to see?"

At this, Helaine threw a bar towel at her husband and stormed out the front door. Ben and Umberto shook their heads at each other—but each for a different reason. Umberto wondered who Helaine would be meeting that night. Ben wondered who would be doing his mom's share of the work during the "After-Wort Clean-up" that night. Thor just smiled and thought that he would never speak to Katharine Holmeier that way, *if* he ever got the chance.

After stopping at home for about an hour to pack a few things, Helaine drove at top speed out of town and along the road to Wright Lake. Her route took her right past Julien's house. She stepped on the accelerator as she passed by and snarled, "Julien Pidgeon, I hope your pesto makes you very, very, very sick!"

Joe Ivan left the Magpie about thirty minutes after Helaine. He needed to do some logistical work before his plan went into action that evening. While he was driving around checking times and distances, he saw Helaine turn onto Railroad Highway. Wasn't that the way to Julien's cabin? Was she really going to have dinner with Julien after all?

Chapter 8

JUNE 27, 2015 SATURDAY

Julien Pidgeon's regular Saturday evening activity was cooking at home, and this Saturday was no exception. He couldn't wait for Helaine to arrive and tell him that his green garlic pesto was amazing.

"No—it's more than amazing!" he told himself out loud. He loved talking to himself. "It's fantastic—really five-star! Helaine and Umberto will have to let me cook at the Magpie. Now, just a few more finishing touches...and I'd better write these down. This recipe could be gold some day!" That thought caused him to burst into a loud "'Che La Luna Mezzo Mare.'"

The singing went on until, "Whoa! It's 7:30 already. She's late! She promised to come at six. Oops, I need to change into my special chef pants. Helaine will *love* them! She won't be able to resist the pesto...or me!"

Finally, the doorbell chimed. Julien quickly washed his hands and started to sing "My Way" in his best Frank Sinatra. Women, he believed, loved men who could sing Frank Sinatra songs.

He opened the door with panache, or so he believed, and said in surprise, "What? Where is Helaine? Oh! Of course, of course, sure, you can come in. But what happened to Helaine? Oh, that's terrible! Thank you for letting me know. I'll call her tomorrow. Sure, sure. You brought wine? Great! Come in and try the pesto!"

The new guest whispered too softly for Julien to hear, "That was an ill-fated gesture of hospitality if there ever was one!"

Six or seven hours later, Helaine finally decided that she had better return home. Driving back along Railroad Highway, she passed a car partially hidden in a construction turnoff a little past Julien's cabin. Her headlights caught the profile of the driver for a moment.

"Hmmm," she said aloud to herself. "Who *was* that? I've seen that car and driver profile somewhere before. Recently. I just can't remember when or where. Who would be waiting there at this hour? A birder? Hah! Probably looking for owls." *Oh, well*, she thought. She had more important things to occupy her mind right then. *I hope Umberto is asleep.*

Once at home, Helaine quietly walked into the bedroom, took off a few things, and lay down next to the snoring Umberto. She remained that way, on her side, eyes open but unfocused, for a long while.

Sunday morning and afternoon went by quickly. Sunday night, however, seemed to last forever. Helaine spent many of her nighttime hours thinking about Julien and what she should do about his reckless lack of attention to his tuberculosis. Her sighs, twists, and turns finally woke up Umberto.

"Helaine, my love. What is all this unhappiness? I know you love me, and I will try not to be so angry. I am sorry."

"I *do* love you!" she cried. "It's just this Julien Pidgeon thing. I don't know what to do!"

"Go and tell him what you think in the morning. Try one more time with all your heart. You are good at that. If that doesn't work, I will try my own way, my family's way. Now go to sleep and do not worry."

"I *will* go see him early tomorrow and talk to him, my love." But she suspected that it was much too late for *that* plan to work.

Chapter 9

JUNE 29, 2015 MONDAY

E ven before the first American Crow had landed in the Pia's backyard white pine tree to act as a sentinel for its many brothers and sisters, Helaine was in her car heading for Railroad Highway. By the time she turned into Julien's driveway, she was feeling fairly confident that she could resolve the Julien Pidgeon problem.

So, with no hesitation, she walked up the steps and knocked on his door. She waited and then knocked again. Nothing. Not wanting to give up too soon, she walked around the house looking in the windows. When she looked through the small window on the side of the garage, she thought she saw Julien in the driver's seat of his car with his head resting at an odd angle against the headrest support. She banged on the window. He didn't move. He appeared to be unconscious or even dead.

She realized that a nobler person might have broken the window and rushed in to try and save him. But this wasn't one of her finer moments. She went back to her car, called 911, and asked the dispatcher to call Deputy Miso, not the sheriff. Then she spent the next fifteen minutes feeling both guilty and relieved that no one might ever need to talk to Julien Pidgeon about anything ever again.

Deputy Missoula Marquart was someone Helaine trusted. She had known him growing up and was always happy to see his rough-cut, easygoing form walk into her bar. She liked the little hint of cowboy about him that came from his summers working on his uncle's ranch in Montana. The whole town liked him and affectionately called him Deputy Miso—he was a rare Montanan vegetarian as well as a Missoula. When he was out of uniform and into a plaid shirt, jeans, and boots, he was nearly irresistible.

Deputy Miso arrived about ten minutes after the paramedics. He found Helaine sitting on the porch steps. Worried most about Helaine, he went over to check on her before going to look in the garage. He already knew that Julien was dead. The dispatcher had relayed the news to him in the same excited voice that she used to report free pancakes at Cedar House. Julien's passing, it seemed, would not invoke great sorrow in the town of Wildcreek or its surrounding populated areas.

"Helaine, are you okay?" Helaine looked up at Miso but didn't respond. "I heard you were the one who called 911. What happened?" Helaine sighed and began talking. Wisely, Miso did not interrupt.

"I needed to talk to Julien. You know that I was supposed to have dinner here on Saturday. Everybody seems to know that. But he called and canceled the dinner, so I went birding instead. I was happy he canceled because I didn't want to eat with him. I just wanted to talk with him.

"Umberto urged me to come here this morning and talk to Julien. Julien wanted me to help him get a chef position in our restaurant and that just couldn't happen. So, early this morning I drove here to try and make him listen. I banged on the window, but he didn't move. Now, I guess it's too late."

"Too late for what, Helaine?" Miso had heard about the green garlic dinner, but he didn't think that missing a talk with Julien about green garlic would be enough to upset Helaine so much. "I still don't understand, Helaine. Why did you need to talk with him?"

Helaine shook her head and began explaining slowly as if Miso had missed something obvious.

"Because... he... has... antibiotic... resistant... tuberculosis, and he won't follow the prescribed protocols or go to The Clinic for treatment like he's supposed to! So, you see why he can't be in our kitchen! Or anybody's kitchen. Two of my uncles died of tuberculosis. They had silicosis from working in the mines and couldn't fight it; there are still people around here who are vulnerable. Julien is, um, I mean was... he was like a murderer walking around!" Helaine was crying now.

All this was news to Deputy Miso. Why hadn't anyone from The Clinic complained to the Sheriff's Office? "Okay, okay, Helaine. Now I get it." He tried to remember who all was at the Magpie on St. John's Wort Day. He was there for a short while—and Umberto, Helaine, Ben, Thor, Rascal and Sarah, Myra, Katharine, Afton Laurie, Greg Alatza, and some red-haired guy who sat in a corner all night. There were others, too. He would need to interview everyone who knew about the green garlic dinner.

"Helaine, how did you find out about the tuberculosis? It seems like I would have heard something."

Helaine said, "I don't remember," but her answer sounded to Miso more like, *I'm not going to tell you.*

Helaine's mention of "The Clinic", however, gave Miso a pretty good idea about where the information had come from. Nurse Wanda Darling, head nurse at the Sunray Clinic and Trauma Center, otherwise known as "The Clinic," had never heard of HIPAA. Or if she had, she thought it had something to do with loose hips, not loose lips. Nurse Darling was a gossip, not too bright, and a serious flirt. Miso dreaded interviewing her. Maybe he would send Deputy Buttars to take care of that chore.

"Just one more thing, and then you can go." Miso did his best to be reassuring. Helaine almost smiled. "Tell me where you went after you left the Magpie on Saturday." Helaine repeated her story about going birding.

Miso asked, "By yourself?" Miso had heard some stories about Helaine's birding excursions. The question was whether they involved birding at all.

Helaine responded by asking, "By myself?" Then, after an awkward moment, she said, "Yes, of course by myself".

"Do you need someone to drive you home?"

"No, no thanks. I have my car here. I'll be fine." With that, she stood up and walked a little unsteadily to her car. She thought she might stop for coffee rather than go home right away and talk to Umberto. Could this have been the result of "family business"? She didn't want to think about that.

Robotically, Helaine fastened her seatbelt and put her key in the ignition. Then she looked over to check the passenger side rearview mirror and felt a jolt of electricity race down her spine. A handwritten map and a note addressed to her were laying on the passenger seat. Helaine quickly shoved them into the glovebox—well under the rest of the papers there. As she started the car, she asked herself, "Now why did I do that?" Without conviction, she answered herself, "I don't have anything to hide, really, I don't."

Chapter 10

JUNE 29, 2015 MONDAY

After Helaine was safely on her way, Deputy Miso donned his protective suit, gloves, and booties and went into the garage. Julien's body was still in the driver's seat. It slumped back in the corner made by the seat and the door. A thin trail of dried pink foam ran from the corner of the mouth down into the shirt collar. The hair looked like it had dried drenched in sweat. The feet were somewhat tangled in the floor mat that had been lifted and pushed to the side.

Because the body had been in the warm car for an estimated day and a half, Miso decided not to get too close. The forensic pathologist, Dr. Edward Gadsberry was excellent, a surprisingly good find for rural Bonner County, and Miso knew that the death details were best left to a professional.

"At first glance, it looks like death was probably the result of some kind of poison." Doctor Gadsberry was not reluctant to provide detectives with preliminary information if he could. "I'll let you know more after the autopsy and tox screens."

"Any idea what kind of poison killed him or how it was administered?" Miso asked, hoping for a little more.

"Not really. Not yet. And I can't rule out homicide, so be careful what you tell the sheriff."

Miso nodded grimly and said, "Okay, no suicide or accident yet. And just an FYI—Helaine Pia told me that Julien Pidgeon had XDR TB. I'm not clear on how she knows that, but she seemed certain."

Next, Miso turned to the interior of the house. He changed his booties and gloves and entered the kitchen through the adjoining door from the garage. He watched the forensic team collect samples from the trash, two re-branded wine bottles with new Magpie labels, various items of tableware, and samples of mysterious puddles and splashes that showed up in the bathroom as well. On the floor, stuck to a drying pool of green liquid, was a handwritten recipe for green garlic pesto.

One of the techs was bagging a cell phone and a set of keys. "Where did you find those?" Miso asked.

"They were under a couch cushion, sir. The key looks like it belongs to the car in the garage, and the cell phone isn't damaged, so we should be able to get something from it."

Miso hoped so, too. "Make sure you get every scrap of paper—financial, personal, and especially medical. I have a feeling that we are going to find way too many motives if this turns out to be a homicide. Oh, and take all the garbage bags and any CSA-related stuff. This green garlic dinner either happened or didn't happen, but, either way, it may be important."

Just then, a tech called from the garage, "We're taking the body and the car now, sir. We're using the key that we found under the cushion. A little odd. No spare anywhere. But we did find an extra key to the house in the hallway drawer."

An hour later, after looking at the body again, talking with the forensic pathologist a little more, and securing the scene, an exhausted Deputy Missoula Marquart departed. Instead of heading to the office, however, he drove straight to Cedar House. Thanks to all that was well and good in the world, Helaine had found Julien Pidgeon on free pancake day, and Miso needed pancakes badly.

Chapter 11

June 29, 2015 Monday

Deputy Miso finished his third plate-sized Scottish orange oatmeal pancake and wondered what he should do next. He knew that he should report to the sheriff, but he didn't want to ruin his day just yet. The pancakes had raised his spirits considerably.

So, he decided to visit Greengrocers to check out the CSA bag and green garlic situation. Perhaps there would be time for a pleasant conversation with Myra as well. After all, Julien's death might just turn out to be an unhappy, or in the opinions of some Wildcreek residents, happy accident.

Pleased with this idea, Miso hummed "June is Bustin' Out All Over" all the way to Greengrocers. Anyone who knew Miso well knew that his mother had been a great admirer of Rodgers and Hammerstein. Thus, Miso grew up with an arsenal of songs to deal with every occasion.

His optimism evaporated, however, when he arrived at Greengrocers and found that it was closed. What? On a Monday morning?

Things were not looking good. Now, with nothing left to do but go back to the office, he shaved in his truck and prepared to suffer through a meeting with his boss, Sheriff Cannon.

Sheriff Kimball D'Frank Cannon served the citizens of Wildcreek with "Truth, Dignity, Courage, and Loyalty." At least that was how he viewed his long tenure as head of the Wildcreek Police Department. Other people, more grounded in reality, viewed his extended service as the result of outlandish publicity gimmicks like printing his face on T-shirts for inmates, as well as extensive family and business contacts, and low public interest in voting.

One of those gimmicks was changing his title from Chief of Police to Sheriff of Wildcreek. Kimball D'Frank Cannon greatly admired the famous Arizona sheriff, Joe Arpaio, and sought to emulate his hero, Sheriff Joe.

Originally, most of Kimball d'Frank Cannon's constituency just called him D'Frank because that was what he called himself during his first few years as head of the Wildcreek Police Department. Unfortunately, the name often came out sounding like "Duh, Frank." The latter soon gained popularity with the local press, critical of his performance as Chief of Police, and Duh Frank soon became Chief Duh Frank.

He began to suspect that these nicknames were not really terms of endearment or respect and started trying to make everyone call him "Sheriff Cannon" or "Sheriff". After all, he argued, some chiefs of police in early Idaho were called Marshalls, so why not a sheriff for Wildcreek Police Department?

"Deputy Miso!" Sheriff Cannon bellowed. "Where have you been all this time? I've been waiting for you to confirm that Julien Pidgeon committed suicide. I need to call a press conference right away."

"Sir, I don't think we can really say it was suicide yet. The forensic pathologist thought it might have been some kind of poison. From what I saw, I think he could be right." Miso knew this would not please the sheriff.

"If it wasn't suicide, then it must have been an accident. We do not have murders in Wildcreek. Everybody, even you, Deputy Missed-the-Mark Miso, knows he probably choked on that damn green garlic." The use of "damn" was the only allowed way to swear in the Wildcreek Police Department. All other such words were strictly prohibited by the sheriff's wife, who served unofficially as Chief Deputy. Unfortunately, insulting nicknames, like "Missed-the-Mark Miso", were not at all prohibited.

"That forensic pathological-ist," sputtered the sheriff. "What does he know? He's just a baby! He has no experience in Wildcreek, and he thinks he knows everything just because he has some fancy East Coast education. Even Wanda Darling could do a better job!" The sheriff's complexion was beginning to change from its usual red flush to purple.

Sheriff Cannon was well aware that Dr. Edward Gadsberry, a forensic pathologist for Inland Pacific Medical Investigations, had been investigating suspicious deaths for more than fifteen years and that Dr. Gadsberry often worked with the County Coroner on Wildcreek's more complex cases.

Moreover, because the sheriff had been a member of the committee that hired Dr. Gadsberry, he knew that the doctor was both well-educated and had extensive experience in forensic pathology. He had earned his bachelor's degree in Anthropology from the University of Tennessee in Knoxville and then attended medical school at the University of North Carolina at Chapel Hill. After that, he completed an Anatomic Pathology Residency at Brigham and Women's Hospital in Boston and a Forensic Pathology Fellowship at the University of New Mexico School of Medicine.

Done with school, Dr. Gadsberry took a position as an Assistant Medical Examiner in Pima County, Arizona, and lasted eight years. When the workload and the heat got to be too much for him, he packed his bags and moved to Wildcreek. The smaller workload left him time to do a lot of the things he loved—flying, fishing, skiing, and logrolling—just to name a few.

However, the sheriff was not one to let facts get in the way of the Truth he served. "Miso, I want you to go back out to the scene and find the evidence that we all know is there, namely that Julien Pidgeon committed suicide by choking on his own dinner. And do it now! I want to make a statement for the evening news."

Deputy Miso wondered how he was going to conduct a professional investigation. "Sheriff, don't you think we should wait for the lab report? It would be embarrassing if you told the press that Julien Pidgeon choked to death, and then it turned out that he died from poison." To placate the sheriff, Miso added, "Of course, some poisons *do* cause choking. We just need to wait for the autopsy."

At this, the sheriff's complexion started to return to normal. He nodded once and waved his hand in acquiescence. Miso felt he was gaining ground. This was definitely *not* the time to mention XDR TB.

To make sure that the sheriff didn't change his mind and issue any more questionable orders, Miso decided to enlist the help of Deputy Brodie Buttars, whose desk faced the sheriff's desk and who openly listened to everything the sheriff said. His primary responsibility, in fact, was to waylay as many of the sheriff's bizarre commands as possible. He did this in many ways, including creating diversions at opportune times. Miso's urgent glance told Buttars that now was an opportune time.

Buttars nodded, and a loud booming sound began immediately. Unfortunately for the sheriff and fortunately for everyone else, no one could hear what he was saying. Miso and Buttars shook their heads and made shrugging motions. Miso pointed to the door to indicate he was leaving. The sheriff started shaking his head and stomping his feet on the floor. The floor happened to be directly above the shooting range in the basement, where the sheriff believed the noise originated.

Miso made a hasty retreat, smiling at Buttars on the way out. Buttars smiled back and made a surreptitious peace sign with his right hand. Then, Buttars looked down and attended to the complicated button assembly occupying the second drawer down on his right-hand side. Fixed into the drawer were five red buttons with the labels: "Firearms Testing," the button recently employed, "Fried Chicken Delivery", "Google Name Alerts", "Sgt. Skew", and "Service Animal". Buttars was careful not to use them too often and always kept the drawer locked until it was needed.

With the recorded sound of firearms practice still ringing in his ears, Miso made his way to his own office and started making telephone calls. He called all the possible witnesses on his list and asked them for appointments as soon as possible. He had to leave voicemail messages for most of them, but when he called The Clinic, he was surprised to get the doctor who treated Julien for XDR TB. The doctor, however, refused to discuss Julien's case and transferred the call to The Clinic's legal services office in New Mexico. After more than fifteen minutes of waiting on hold, the cloying tones of Nurse Wanda Darling's voice interrupted the call.

"Miso, my lovely Miso, how are you? Why didn't you call me first? You should have called my cell! You have the number, don't you sweetheart?" Deputy Miso guessed that the extra familiarity meant that she was playing to an audience of co-workers. He cut to the chase.

"Nurse Darling, I was just thinking about calling you. I was wondering if you were available to talk about a few things. The subject matter might be a little sensitive, so The Clinic might not be the best place. What about tomorrow sometime at WPD?"

"Tomorrow! My shift ends in an hour. The Bed Pantry, dear. I'll see you there at 3:15. Don't keep a girl waiting. And don't call me Nurse Darling! I'm just 'Darling' to you." On that note, and not giving him any chance to object, she ended the call.

Miso was not happy about going to the Bed Pantry. The tiny café would be packed with Clinic employees ready to be witnesses to Wanda's staged "liaison". He thought about calling her back to suggest a different location, but, in the end, Miso decided to get the interview out of the way quickly before "Darling" changed her mind and insisted on meeting at her apartment.

After listening to the sheriff's recent tirade, Miso suspected that Nurse Darling was somehow involved in Sheriff Cannon's insistence on suicide by choking. She would have been the first person the sheriff called if he needed confirmation of a self-serving medical theory. Unlike the forensic team, Nurse D was more than accommodating and would have told the sheriff whatever he wanted to hear. She was probably "Darling" to the sheriff, too.

Chapter 12

JUNE 29, 2015 MONDAY

The meeting with Miso could not come too soon for Nurse Darling. The minute her shift was over, she rushed into the nurses' lounge to re-apply her makeup and brush out her work ponytail. All the while she hummed Chuck Berry's "Brown Eyed Handsome Man" and twirled to check out her back view in the full-length mirror. At last, she nodded in satisfaction and, with a final master stroke, undid the top two buttons of her nurse's uniform. She firmly believed that men liked a woman in uniform.

Nurse Darling was already waiting at the Bed Pantry when Miso arrived. She knew that he liked strawberry lemonade and had ordered a large glass for him.

"Miso Piso! It's so nice to see you!" she gushed, raising her voice an octave. He smiled, but inwardly he wished she would stop making up names for him. He also admonished himself to be patient. Nurse Darling had information, and he needed it.

"Wanda... Darling." He spoke her full name with just a little pause between her first and last name—an attempt at flirtation. An unnecessary effort. Wanda gave him a radiant smile. Too much radiance, in fact. Now he suspected that the information he needed would cost him a dinner at the Magpie. *Oh well*, he had known that might happen.

"Wanda, I know I can trust you to be discreet." This was a lie, and they both knew it. "But I need a little information about Julien Pidgeon. I heard that he was a patient at The Clinic. No one seems to know much about him."

"Is that an order, deputy? I *know* how to follow orders. I like to follow orders." Wanda sat up straight, arched her back and pointed her large breasts right at him.

"It's like this, Deputy. Back in 2009, Julien Pidgeon came to Wildcreek by court order to resume treatment for XDR TB. You know, Extensively Drug-Resistant Tuberculosis. Apparently, he was kicked out of the treatment program at the University of Virginia Hospital in Charlottesville. I think one of the doctors at The Clinic agreed to take him on as a favor for a doctor friend in Virginia. Anyway, it was either jail or Wildcreek. Do you want another lemonade, honey?"

Miso shook his head. "Just the facts, ma'am." Nurse D loved that kind of talk.

"So, he's been here ever since. He was on something like medical probation. If he didn't follow a specified treatment protocol, he would have to go back to Virginia and possibly to jail. For instance, he was supposed to be tested once a month and wear a mask in public.

"For a few months, he was a model patient. Then, he stopped wearing the mask except on days when he had a Clinic appointment. A year ago, he stopped coming to The Clinic altogether. The Clinic has been trying to send him back to Virginia, but there just doesn't seem to be a way to do that.

"Julien signed an agreement to comply with testing and the other protocol requirements, but The Clinic's lawyers don't seem to be able to find a way to enforce it. The Clinic has kept the whole thing quiet to avoid panic in the town.

"There really isn't much of a reason to panic, though. Julien was probably not too much of a hazard to healthy people. Only to people with weakened immune systems or lung disease.

"But he was hazardous in *many* other ways." Nurse Darling stretched out the word "many" for several seconds. "He was always looking for ways to embarrass people and hinting that he knew secrets about them. And he insulted everybody at The Clinic, even me!" Miso adopted an exaggerated expression of shock. "Yes, even me!" she repeated with a glimmer of tears in her eyes. Miso switched to a shocked expression with additional overtones of outrage and shook his head in support.

"That's terrible, Wanda. You're truly the Florence Nightingale of Wildcreek. We all owe you so much." These words seemed to forestall any crying that was about to occur. "And by the way, did you happen to mention the XDR TB to anyone? Helaine Pia, for example?"

"Oh no, deputy, that information is confidential! Of course, the information is available to law enforcement... " At this point she gave Miso her most brilliant and frightening smile. "In fact, I think I might have more to say, but it's all a bit fuzzy right now. I might be able to remember things more clearly at the Magpie... perhaps after a plate of Umberto's spaghetti with white clam sauce?"

In hopes of learning more, Miso agreed to dinner but not at the Magpie. Dining at the Magpie with Nurse Darling would start even more rumors. They settled on Mike's BBQ at 7 p.m. Later, at Mike's,

Miso used all his wit and charm, a considerable performance, to keep the conversation on the topic of Julien. He also managed to avoid going to Wanda's for drinks afterward. Unfortunately, however, despite Miso's many and best efforts, Nurse Darling had nothing else useful to say the rest of the evening.

Chapter 13

JUNE 30, 2015 TUESDAY

The next morning, Sheriff Cannon got to work early. A copy of the *Wildcreek Wing* was on his chair. He was so curious about the Julien Pidgeon coverage that he forgot his usual morning ritual of first sitting on his copy of the local newspaper until it was badly wrinkled. Sheriff Cannon enjoyed this little ritual of contempt for the media, even though he made nearly all his decisions with the press in mind.

"Buttars! Call Miso! I want him now!" The sheriff was bellowing—a very bad sign. "The *Wing Ding* reports 'unofficially' that the Pidgeon fellow most likely died of poisoning. What kind of poison? They don't know. And, do you know what else?" Buttars knew better than to answer this question. "It says that Julien Pidgeon had TB and that he was not following his protocol and that he was supposed to be wearing a mask in public. It's asking why the WPD hadn't done anything!" By this time the sheriff was wadding up newsprint into balls and throwing them at the wall.

Miso arrived just as the sheriff was shredding the last page of the morning paper. "Deputy Marquart, you told me this was a suicide!"

Miso removed his hat to use as a shield. "No Sheriff, *you* told *me* this was a suicide."

The sheriff roared, "You know very well that the dead guy was going to our church suppers every month. Why didn't you tell me he had incurable tuberculosis?"

Miso shook his head and tried to use a soothing voice, "Sheriff, why would I go to those dinners, too, if I knew about the XDR TB? I really had no idea."

Miso knew why the sheriff was especially upset. Julien didn't just attend the dinners. He also engaged in what most people called the "MacMarton Maneuver" or "M&M". The MacMartons were a family of two parents and eight children who came to church suppers, ate like locusts, and left with pockets full of every dish on the serving table. Julien, who also made a habit of taking things, always wore cargo pants and, like the MacMarton children, put his hands in all the food.

"Are you trying to kill me? This article is causing an uproar! The phone is ringing off the hook!" Miso looked back at Buttars who was shaking his head negatively. The phone was not ringing off the hook. "The mayor has ordered N95 Peculiar Expiration Masks for himself and the Town Council. Buttars!..."

Buttars interrupted, "I think you mean Particulate Respirator Masks, sir."

"Just order as many as you can, Buttars. Use the ammo budget. If everyone dies of tuberculosis there won't be anybody left to shoot!"

The sheriff frowned. He wasn't done ranting. "People are more upset about this XYZ TB than the murder. No one really liked what's-his-name, anyway. So, Miso, go wrap this up as a suicide right away. Now! And get Sergeant Skew. I need her to write a letter to the *Wing Ding* editor."

Apparently Buttars had had enough of this tirade. He shouted, "It's XDR TB, sir!" And then, before the sheriff could reply, the deafening sound of fireworks drowned out any further pronouncements from Wildcreek's chief law enforcement officer.

Miso smiled. Buttars must have added a new sound effect. After a few seconds of this, the sheriff swore and threw his "medicine" flask at the wall, leaving a Jack Daniels stain that resembled his posterior. Sgt. Skew came running into the room.

Miso mumbled, "I have to go do a few interviews... " He quickly ducked out the door and ran to his car to meet with Myra Briney as arranged the day before.

Chapter 14

Myra was late getting to the store. She dreaded the meeting with Deputy Miso. Should she tell him that Katharine was missing? That Katharine did not come home from the store on Saturday? That she had not called? Myra had been hoping all day Sunday that Katharine simply had spent the weekend with friends and forgotten to let Myra know.

Worry had become outright fear on Monday morning when Myra arrived at the store and saw that Katharine's car was still parked on the street where she'd left it on Saturday. Rather than call the WPD, Myra left the "Closed" sign facing the street, moved Katharine's car to the back, and spent the day looking for her friend. When she heard that Julien had died on Saturday night, she panicked. Had Katharine confronted Julien about his menacing requests for money? Myra didn't want to get Katharine into trouble needlessly. Why didn't Katharine call?

Deputy Miso was waiting outside Greengrocers when Myra arrived at 9:15 a.m. Unfortunately, a few customers were also waiting at the door. Myra addressed the small gathering, "I'm sorry everybody! It's just that I haven't been feeling well these last few days. I'll be opening at noon today." In response to questions about Katharine and bread, she mumbled, "Katharine... not... maybe tomorrow... no bread today." Myra looked terrible. Her reddened eyes and rumpled clothes told her customers that any additional questions would be fruitless. They headed for their cars without complaint, except for Miso, who followed Myra inside.

Deputy Miso noticed Myra's disheveled state but decided not to mention it. After sitting down at one of the tables near the bakery counter, Miso began, "Myra, are you sure you're okay?" Myra nodded.

"I just need you to tell me a little about how the store prepares the CSA bags. You've probably heard that Julien Pidgeon was found dead in his garage yesterday. Well, it looks like he prepared a meal Saturday evening from some of Saturday's CSA bag ingredients. I just need to know a little about the process. Of course, the meal may have had nothing to do with his death. I'm just trying to get a complete picture of his day on Saturday."

Myra sighed, "Well, I do all the packing early on Saturday morning before the store opens. Then I put name tags on each bag, and I slip a recipe or newsletter inside the bag as well. And an uplifting message if I find one during the week that I like. Oh, and I list the contents of the bag on an insert, too. The same insert is posted on the store's outside bulletin board the Monday before pickup. People can call me and ask about the contents, too."

"Do you have an insert from the Saturday bags that I could keep?" Myra got up, went behind the counter, opened a drawer, and pulled out a packet of bright pink computer paper. She brought a sheet back to Miso. After reading it slowly, he asked, "Could any of the items in this list cause an allergic reaction? Or possibly be poisonous?"

"No!" Myra's voice was now nearly two octaves higher. "Mostly I get them from the organic vendors at the Farmers' Market. Some things I grow in my own garden behind the store. No one has ever, ever complained about the quality of the ingredients. I definitely know poisonous plants from edible ones!"

Miso asked, "Would you make a list of your suppliers for the items in last Saturday's bags... please?" He tried to sound non-accusatory. "Just routine. I'll have to check up on all the sources. When you get time. Just call Deputy Buttars, and he'll come pick it up. Oh, and are there ever any bags that don't get picked up? What happens to them?"

Myra cringed at this question. Deputy Miso would need to interview Davina Binns! Myra hoped that Morris wouldn't try to be helpful.

Myra asked, "Do you know Davina Binns?" Miso nodded reluctantly. A slight tic appeared in his left eye. Myra continued, "She comes over to the store at lunchtime on Saturdays and covers so that Katharine and I can go to lunch. When she gets here, she puts the leftover bags in the storeroom and then takes them home with her when we get back from lunch. That's sort of her pay for minding the store.

"Oh, and she makes a list of the people who don't pick up their bags. They don't get credit or anything, but we just like to know." Miso asked for the list.

"Here's the list from last Saturday," she told him, handing him another piece of pink paper. "Only one remaining bag, and it didn't have a nametag. Very odd, because I'm sure I tagged all the bags."

"Just a few more questions, Myra. Did Julien Pidgeon pick up a CSA bag on Saturday morning?"

"Yes, he did. He arrived just after Thor left, about an hour before lunch. He was his usual self. He insulted people, talked about his green garlic pesto dinner with Helaine, and took things without paying. Then he left."

"Did he seem ill to you?"

"No, not *physically* ill if that's what you mean." Myra had no problem speaking ill of the dead, especially on this occasion.

"Do you remember who came into the store up until the time that Julien left?"

"Well, Mrs. Moser came in first for some apricot jelly, then Afton Laurie, then Joe Ivan, who introduced himself and asked us all about our store and how we started it, and if we made a good profit. I think he just wanted to spend time talking with Katharine. Thor came in and out of the store a lot because he was delivering St. John's Wort flower bundles. He was using old CSA bags and getting the flowers all mixed up with the weekly bags. That's all I can remember right now."

Miso closed his notebook to signal the end of the interview. He looked around. "Hey, I don't see Katharine here today. Is she at home?" Miso was hoping to interview Katharine, too, even though she hadn't answered when he called her for an appointment.

Miso watched as Myra stopped moving. She appeared to be holding her breath. Her eyes didn't blink. Could people really turn to stone? Miso wasn't sure what had just happened.

Then Myra's lips began to tremble, and her words tumbled out in great sobs. "Katharine... is not... at home." Several seconds went by. "She... she... I haven't seen her since Saturday afternoon." The rest was unintelligible.

It took another twenty minutes or so for Miso to get the full story, such as it was. Myra left the store around 5 p.m. on Saturday. Katharine stayed to prepare for Monday's baking and to lock up. That was the usual routine. Katharine stayed, and Myra went home to get dinner ready.

But Katharine never came home. Myra called Katharine's cell phone all evening, but Katharine never called back. Myra's cell phone log showed ten calls on Saturday evening, and twice that on Sunday and Monday.

After unburdening herself, Myra took Miso behind the store and showed him Katharine's car. "I have a key, so when I saw it on the street Monday morning, I decided to drive it around to the back to keep it safe."

Miso asked for the key and did a quick search of the car and trunk. "Did you find her purse or phone anywhere?" Myra shook her head. "Did you take anything from the car or the store?" Myra again shook her head. "Did you make any calls to find her other than the ones you made to her cell phone?" Myra looked down at her knees and shook her head for a third time.

Finally, Myra looked up and added, "Really, Miso, the car was parked exactly where Katharine left it on Saturday morning. When I got inside to drive it, everything seemed to be fine. It looked like nothing had been touched. The store, too, was just like she would have left it on a Saturday evening. Preparations for Monday's bread baking were done, and the doors were locked.

"I went to the store early on Monday, parked Katharine's car in the back, and made sure the 'Closed' sign was still on the door. Then I went home again and spent the rest of the day at home waiting for her to call."

Miso asked whether Katharine had problems with anyone. "Come on, Miso! You know everyone loves Katharine. Some people are even *in love* with Katharine—like Thor and maybe that red-haired guy, Joe Ivan.

"Most people love her for her bread. But nobody hates her or even dislikes her. You know that." Myra repeatedly and emphatically told him again how much everyone loved Katharine.

Miso had to agree. Katharine was attractive, smart, pleasant, and she baked delicious bread. On occasion, he had even imagined what it would be like to be married to someone like Katharine. But he never had the courage to do more than just imagine.

Nonetheless, coming back to reality, Miso thought Myra's behavior during the interview had been strange. Her account of her actions on Monday seemed incomplete somehow. Maybe Myra wasn't telling him everything she knew about Katharine. Even so, she clearly cared for her friend deeply and seemed baffled by her disappearance.

After the interview, Miso called the station from his car and asked for Buttars. "Hey, would you open a missing persons investigation for Katharine Holmeier? No one has seen her since Saturday afternoon, apparently. And would you stop by Greengrocers and pick up the complete list of CSA suppliers from Myra Briney tomorrow afternoon? Oh, and would you check with the hotels in town and find out if a guy named Joe Ivan is staying in any of them? I may be out doing interviews all day tomorrow. Thanks." Miso did not intend to return to the office and talk with the sheriff if he could at all avoid it.

Chapter 15

June 30, 2015 Tuesday

After leaving Greengrocers and calling Buttars, Miso decided to go to the Magpie next and try to catch Ben and Umberto before the lunch crowd arrived. Ben saw him and met him at the door. "Hi, Miso! Do you want to talk to my dad?"

"Sure, but I'd like to ask you about a couple of things, too. What do you know about this green garlic dinner? I heard that your mom was supposed to go to Julien Pidgeon's house on Saturday to try some new dish that Julien invented."

"Yeah, he was telling everybody that he created a fantastic new pesto made with green garlic. My mom told him she would try it, but he canceled the dinner. I took the call."

Miso asked, "Are you sure it was Julien? What exactly did he say?"

"He just asked me to tell my mom that he couldn't make dinner on Saturday. He said that he would let her know when he was ready to try it again. He said 'again' in his, you know, in his long, drawn-out way, like he was from the South or something. He coughed a lot, though. I can't tell you his exact words."

"How did your mom seem when she heard the news?"

Ben closed his eyes in an attempt to recall. "She said she was disappointed, but I think she was relieved. I'm pretty sure that she promised to go to his dinner just to get him out of the Magpie's kitchen on St. John's Wort Day. I expected her to be the one to cancel. She was never going to eat anything that he cooked."

"Okay, thanks a lot, Ben. Is your dad around?"

"Yeah, he's in the kitchen. Just a minute. I'll go get him." Ben almost ran back to the kitchen. Being questioned by Deputy Miso about a murdered guy was the highlight of his week. He had some texting to do.

Umberto came out of the kitchen wiping his hands on a towel. He explained that Helaine was concerned about Julien's XDR TB and that she was planning to go to Julien's for dinner to talk with him about it. She was disappointed when he canceled the evening.

Miso asked, "How did she find out about his tuberculosis?"

"I don't know. Some of Helaine's relatives died from TB complicated by silicosis, and she felt it was her duty to try and persuade Julien to be more careful. Personally, I think he would only laugh at her story and try to make her even more upset. He would never help her or listen to her. He thinks about himself only."

"Umberto, do you know where Helaine was on Saturday evening?"

Umberto's face darkened as he replied, "I don't know where she was, but she was not here helping us with the deep cleaning. We always close at 9 p.m on the day after the St. John's Wort Celebration to clean, and she was not here. I can tell you what she *said* she was doing. She said she was birdwatching! All night she was birdwatching! Who does that? But yes, she was at home when I woke up around five o'clock on Sunday."

Ben came out of the kitchen to join his dad. Clearly, he had been listening at the doorway. "Mom goes birdwatching a lot." Ben watched his dad look down at the floor.

"Is Helaine here by any chance?" asked Miso, thinking that he had better clear up a few things.

"No," said Ben and Umberto in unison. "She's out birdwatching!"

"Umberto, some people think that Helaine and Julien were romantically involved. Could that be true?" Miso hated to ask, but it could be important.

"No, that could not be true," Umberto answered, smiling. "Helaine prefers Boreal Owls." Umberto's smile could not be called pleasant.

Miso left the Magpie and spent the rest of his afternoon making several fruitless attempts to track down Helaine, find Katharine, and figure out exactly where the red-haired guy, who had been seen around town for a few weeks, was right now and what he was doing on Saturday night. He hoped Buttars would have better luck.

Finally, after several hours of investigating to no avail, Miso gave up and returned to the Magpie. If Umberto had a Cold Smoke Scotch Ale in stock, he would consider himself lucky. In fact, he found more than that. He found Thor sitting at the bar drinking another of Umberto's signature drinks, the Black and White with Feathers. And even better than finding the ale and another witness to interview, it just happened that Umberto was serving one of his impromptu "Taste of Corsica" evenings. The food promised to be extraordinary.

"Thor, do you have time to talk? I'm trying to learn all I can about Julien Pidgeon's activities for the last few weeks. Did you see him at the St. John's Wort Celebration?" Thor nodded at his drink.

"Well, did you hear him say anything about a green garlic dinner?" Again, Thor nodded at his drink.

"What exactly did you hear?" This time, Miso was not taking *nod* for an answer.

"Deputy, you were there at the Magpie, too. Don't you remember?" Miso was tempted to mimic Thor with a nod.

"Thor, I know what I remember, but I want to know what *you* remember. The sooner you answer my questions, the sooner I'll move over to the corner with a plate full of grilled *lonzu* and chestnut polenta and leave you alone."

"Fair enough, Deputy. Yes, I did hear that lowlife ask Helaine to come to his house for dinner on Saturday night. He was his usual lecherous self, and I couldn't believe she agreed. I figured she was lying to him to get him out of the Magpie. That was a service to us all as it turned out. I just hope Julien didn't cough in the beer."

Thor took a long swallow of his Feathered B&W, looked into its depths but didn't seem to find what he was looking for, and continued, "And I saw him Saturday morning at Greengrocers. He was coming in just as I was going out. That's all I can say, we didn't speak."

"Why don't you just go ahead and tell me what you did with the rest of your day after Greengrocers, Thor." Deputy Miso immediately regretted the way he phrased the question.

"I don't know why I don't *just* go ahead, Deputy. Or do you *just* want to know what I did?" Thor wasn't in the mood for law enforcement questioning. He had come to the Magpie to relax and drink.

But Miso sat there, not moving, so Thor finally continued. "Okay, then, sir. I went back to the farm, unloaded the truck, and read a book for a while. Then I went back to the Magpie for Happy Hour. I stayed until about 1 a.m., closing time. I always leave at closing time on Saturdays. And then I went home and went to sleep."

"Did anyone see you after you left the Magpie? Rascal and Sarah, for instance?"

"I doubt it, Deputy. Rascal and Sarah go to bed early. I didn't see them, and I didn't see anybody else, either."

"Was Helaine at the Magpie during Happy Hour?" Miso just had a few more questions.

"Sure she was. I saw her leave around 4 p.m. and thought she might be going to Julien's house. She was headed in his direction. I heard her tell Umberto and Ben that she was going 'birding.'"

"One last thing, Thor. Do you get CSA bags from Greengrocers?" Thor nodded at his empty glass. "Did you get one last Saturday?" Another nod. "Was anything wrong with it?" At this, Thor swung around to look at Miso.

"Like what, Deputy? My bag was fine. Myra knows what she's doing. Next to me, she knows more about organic gardening than anyone else in the county. Anyway, I always give my bag to Sarah and Rascal, and Sarah does the cooking. All three of us, Sarah, Rascal, and myself ate from the bag last week, and we're still here to answer your questions about it. Anything else?"

"Yes, as a matter of fact." Miso was tired of Thor's attitude. "Did you know that Katharine Holmeier is missing?" Thor's eyes widened and his mouth dropped open.

"What makes you think that, Miso?" Thor's unfriendly posture instantly disappeared. "I saw her on Saturday morning. She seemed fine. We talked a little." Thor looked worried and alarmed. Everyone knew that Thor had a thing for Katharine.

"Myra told me today that Katharine has been missing since Saturday evening." Miso's patience was growing thin.

"Did Julien Pidgeon have anything to do with that?" Thor's eyes were burning with intensity.

"We're looking for her, Thor. We don't know anything yet."

Thor drained his glass and stared. The ice in Thor's glass began to tinkle loudly as Thor tried to control his shaking hand. Miso, seeing Thor's distress, ordered him another Black and White with Feathers. He laid a ten-dollar bill on the bar and moved over to the rear corner to wait for the night's first tasting course. He left the Magpie without asking Thor any more questions.

Chapter 16

While Deputy Miso was interviewing Thor, Afton was sitting at the peninsula bar in her kitchen wondering whether collecting seeds from her garden was worth the effort. For the past three hours, Afton had been harvesting, sorting, and labeling seeds from her garden. She was planning to take them to the County Regional Library's seed library, but now she was worried about cross pollination, unknown variations, and non-native species. The whole idea of sharing seeds was starting to lose its joy. Maybe she should just mix them all together and call it her own brand of mesclun? At any rate, it was time for a break from seed sorting.

First, she checked her phone and found a voicemail from Deputy Miso. The phone was still in silent mode from the day before. Oops. She decided to wait until tomorrow to call Miso back.

Then she went out to get her mail and the local newspaper, the *Wildcreek Wing*. Most of the mail was addressed to Current Resident, and she tossed it into the recycling bin. One official-looking letter she tore into shreds with relish. A surge of anger and a sense of helplessness overcame her every time she saw mail with a Brewster County return address. Even though tearing paper wasn't much of a remedy for the way she'd been treated there, it did provide a brief moment of satisfaction.

Finally, she glanced at the *Wildcreek Wing* and saw the article about Julien Pidgeon who seemingly died from poisoning. "You know, Ralph, dying by poison is a terrible thing, but I don't think many people are going to miss Julien Pidgeon. I wonder if it was an accident? Maybe it was something he ate—like that green garlic pesto he was always talking about." Ralph did not have a perfect command of the English language, but he did know the verb "to eat" and all its conjugations. He got up and went over to his food bowl.

"No, Ralph, it's too early to eat." Ralph turned his starving eyes upon her. "You have to wait another thirty minutes!" Ralph rested his head on his dish—too weak to hold it up any longer. After a few minutes, Afton gave in. "Oh fine. I'll feed you now. But tomorrow night, you absolutely have to wait for dinner until at least 6 p.m." Then she added, "I'm only feeding you early because I'm thinking about eating at the Short List tonight." Ralph yawned to show he didn't care. He hated Short List leftovers.

Chapter 17

JUNE 30, 2015 TUESDAY

The Short List, once a stopping point for railroad employees who worked on the network of rails around Lake Pend Oreille, now served only the small population of farms and cabins, Afton's among them, that stretched upward and north of the railroad tracks. The diminutive structure resembled a green wooden dacha with ornately carved, white-painted trim around the windows, eaves, and door. The thickly growing white pines interspersed with blue spruce intensified its ancient fairytale appearance. The menu, also whimsical, was different every day. Only two entrees were offered, but the vast amounts of alcohol available made up for the chef's fantastical alimentary creations. And, of course, the expansive view of the big lake and the Monarch Mountains was more than exhilarating.

Tuesday was not a big night for the Short List, so it was fairly empty when Afton arrived. She found her usual table against the back wall and started looking at the evening's offerings. The first was Brunswickian Stew, no indication of the ingredients, except that it was gluten-free, with Honeycrisp apple slices. The second was fried fish with sweet potato fries and kimchee slaw "no substitutions."

The waitress came with unsweetened iced tea. She knew it would be Afton's choice. "Is there okra in the Brunswickian Stew?" Afton asked.

The waitress smiled and replied, "I don't know, and you know the rules. If you don't think you'll like it, you can have free pancakes. So, what do you want? Pick one."

Afton sighed. She had been coming regularly to the Short List for a year and still was not sure whether she was welcome. In this north land, acceptance was often hard won and long in coming—or at least hard to recognize.

"I'll try the stew." She couldn't tell from the waitress' expression whether this was a good idea or not. Just as she was regretting her decision, she heard a loud "Hey, hey, hey, hey!" and looked up to see her neighbor, Greg Alatza, walk into the restaurant.

He was standing in the doorway with his arms wide open. Not surprisingly, he seemed to be focused on the two young waitresses. Afton, out of an abundance of caution, slumped down behind her flimsy large-sized menu just in case the waitresses managed to get away—leaving Greg to look around for new prey. After thirty seconds or so, she looked up from behind the menu to see Greg standing right in front of her.

"Good evening, Clarice." Greg always treated Afton as if she were an FBI agent despite the fact that her law enforcement experience was far from anything like the FBI. So, with no escape in sight, there was nothing left to do but invite Greg to join her.

With a smile, she said, "'Whenever feasible, one should always try to seat the rude.' Please sit down, Greg."

Chapter 18

JUNE 30, 2015 TUESDAY

While Greg ordered and one-sidedly flirted with the waitress, Afton cautiously worked her way through her stew. She had not yet detected any unusual animal, vegetable, or mineral in its murky depths, but she continued to pick up bits with her spoon and examine them while Greg talked and talked.

Her caution and Greg's loquaciousness made dinner a lengthy process. Greg, in fact, had eaten barely a quarter of his free stack of pancakes and was only just getting started on his substantial store of Wildcreek news and gossip.

Too much talking and not enough eating was a Greg-behavior familiar to Afton. She had spent many, many hours at the table with her neighbor. He often called her in the evening to tell her that he had made dinner for a date, but the date had been canceled. Could Afton come instead? Yes, most of the time she could. Greg, whose father owned several restaurants, turned out to be an excellent, albeit limited, chef.

To be precise, she knew that Greg had only three dinners in his repertoire—spaghetti with mushroom sauce and salad, chicken breasts on the grill with teriyaki sauce over a bed of asparagus, and scallops with sautéed spinach. Because none of his liaisons had ever made it past three dates, Greg had never felt the need to expand. His need to expound, on the other hand, was unceasing.

Afton's mind started to drift as Greg plunged into one of his favorite stories. She had heard this one at least five times. "Afton, you probably won't believe this, but I played Jerry-slash-Daphne in *Some Like It Hot* at the Wurlitzer Theater three years ago." The Wurlitzer was a charmingly restored playhouse in town.

"I *would* believe it, Greg. No doubt you were great!" Afton thought she could save some time by acknowledging his greatness. That way, he would not have to tell her. Unfortunately, no time was saved.

"The *Wildcreek Wing* loved me! The reviewer said that my comedic talents were mind boggling!" Afton wasn't sure the review was meant to be complimentary. "And Alicia Dexter, the director, told me my performance was second only to Jack Lemmon! If you think about it, playing both Jerry and Daphne made me the odd couple all by myself!" Afton stopped listening completely at this point.

Suddenly, however, Afton's attention snapped back to Greg. He had finished with his acting career and was now talking about the recent death of Julien Pidgeon. "… he might have been poisoned by the contents of his CSA bag. Did you eat from your bag, Afton? I ate most of mine, and I'm fine. But I didn't get parsley, did you get any? Myra forgot it."

Greg took a bite of pancake and continued with his mouth full, "And I needed it for my spaghetti dinner with Amy last week. Without parsley the spaghetti sauce was terrible, and I'm sure that's why she won't call me back." Afton had serious doubts about that.

Wanting to defend Myra, Afton said, "Greg, I didn't get parsley either. At Greengrocers on Saturday, Myra told me that there is a shortage of parsley, that an invasion of parsley worms destroyed most of it, and that she couldn't get enough to fill the bags. She just forgot to cross it out on the tag."

"Well, she should have called everybody. I would have made chicken on the grill, instead." Greg, now certain that Amy's lack of communication was Myra's fault, resumed his critique of the CSA bag. "I decided not to eat the green garlic, though. Did you eat it? Julien talked about his green garlic pesto so much that I just tossed it out into the garden. Let's see how the deer like that!" Afton had never seen deer eat garlic.

"Another thing about Julien," Greg continued. "He had some kind of extreme TB." Greg coughed dramatically to call attention to this pronouncement. Afton was not amused. Greg, predictably, had more to say on the subject.

"My friend, Wanda Darling—you know, Wanda, she's a nurse at The Clinic. Anyway, Wanda told me that Julien was supposed to wear a mask in public, but he never did. And he refused to get chest x-rays. She said she wasn't sorry he died. Yeah, she really *said* that. There aren't many men Wanda would *ever* say that about."

Afton was thinking that there weren't many people that Wanda Darling wouldn't say everything about. Wanda, like Greg, loved the thrill of spreading any tidbit of information she acquired. Especially information that caused embarrassment, shock, or horror. Unlike Wanda, however, Greg Alatza was usually a dependable source. Afton was careful to keep her secrets well hidden.

"Now don't tell anybody," Greg continued, "but I found out that Katharine Holmeier is missing. Melina Moser told me this morning that all of the baked goods at Greengrocers are being shipped in from

Krillo." This was literally true because Krillo was on the other side of the lake, and a ferry regularly ran between Krillo and Wildcreek. "Melina also told me that she was contributing baked goods to help Myra. I mean, who doesn't love Melina's apricot dumplings! I hope she makes *Sachertorte*, too."

Finally, and none too soon, Greg took his last bite of pancake. Afton had been done with her Brunswickian Stew and apples for quite a while. To her delight, he stood up, and with a rolling flourish of his right hand, announced, "Well, it's time to go home. *L.A. Confidential* is showing on TMC in about twenty minutes. 'We'll do the town one night on me,'" he quoted. And with that, he was out the door .

To Greg's quickly retreating back, Afton quoted in response, "'I'll bring my wallet just in case.'" When she looked back down at the table, she was not really surprised to see his unpaid bar tab. The receipt for free pancakes with the waitress' intentionally fake phone number, however, had disappeared. Afton paid, as usual.

That was another Greg trait. When he wasn't out scouting for his next dinner date, looking for treasures at yard sales, or generally spreading himself around, he was watching old movies. His conversation was always sprinkled with quotes and misquotes from film and television.

At least tonight he refrained from using Afton's least favorite line from *L.A Confidential*—"Well, off to get an ex-hooker and a trip to Arizona!" he would say. Then, he would add, "*Brewster County*, Arizona!" Afton wanted to tell him that there might be a reason why he never got past three dates—and it wasn't for lack of parsley.

Back at home from the Shortlist, Afton checked to see that Ralph had eaten his dinner and had plenty of water. Then, she changed into pajamas, poured a glass of red wine, and got into bed. She continued reading at the place she'd left off the night before—the life cycle of puffballs. The strange fungi were appearing all along her driveway, and she was wondering if she could eat them. Myra might know. She would ask Myra tomorrow.

Chapter 19

June 30, 2015 Tuesday

Far away from the Shortlist, Joe Ivan walked into the main room of the hunter's forest cabin and locked the door behind him. Katharine, looking worn and tired, asked, "Are you going to kill me?"

Joe Ivan wanted, with all his heart, to say, "Of course, not! I could never do that. I want you to like me! I bought roses for you, and they are in the car." They were.

But instead, he said, "Me? No, I am not going to kill you, Katharine. I am only going to tell you a story."

Katharine wasn't sure what was happening and continued to make small, sobbing sounds. She could move around the cabin, but there was no way out.

"I am going to tell you the story of two young women, Kelly and Mary, who worked in a Seattle bakery that shared an alley with a rundown three-story apartment complex. One of the young women, probably Kelly..."

At this point he gave his captive a piercing look. Katharine froze. "Kelly walked out of the back of the bakery to the waste bin in the alley and noticed smoke leaking from an upstairs window of the apartment building. It smelled very strongly of marijuana. This was not surprising to her. She had seen the same thing from that window many times.

"No, the surprise was the rental truck parked below the smoking window. The back of the truck was open, and the ramp was down. Inside sat a large block of what looked like cash wrapped in shrink wrap. The young woman, Kelly, approached for a closer look. It was cash.

"She hurried back inside the bakery and came out again with another young woman. Her name was Mary. They looked around and saw a dolly at the end of the alley and across the street at the Stroud's Paper Company's storage entrance. One of them—it doesn't matter who—retrieved the dolly and brought it back to the rental truck. With it, they managed to get the cash out of the truck, and into a hiding place. Does this sound like a good story so far?"

Katharine nodded but made no sound.

"Then, they pushed the dolly back to the paper company, leaving a little piece of torn shrink wrap on the frame. Were they wearing gloves, or did they wipe all their fingerprints off? No one knows that part of the story. Well, the two young women know, of course."

Joe paused, watched Katharine intently, and then continued, "But we do know that the two young women continued to work at the bakery as if nothing had happened. The police spent many months investigating the employees of the paper company, the bakery, the apartments, but the money was never found. This is the end of the story. Did you like it? You don't know? So... now I will tell you what is *not* a story. I will tell you what I *know*."

Joe went on to explain, "According to police reports, someone—was it one of the bakers? —made a complaint about the marijuana smoke in the alley. The police arrived, and the truck was found along with the man who rented it. That man was passed out in the apartment issuing the offending marijuana smoke. Thinking that the police had found the cash in the truck, he admitted that he and four others stole a large block of cash earmarked for destruction from a hangar at Sea Tac airport. It turned out to be three million dollars in old hundred-dollar bills. That weighs about sixty-six pounds. I think two women could move a package weighing sixty-six pounds. Don't you?"

Katharine uttered a barely audible "...Yes."

"One of the four men was my brother, Pavel. Pavel was convicted of theft and sentenced to prison. The money never surfaced. Of course, there were several bakers at the bakery and all of them were questioned. They all said they had not seen or heard anything. Two of them probably laughed and said, 'Why would we still be working in this bakery if we had three million dollars?' Do you think that was funny, Katharine?" Katharine shook her head from side to side.

"Many years later my brother Pavel died from the Hepatitis C that he contracted in prison. By that time, I had finished my education and was working in a large bank. During my last visit with Pavel, he asked me to find the ones who took the money and make them suffer like he had suffered. Do you think I could do such a thing, Katharine?"

Katharine, trying to be hopeful, said, "No, I think you are a good person."

"You are correct. I am a good person. I do not want to hurt anyone. I told Pavel so. Pavel was always wild. When we left Russia and moved to Seattle, he would not go to school. He would not obey our parents. His friends were always in trouble, and soon he was in trouble, too.

But he was my brother, and stealing from a thief is still stealing. Pavel argued that such stealing should receive the same punishment, so I told Pavel that I would find the money and hold the thieves accountable. Do you agree, Katharine?"

This time Katharine remained silent. She was starting to fear the worst.

"My position at the bank allowed me many avenues of investigation. I began to believe that two of the bakers were the key to the puzzle. One of them left the bakery six months after the theft, and the other left less than three months later. For many years I looked for possible ways two bakers might use three million dollars. Of course, the money and the ones who took it might be anywhere. In fact, I may have been completely wrong. The two bakers may have been telling the police the truth—that they were innocent of theft. So much searching and uncertainty made me weary, but I continued because of my promise to my brother.

"Now I have found my way to Wildcreek. I told myself that this would be my last search. If I find nothing, then I go home and consider my promise to Pavel fulfilled. He would be happy with my efforts, I know. So, what happened? Just when I have decided to rest from my hunting, I find a trail.

"Greengrocers, I discovered, opened near the time that the money disappeared. The Magpie is another business that opened around that time, but no one at the Magpie looks like the two bakers. Yes, Katharine, I have photographs of the two young bakers. Do you know something? Kelly and Mary look very much like Katharine and Myra of Greengrocers.

"So, now for my big question, Katharine. Why did Myra ask you 'should we move it?' last Saturday at the Magpie? What is it that you might need to move, Katharine?"

Chapter 20

JULY 1, 2015 WEDNESDAY

Deputy Miso got up Wednesday morning and reaffirmed his intention not to check in at the station, or with the sheriff, before driving north to Bullhead Farm to interview Sarah and Rascal. Maybe Thor would be there, too. Sober this time. If all went well, he might even be able to catch Afton Laurie on his way back to Wildcreek. First, though, he had a phone call to make.

"Hi, Buttars? How's the sheriff?"

"Not good, Miso. He wants me to let him know the minute you get here. If I were you, I would find other things to do."

"That's my plan, Buttars. I'm going out to Bullhead Lake to interview some people. Did you open a missing persons case on Katharine Holmeier?"

"Yeah, and I found an open criminal traffic and failure to appear warrant out for her. If we find her, we can arrest her.

"And I called around to try and find Joe Ivan. The clerk at the Bountiful Arms told me that he checked out last Saturday at about

4:30 in the afternoon. He told her that he hadn't been able to find what he was looking for and wanted to know whether there were any small towns nearby that might be a good location for starting a food-related business.

"She got the impression he was headed out of town. She saw a lot of provisions in his trunk like water and toilet paper. Oh, and he asked her for the name of a place to buy roses. She told him the Florabella shop on Railroad Highway.

"Right now I'm leaving to pick up those documents from Myra Briney. Then *I'm* going to find some other things to do, too. Good luck, Miso!"

"Good luck to you, too, Buttars."

It was a fine, cloudless day, a good day to drive up into the forested hills and lakes north of Wildcreek. Miso was feeling optimistic. Hopefully, he could make some real progress in the investigation. Before long, he was singing "Oh What a Beautiful Mornin" in his best Gordon MacRae imitation. *Oklahoma* was one of his mother's favorite musicals.

As he was pulling up to the house at Bullhead Farm, Sarah opened the door and waved him in. "Come on in, Miso. Want some coffee? I have some huckleberry scones, too. We trade spinach for a dozen of Katharine's scones every week because Katharine's scones are the best!" Sarah hadn't noticed that the scones she received on Tuesday afternoon were from Greengrocers' freezer.

"Thanks, Sarah, I think I'll have both." Miso was thinking this really was a beautiful morning. Coffee *and* scones. Miso tried to suppress a small twinge of guilt as he took a second scone. He made a mental note not to tell Sarah that Katharine might not be baking scones next week. No one seemed to know where she was.

"Is Rascal around? I was hoping to talk with him, too."

"Oh, yeah, he's just out in the field cutting and washing the arugula for this afternoon's Farmers' Market. He'll be bringing it back here soon, so I can bag and label it. And Thor might be in his cabin, I'm not sure."

"Okay, Sarah, let's get started. Were you at the Magpie Café on June 26th for the St. John's Wort Celebration?"

"Sure, we were all there, Rascal, Thor and I. We saw you there, too. We had to be there because we produce most of the St. John's Wort sold around Wildcreek."

"Do you remember seeing Julien Pidgeon there? Do you remember hearing anything that he said?"

"Yeah, I saw him. He was giving Helaine a hard time, but I don't remember anything specific. He was really drunk!" Miso remained silent, but Sarah's memory didn't improve.

"Can you think of anyone who might have wanted to kill him?"

Sarah choked on a bit of scone. "Are you serious, Miso? Everyone wanted to kill him!"

Miso continued asking questions but didn't get any more helpful information about who might want to kill Julien Pidgeon. Sarah told him that she and Rascal had been on the phone all Saturday night dealing with her mother's medical issues. Neither of them knew what Thor had been doing.

Finally, contrary to his earlier resolution, Miso revealed that Katharine Holmeier was missing. At that, Sarah's last bit of scone stopped on its way to her open mouth. She didn't seem to be breathing, and Miso worried she might be turning blue soon.

After about fifteen seconds, she recovered and said, "Since when?"

"We think sometime Saturday evening."

"Oh no! Thor will be heartbroken. Rascal and I think he's in love with her. He will be devastated. We don't think Katharine feels the same way, but she's always so nice and kind to him. She has tried to tell him a few times that she's not interested in working on a farm, but Thor keeps trying anyway. Hopefully, he won't give up farming for her. Rascal and I need him to keep working here!"

"How long have you and Rascal owned this place?"

Sarah hesitated, pulled the basket of scones from Miso's reach, and then rather stiffly answered, "Rascal and I bought Bullhead Farm in March of 2008."

"So, for a little more than seven years?" Sarah treated this question as rhetorical and looked at her plate. She pushed around a few crumbs with her right forefinger until Miso asked another question.

"Thor told me that he usually gives you his CSA bag. Did he give you one last Saturday? Was there anything unusual about it?" He wondered why Sarah seemed to be shutting down.

"Probably. I don't really remember. We've been so busy with the St. John's Wort season. Sometimes Thor gives it away, especially if it contains beets or turnips. Rascal hates all vegetables, especially root vegetables—except potatoes, of course. Sometimes, he will eat raw carrots and celery if they come with pizza. Don't even mention lentils…"

Miso needed a way to steer the conversation away from Rascal's eating habits. As if on cue, Rascal came walking through the door with several large bags of leafy greens—spinach, mustard, and arugula.

Sarah called, "Hey, Rascal! Deputy Miso has a few questions for you about Julien Pidgeon."

Rascal made a sour face. "I'm busy, and I don't know anything about that uh... mmm... guy." Rascal did not like Julien Pidgeon.

Sarah tried again, "Why don't we all go outside and talk. I can bag and label while Rascal loads the coolers in the truck. Rascal can talk while he loads."

Miso and Rascal both nodded obediently. They recognized the Fire Lieutenant voice that Sarah had used in her old life before organic farming. She and Rascal had retired from the Hackensack Fire Department in New Jersey and moved to Bullhead Farm to fulfill Sarah's dream to someday live on an organic farm with lots of animals and healthy food.

"So, Rascal, how well did you know Julien?"

Rascal was a little wet, a little dirty, and a little surly. "Not well. Not a fan."

"Why not?"

"Nothing about the man to like".

"When was the last time you saw Julien?"

"Probably at the Magpie on the 26th."

"Do you know whether Julien had any enemies?" Miso was starting to feel trapped inside a TV crime drama dialogue. He couldn't seem to find a hook to pull Rascal out of his shell.

"Just about the whole town."

"Why was that?"

"He was an ass, that's why."

Miso changed the subject. "Did you grow any of the produce in the June 27th CSA bags?"

"No, we don't sell to Myra, except for the St. John's Wort. Thor handles that. We do a little trading with Katharine for bakery goods. Otherwise, we sell our produce at the Farmers' Market and to a few neighbors."

"So, you have nothing to do with Greengrocers?"

"Nope. I just told you that." Rascal pointed toward Thor's cabin, "He's not there." Then Rascal turned away. Conversation over, apparently.

Miso gave up and walked down to the cabin. He wondered what was going on. Sarah and Rascal were usually a lot friendlier. They normally could be counted on to pass along information they gleaned from their customers at the Farmers' Market. Miso, the information gatherer, had been hoping for a better harvest.

The deputy's luck was no better when he got to Thor's cabin. No one answered the door, and Thor's truck was nowhere to be seen. When Miso looked in the side window, all he could see were tools, papers, an old photo album, and a silver dish of some sort on the kitchen table. More of the same littered the counters. Dishes sprouted from the sink haphazardly while the usual assortment of chairs, a couch, a coffee table and a television filled the rest of the room. Other than that room, there were only a bedroom and a bathroom—both seemingly unoccupied. The doors, of course, were locked.

Sarah and Rascal had already left for the Farmers' Market by the time Miso got back to his car. He was almost certain that everyone they met that afternoon would hear Bullhead Farm's version of being questioned about the murder of Julien Pidgeon. Who knows what the story would be like by the time it got around to Thor?

Miso pulled out his phone and tried calling Afton Laurie one more time. He had already left several messages for her but had not heard back. Finally, Afton answered. Not giving her time to think up an excuse, Miso used his deputy voice to tell her, "Hello, Ms. Laurie. This is Deputy Marquart. I'm on the way to your place now. I should get there in about ten. I just have a few questions for you."

Fortunately for Miso, Afton was at home. Miso arrived at Afton's cabin just about on time. He had never been there before. The cedar-sided square house sat on a slight rise above a looping gravel drive. A two-car garage jutted out from one side of the square. A covered porch stretched across the front until it met the side of the garage. Instead of the usual forest green trim around the windows, Miso was surprised to see ornate white shutters and carving above the front door. Matching ornate carving stretched along the eaves above the porch.

As soon as he opened his car door, his ears were assaulted by loud booming barking sounds coming from the house. When the front door opened, chaos ensued. Miso's adrenaline spiked as an enormous Old English Sheepdog came bounding down the porch steps heading straight for him. Abruptly, the dog stopped just two feet away from the toes of his boots but continued to bark. Several stern repetitions of "Quiet, Ralph!" and "It's okay!" brought the din to a halt. After that, Ralph seemed to settle for making only a few intermittent huffing sounds.

Right behind Ralph came a tall, striking woman with auburn hair, a wide smile, and eyes, as he would later conclude, of an indeterminate color. "Hi. You must be Deputy Marquart. I'm Afton Laurie. We've never been properly introduced, I guess."

He said, "Hi. Uh, That's right. I'm Deputy Missoula Marquart. I have a few questions for you... if Ralph doesn't mind..." Ralph stepped forward and nosed Miso's slightly shaking hand with approval.

Introductions completed, Miso went into the house without any trouble. Unfortunately, Afton had no new information for him. In fact, she managed to learn everything *he* knew about Julien Pidgeon's death and Katharine Holmeier's disappearance. Afterward, he found himself wondering why he had shared so much information. He usually didn't talk so much.

Chapter 21

July 2, 2015 Thursday

The following afternoon found Nurse Darling sitting at her usual window table in the Bed Pantry relaxing from a long day at The Clinic. The tiny café got its name, Bed Pantry, from the fact that a mattress store occupied the back portion of the Bed Pantry's space. Only a wall with an arched doorway separated the Bed Pantry from the "best deals on twin, full size, queen & king mattresses & more..."

The owner of the Bed Pantry, Mrs. Lorena Oglethorpe-Day, strenuously denied any relationship to bedpans, but the good citizens of Wildcreek disagreed. Due to its proximity to The Clinic, they commonly referred to the café as the "Bedpan Tree". But never within the hearing of Mrs. Oglethorpe-Day.

Most people assumed that Nurse Darling commandeered the window table in order to watch the goings-on in town. Not so. Nurse Darling liked that particular window table because it allowed her to keep an eye on the people who were buying and testing mattresses. On occasion, she had even been known to follow an unsuspecting attractive customer into the back and attempt to strike up a conversation about mattresses... and other things.

Today, however, she was far too engaged in gossip to even notice the mattresses. Mrs. Moser and Greg Alatza had stopped by for coffee. The subject of Helaine Pia had come up.

"That poor girl found the body. So terrible! Was she really having an affair with him?" Mrs. Moser's question showed that, surprisingly, for once, she didn't know everything about everybody.

"Never!" answered Greg. "She wanted Julien to stay out of the restaurant and do something about his coughing."

"Well, I think she *is* seeing someone," Mrs. Moser said. "A number of people mention it when they come into the shop."

Greg added, "I think Umberto suspects something. Thor told me that Helaine and Umberto had an argument about it in the Magpie the other day. And by 'it' I mean the so-called 'birdwatching'". Greg bobbled his eyebrows up and down.

"What day was that?" Nurse Darling asked, leaning forward.

"The day Julien was killed." Greg was pleased with the timing of his delivery.

They all looked at each other, wide-eyed, for a silent moment.

"Horrible man, that useless, thieving you-know-what," mumbled Mrs. Moser. "I must get back to the shop—the pre-July 4th sale tomorrow always brings in a crowd."

"That's right! I've got to go finish my yard sale map for Saturday—the competition is going to get nasty this year. It's war!" Greg Alatza lived for yard sales. His house was full of the "treasures" he had collected over the years.

"Ladies, I must leave. 'I'm a thinkin' it's time to go to the mattresses!'" And, with that quote from *The Godfather* and a wink, he went through the arch and into the mattress store, but only to go out the back door and into the alley where his car was parked.

Chapter 22

JULY 3, 2015 FRIDAY

It was the day before July 4th and the Magpie was packed. Because July 4th was on a Saturday, Friday was the official day off work. Both locals and visitors were celebrating the beginning of a three-day weekend. Helaine was sitting at a table on the back patio taking a well-earned mid-afternoon break. Her legs ached and sweat was collecting along her hairline. She was so tired, in fact, that she almost didn't answer her cell phone when it rang. But she did.

"What are you saying? Slow down! I'm at work. I really can't talk right now." Helaine didn't want to talk just then. She was having trouble convincing Umberto that she wasn't having an affair. Town gossip, she was beginning to suspect, was not on her side.

"I don't think Umberto will like my leaving," Helaine said in a low voice. After a moment's pause, however, her prick of conscience vanished. Umberto should trust her. "Are you sure you need to meet now? I really don't need any more trouble..."

"Okay, I'll be there as soon as I can. Promise you'll wait for me?

Moments later Ben came out onto the patio. Before her son could say anything, Helaine said, "Ben, something has come up, and I have to go. Tell your father that I will be gone for a few hours only. I know it's busy, but this is important!" Helaine rushed into the bar, grabbed her purse and was gone.

Ben was troubled by his mother's rapid exit. He didn't know what to do. He'd overheard only part of her conversation on the patio. He thought he'd heard her say "... I don't think Umberto will like my leaving... are you sure ... I... really need ... you... promise you'll wait for me..."

Ben didn't know what to tell his dad. If he told his dad that his mom rushed out to meet someone, his dad would be livid. Ben was seriously thinking about cleaning the inside of the dumpster until his mom returned. His dad would never look for him there. Fortunately, however, the gods were about to spare young Ben.

Right on cue, Deputy Miso walked into the Magpie. He announced that he wanted to interview nearly everyone. So, nearly everyone rushed to the bar to make it harder for Miso to corner them alone. For the next two hours, Umberto and Ben were far too busy to discuss Helaine's whereabouts.

Chapter 23

JULY 4, 2015 SATURDAY

Joe Ivan was not surprised to find no one home at Katharine and Myra's house on the night of July 4th. After all, he knew that Katharine wouldn't be there. And, according to Katharine, July 4th was a big holiday in Thompson Park—the location of the Farmers' Market on Saturdays, except for this particular Saturday—with fireworks going off well past midnight. On the other hand, he was surprised to find the front door unlocked. Myra, he thought, should be a lot more careful.

So far, Joe had not been able to get any information about the stolen money from Katharine. She had been his unwilling housemate for a week. He had expected Katharine to be terrified and tell him everything right away. The whole thing was going wrong. Now he was desperate. His brother Pavel would have hurt Katharine. Joe couldn't do that. He needed a plan. Especially one that would end with Katharine liking him—or at least not hating him.

Joe spent over an hour searching the house carefully for anything that might be a clue to the location of the money. Unfortunately, all he managed to do was find an extremely offended cat. He started to leave and then thought, *What if Katharine cares about the cat? What if she loves the cat?*

Joe turned around and spent another hour chasing and containing the fierce and uncooperative miniature tiger, who, instead of a warning label, was wearing a collar embroidered with the deceptively friendly name "Cat".

Completely exhausted and bleeding from a large number of scratches, Joe left the house and locked the door behind him. He told Cat, "We are going to see Katharine now, and I am going to tell her that she has one week to tell me where the money is, or I will kill you!" Joe couldn't believe he said that—even to an ill-tempered cat.

Chapter 24

July 5, 2015 Sunday

On Sunday morning Afton woke early, largely due to the violent rocking of the mattress on her left side. Ralph wanted breakfast. Reluctantly, she got out of bed, endured more nose prodding about the knees, and made her way to the kitchen where she filled Ralph's dish and relieved his anxiety about possibly starving to death.

While he was eating, she weighed herself, was not pleased, and decided against going to The Shortlist for breakfast. Instead, she dressed, took Ralph out to the end of the lane and back, made a pot of coffee, and settled down to read the online version of the *Wildcreek Wing*.

"Hey, Ralph, there's a new article about the man who died a couple of weeks ago. The *Wing* says that he died as a result of eating two different poisonous plants—death camas and low larkspur. What is death camas? I've never heard of it. I'm almost sure they didn't have anything like that in Brewster County."

"Uh oh... the *Wing* also says that remnants of both plants were found in Julien Pidgeon's CSA bag. That must be his bag from Greengrocers! Cooked parts of the plants were found in his leftover pesto. The article goes on to warn that death camas, when not flowering, can look a lot like green garlic or spring onions. Low Larkspur can resemble parsley.

"Ralph, I ate some of the green garlic from my CSA bag a few days ago. Remember when I said I felt a little sick but thought it was due to the Brunswickian Stew from The Shortlist?" Ralph seemed uninterested in Afton's thoughts on pesto, green garlic or CSA bags, but his ears perked up at the mention of stew.

"Ralph, we still have some of that green garlic in the refrigerator!" Afton got up quickly and opened the refrigerator door. Ralph managed to get his head into the open space in front of her and began inspecting the refrigerator shelves for something to eat. Not finding anything he wanted, Ralph padded over to the sliding glass doors to look out for trespassing quail.

Afton stayed in the kitchen and began pulling the remaining green garlic out of the crisper bin and bagging it. She would take it to Myra for inspection later. She didn't believe for a minute that Myra, an expert on plants, could mistake a poisonous plant for a benign one. And she needed to ask Myra about the puffballs.

Breakfast accomplished and Ralph at peace, Afton was finally able to go back to reading the article about Julien Pidgeon's death. Greengrocers was identified as the source of the CSA bag containing the death camas and low larkspur. Were these local plants? The article said no more about what the plants looked like or where they were found, so Afton turned to the internet.

First, she searched "death camas". Apparently, death camas "looks like green garlic or spring onions." *Zigadenus venenosus*, or *Toxicoscordion venenosum,* otherwise known as meadow death camas, white camas, or poison onion, grew in some parts of western North America and might easily be confused with edible wild onions. All parts of the plant were highly toxic and potentially fatal. The plant contained the neurotoxic steroidal alkaloid, zygacine, and "could remain toxic in dried form for at least 20 years."

"Ralph, listen to this!" Afton read to him from a website, "'Especially interesting to people living along the route of Lewis and Clark, death camas may have been the cause of the mysterious illnesses that troubled the expedition. According to food historian, Elaine Nelson McIntosh, food was scarce in 1805, and the explorers were desperate for provisions. They managed to find fish and some bulbs of a plant they believed was blue onion. Blue onions were wild edible plants that looked like death camas but had blue flowers instead of white flowers. Unfortunately, at that time of year, the plants were not blooming. After eating the bulbs, the group became terribly ill for weeks. They had to eat their *dogs* to survive!'"

Ralph, predictably alarmed, immediately rolled over onto his back and tried to look too cute to be eaten.

Afton began a new search. Low larkspur was a member of the buttercup family Ranunculaceae, genus *Delphinium*. It commonly grew in the same places as death camas and, when not in bloom, the lower leaves looked a little like flat parsley. The entirety of all delphiniums, including low larkspur, were toxic to humans. The main toxins in low larkspur included methyllycaconitine and nudicauline.

As she continued to browse, she came across an article from 2003 that indicated that low larkspur enhanced the poisonous effect of death camas. However, articles written ten years later contradicted that theory. Nonetheless, both plants, together or separately, could cause serious harm to people.

She had spent too much time reading about poisons. Ralph, who was now curled up on his enormous dog cushion with a sandal between his paws, was looking dangerously bored. She feared that the sandal might not be enough to keep him out of trouble.

"Ralph! Let's go outside! Let's go for a walk down the creek!" Those were the magic words. Both she and Ralph were soon hiking down the wild edges of their favorite place.

Littlecatch Creek ran south along the western boundary of her property on its way to Lake Pend Oreille. The inhabitants of this slow-moving, pool-filled creek included not only turtles, like painted turtles, but also the spawn of bull trout and kokanee salmon, wood frogs, and common garter snakes.

She had only seen a wood frog once, but she loved how it adapted to the extreme cold of North Idaho winters. Wood frogs froze solid! Well, almost. The sugars in their blood settled in the heart, brain, liver, and other organs and acted like anti-freeze. In the spring, the frosty little frog-cubes thawed out and went about their froggy business.

Chapter 25

JULY 5, 2015 SUNDAY

While Afton was dealing with the threat posed by a bored Old English Sheepdog, Joe Ivan was dealing with a different sort of threat—his threat to kill Katharine's cat in one week if she continued to refuse to tell him the location of the money. The situation was complicated by the fact that he was falling in love with Katharine, and he was beginning to like her cat.

Joe sat outside the hunter's cabin in his car talking to himself and Cat. "Why is everything going wrong? The plan was simple. Find the two women who took the money. Take one of them and scare her into telling me where it is. Go get it. Leave and start a new life. But, little Koshka, after threatening to kill you, I'm still no closer to finding the money. Why is your mistress so stubborn?" Koshka had no answers for him.

Suddenly, an idea came to him. "I'll make a grand dinner for her tomorrow—salmon mousse, beef stroganoff, a spicy salad and a crisp rosé wine. Chocolate ice cream for dessert. I like this idea. When

Katharine is feeling happy and safe, I will tell her more about Pavel and the promise I made to him.

"I know that after she hears this sad story, she will feel terribly sorry for me and tell me where the money is hidden. Then I will let her go and disappear." But, could he really let her go? He hoped and hoped his plan would work. It was time to launch Project Dinner!

"Katharine! Wake up!" Joe gently pulled Katharine's hand. She had been sleeping a lot lately, and he was worried about her. "I think you need some good food to help you decide the right thing to do. I am going to make you good food. You are going to feel better and understand why you must tell me about the money.

"You have seven days until next Sunday, the deadline. After you tell me what I need to know, you will be happy and your little koshka can go home." Katharine looked up into his eyes, and much to his surprise, she smiled a very small, very wise smile. But she didn't tell him anything. She went back to sleep.

Joe Ivan panicked. Why had he taken the cat? He only had a week to figure something out.

Chapter 26

JULY 6, 2015 MONDAY

Monday morning at the WPD headquarters started off with more than the usual pandemonium. Sheriff Cannon was looking out the window and shouting into his cell phone, "Buttars! Where *are* you? You need to get in here right away. Have you seen this effing excuse for a newspaper? No wonder everyone calls it *The Wingding*!"

Sheriff Cannon swished a handful of newsprint back and forth in front of his cell phone as if it were visible to the person on the other end of the call. "Yes, Buttars, I damn well know there's a rule about not saying 'effing' at work," the sheriff roared. "But that's Fonda Dan's rule, not mine. I'm suspending it!" Fonda Dan was the Chief Deputy *and* the sheriff's formidable wife of 40 years.

"Actually, Sheriff, I'm right over here. Just turn around." Deputy Buttars had been sitting at his desk across from the sheriff for at least half an hour—a delightfully peaceful half hour until the sheriff discovered him.

Buttars wasn't surprised that the Monday morning story in the *Wildcreek Wing* had enraged the sheriff. Someone had leaked the story about the forensic pathologist's preliminary findings—including the details about the pesto, the CSA bag, and the lack of any fingerprints on the wine bottle and the unwashed dishes. The crime scene had been wiped. And, unfortunately for Myra Briney, Greengrocers was mentioned as the source of the CSA bag in question.

Of course, Sheriff Cannon would be seeking revenge. As everyone at WPD knew, only the sheriff was allowed to leak information—knowingly or unknowingly. Someone had preempted him, and he was furious. Worst of all, the leaked information happened to be true and was nothing like the information the sheriff had intended to leak. In the sheriff's eyes, honest dealing with the press would set a terrible precedent. He believed that transparency was unpatriotic, and moreover, treasonous.

While the sheriff was storming around in his office, Myra Briney was trying to get Greengrocers ready to open for the day. She wasn't making much progress. Mostly she was just moving around and crying in different parts of the store. The *Wildcreek Wing* had all but accused her of poisoning Julien Pidgeon. When she wasn't crying, she was looking out of the streetside window in nervous terror. Deputy Miso wanted to come by and ask more questions. He would arrive any minute.

Two minutes later, Deputy Miso did, in fact, arrive but not alone. He parked the sheriff's SUV right in front of the store for all to see. He and two other deputies walked to the door. Myra opened it and let them in. She was shaking.

"Myra, I've got a warrant to search the store. While Sam and Dave are searching, I'd like to talk with you about a few things. Okay?"

Myra blurted out, "Miso, I didn't put anything but healthy food in those CSA bags, I swear!"

"Okay, okay, Myra. Do you always pack the CSA bags? Does Katharine ever do it?"

"Yes, I always do it. And I make the tags and write any recipes that are included. Katharine never touches them. She handles the bakery."

"Did you pack the CSA bags for Saturday the 27th?"

"Yes, early that morning before we opened. There was *no* death camas *or* parsley *or* low larkspur in any of the CSA bags!" Myra had answered the question a little too loudly. The deputies stopped rooting around behind the counter and looked to see whether Miso needed assistance. Miso waved them back.

"Myra, I've got a tag from Julien's bag that lists parsley."

"There was *no* parsley, Miso. There was *no* parsley anywhere. The worms ate it all. Nobody's got parsley. I just forgot to cross the word 'parsley' off the tag. Julien did not get parsley from me. Go to Safeway and ask the produce manager about parsley. There is no local organic parsley in Wildcreek. None, nada, zip—no parsley!" Deputy Miso made a note on his pad: *DO NOT MENTION PARSLEY TO MYRA EVER AGAIN!*

"Okay, moving on. Are you familiar with death camas or low larkspur?"

Myra nodded. "Of course. Both those plants grow wild in the fields and meadows around here. They can make cattle and sheep sick if they eat too much. The County Extension Service puts on a class every year to teach people about the local poisonous plants and noxious weeds. You should go. Sometimes I help with the program. I would never mistake death camas or low larkspur for food!"

"How well did you know Julien Pidgeon?"

The question surprised Myra. She wasn't sure she should tell Miso that she despised Julien. She definitely wasn't going to tell him the reason for her loathing. "He was a customer, he was rude, and he stole things. That's all. I didn't like him, but I wouldn't kill him just for being obnoxious. I don't think anybody really liked him. He stole things from other people, too."

"Did Katharine have a problem with Julien?"

Myra had been wondering, herself, if Katharine's disappearance could have had something to do with Julien's death. She didn't believe Katharine would do something like that, but Julien might have pushed her too far. She wished she knew what happened to Katharine. Was she safe and just hiding or was she in danger or worse? Finally, Myra replied, "Not really. Julien made unwelcome sexual comments to her, but she just ignored them."

"Have you seen or heard from Katharine since you left her at Greengrocers on Saturday, June 27th?"

"No, nothing." Miso told Myra that there was an outstanding criminal traffic warrant for Katharine.

"Miso, you don't really think that committing a criminal traffic violation makes her a suspect in a murder!"

"No, Myra, but it might help me find her. I might be able to change the warrant to a national warrant. Let me know immediately if you hear from her."

The *Wildcreek Wing* had already written that the sheriff's office was looking for Katharine in connection with Julien Pidgeon's murder. That wasn't true when the story was published, but Miso thought it possible now.

"Who owns Greengrocers?"

"I do. Katharine works in the bakery." Myra did not want to lie. Katharine and Efrain were silent partners—well, more like secret partners. The financial details of Greengrocers were complex and not something Myra wanted to share.

"Well, I would like to see copies of your accounts, sales and purchases for the last year, correspondence, and lists of all the suppliers to the store. And any records related to the opening of Greengrocers."

"That's a lot, Miso! I'll do my best. Katharine keeps some of that information, but I'll try to get you what I have by tomorrow."

"We could start with your store computer. I could get a warrant, but you would have to close until I return with it."

"No problem, Miso. I have nothing to hide." Actually, she did. Myra realized that she needed to call Efrain as soon as possible.

"Do you grow any of the CSA produce yourself?"

"Like I told you last Tuesday, I have a garden behind the store. I sometimes add herbs or flowers to the bags." She had seen the deputies go out the back door. They were probably taking samples of plants. "But I did *not* add any..."

"I know, Myra, you did not add any parsley." Myra started crying again. Miso thought this was probably a good time to leave.

As soon as Miso and the other deputies were gone, Myra called Efrain. "I had nothing to do with Julien's death! Why would I do something like that and draw attention to myself and Katharine? What if they start asking questions about where I got the money to open the store?"

When Myra slowed to take a ragged breath, he interrupted, "Calm down, Myra. We've all been extremely careful. He won't find anything unusual in any of your records. That's what you hired me for. Just get as many of the things he asked for that you can find and then let me check them tomorrow before you hand them over. He's looking for a motive for murdering Julien. That's all. I know you didn't kill anyone. Keep waiting and don't do anything rash—like packing a bag and rushing off to Brazil. Okay?"

Efrain intended that last comment to lighten things up, but when Myra didn't respond, he got the feeling that she might have already started packing.

"Okay, Efrain. I'm just so scared and worried about Katharine. But I'll wait."

"And one more thing, Myra. Call Miso tomorrow and tell him he'll need a warrant for Katharine's personal property. Say that you can't give him Katharine's personal records or possessions without it."

"But that information may help Miso find her! What if she's hurt or in danger!"

"Myra, she may not want to be found. Or possibly arrested. We don't know. She hated Julien, we both know that."

"Katharine despised Julien but wouldn't kill him! Well—maybe in self-defense. Anyone can do that, right?"

Efrain chose not to explain how to kill someone in self-defense. "Katharine may turn up. Let's give her a little bit longer. She may try to contact you. If she does, call me right away."

"Efrain, I moved the money. I moved it the Monday morning after Katharine disappeared. I thought Julien might have taken her. Then I learned that he had been murdered. Oh, I wish so much that Katharine and I had never seen that money."

"Myra, please do not, I repeat, do not go anywhere near your new hiding place. And don't tell anyone, not even me, where it is."

"But now Katharine won't be able to find it if she needs it!"

Efrain spoke soothingly and sincerely. "But she can find *you*, Myra. And she can find me. I'll do my best to help her. You know that. I want to help you both."

Efrain then tried to change the subject. "Myra, I found out that Thor bought Rascal's farm six months ago. The Big House still belongs to Rascal and Sarah, but the farm, cabin, and all the other outbuildings belong to Thor. And there's another odd provision. If Thor dies, the farm transfers back to Rascal and Sarah unless both predecease him. So, do you still want me to approach Thor about buying the farm? I doubt if he wants to sell it. And we know that Katharine would not want to buy it."

Myra made a few sounds of surprise but then resumed listing her fears about Miso's investigation. "Miso is going to ask about the five thousand dollars." Myra would not be diverted from her panic over being arrested. "I gave Julien five thousand dollars from the CSA account to placate him even though I was sure he didn't really know anything."

Efrain winced and was glad that Myra couldn't see him. "I told you not to make any unusual expenditures. They will create questions."

"I listed it as a loan to the store from the CSA account."

"Not good, Myra. By giving him money, you probably just confirmed to Julien that you *did* have money from somewhere. And apparently it didn't work. He wasn't placated. I've heard from other people that Julien made cryptic comments at the store on the day he was murdered. If I've heard those rumors, Miso is going to hear them at some point. too."

"Oh my God, Efrain, am I going to be arrested?" Myra sounded like she was hyperventilating and choking on tears.

"Breathe deeply and count to ten." Efrain didn't know what else to say. After a few moments he continued, "I have an idea. Why don't you call Afton Laurie for help? That's who I call when I need help. A long time ago, she once got me through a situation a little like this. It turned out I wasn't the killer." Efrain's joke fell flat. "Oh, and if she asks about 'the money' just tell her to call me, okay?" Myra didn't respond. Perhaps he should have advised Myra not to talk to Miso at all.

"Myra, I know you didn't kill Julien, and Afton will know it, too. She'll be happy to talk with you." Efrain used his most calming tones trying to get Myra to feel better. Privately, Efrain was worried. He knew that Afton Laurie would not be pleased about getting embroiled in another sensational murder controversy. Not pleased at all.

Chapter 27

July 6, 2015 Monday

As it turned out, Myra didn't have to call Afton after all. Afton, not having the least idea that Efrain had enlisted her to save Myra, had decided to make a quick trip to Greengrocers for more almond butter and to try to find out if her green garlic—she hoped it was green garlic—was okay to eat.

Afton grabbed the bag containing the green garlic out of the refrigerator, threw a dog treat across the room, and then slipped out the door to the garage before Ralph could retrieve the treat and get back. She was surprised the trick worked. Ralph was usually way ahead of her. He *really* liked to ride in the minivan.

As she drove along the east side of Little Catch Creek down toward Wildcreek, she felt again the welcome solitude of the large mountain lake ahead and the peace that her new life had brought to her. She prayed it would continue forever.

At Greengrocers, the sign on the window said "Closed". Afton turned to go back to her car but then thought she heard faint sounds of crying. The muted little sobs led her to the garden behind the store. There, she found Myra sitting in a blue Adirondack chair crying into a kitchen apron that looked like one of Katharine's. Afton felt like an intruder. She knew Myra mostly from words exchanged on occasion at the cash register, and she told herself that Myra might not appreciate a violation of her private sorrow right then. Afton turned around to leave.

Almost immediately her conscience halted her retreat. She realized that rather than comforting Myra, her first instinct had been to quietly turn around, go home, and pretend that she hadn't seen Myra's distress. She was embarrassed to admit that her rule about not getting involved in the problems of other people was turning her into someone she didn't like. Maybe she had done her job of staying out of other people's business *too* well. She felt lonely and selfish. So, she turned back around.

Myra looked up and saw Afton standing a few yards away with green garlic hanging out of a polypropylene grocery bag. She immediately burst into a torrent of tears. Afton stood where she was, paralyzed, wondering what she had done to cause this new outpouring of grief. Myra was staring at the bag. The bag was decorated with various kinds of sushi on a bright blue background. Could Myra be having problems with sushi? What could be so disturbing about the bag?

Afton's questions were answered definitively when Myra jumped up and pulled the green garlic out of Afton's bag. "These grow right here in my own garden. It's garlic—not poison! If you let them continue to grow, you get heads of garlic at the bottom and spirally things at the top called scapes." Myra bit down on one of the bulbs, roots and all.

Afton began to feel somewhat alarmed. Perhaps a few soothing words would not be enough. But before Afton could think of something to say, Myra broke down again. "Oh, Afton," she cried, "Miso wants to arrest me! He thinks I killed Julien Pidgeon. I didn't! Jail is super toxic. It will be the end of me! I will die in jail!"

Afton tried to smile and spoke reassuringly. "Miso is not a bad guy, Myra. Really. I'm sure that Miso will try to do the right thing. But sheriff? I'm not so sure about him. Luckily, Miso seems to be able to work around Sheriff Cannon most of the time. At least that's what I've heard."

Myra, blowing her nose, interrupted. She was blinking back tears and getting shriller by the minute. "It couldn't have been me. I left the parsley out of the bags because I didn't have any, and no one got anything in their bags like parsley from me." Myra kicked at a butterfly as it fluttered past and, as a result, fell backward into the dill section of her garden.

"There was a parsley shortage everywhere," she went on. "It wasn't the black swallowtails... the parsley worms ate it all... the unenlightened worms... the hungry caterpillars...the Pap pillow poly jeans!" The dill fronds in Myra's mouth seemed to be interfering with her speech.

"What? Who is Polly Jeanes? Is she related to Mitchell?" Afton was lost after this turn in the conversation and googled Myra's words on her phone. Maybe she should leave. There didn't seem to be anything she could do.

"The tag said parsley but there wasn't any parsley!" A fresh flood of tears and garden soil were making tracks down Myra's face.

"Did you tell Miso this?" Afton was trying to be helpful.

"No, not about the butterflies. Do you think that would convince him I'm innocent? I saw him write something about parsley in his notes, though—in capital letters!"

Myra began to sob again. Afton could only imagine what kind of notes were in Miso's little book after his interview with Myra.

"The bags are picked up by CSA members on an honor system. No one complained about those bags! People have to pick up their bags by noon or Davina gets them. Ask Davina. She's still alive. And *she* got two bags! One for herself and one that didn't have a tag!

"Everyone but Julien is still alive! Please, Afton! Please help me! Efrain said you had a gift for getting to the bottom of things. You have to find out what happened. For me and for Katharine. I can't go to jail!"

"What's that about Katharine?" Afton asked.

"Katharine's cat is missing! And Katharine is missing, too. And Miso wants all her records. I haven't seen her since I left the store on Saturday." More crying ensued.

Afton's instincts were telling her that Myra did not kill Julien, but she did *not* want to get entangled too deeply in this very messy situation. It seemed like Myra was afraid of a lot more than the possibility of being arrested for Julien's murder. What was Efrain thinking?

"Myra, as far as I can tell from the *Wildcreek Wing* and what you've told me, there doesn't seem to be enough evidence to arrest you or Katharine for Julien's murder. Just follow Efrain's advice you'll be fine." Afton wasn't sure that Myra had heard any of this and wasn't sure, herself, that anything at all would be fine.

"But Efrain told me to follow *your* advice."

Afton tried again and mumbled, "There's really nothing I can do" and "Sorry" and "Everything will work out, everything will be okay".

Afton looked at Myra and felt the emotional tug that always pre-ceded a head-long leap into a morass of murder drama. She struggled to resist. Something about the Julien Pidgeon killing, though, kept drawing her in. The possibility of justice going astray under the direction of Sheriff Cannon made her want to make that leap.

Should she allow the peaceful, anonymous life that she had worked so hard to find be destroyed? *If my gifts can help Myra but I choose not to use them, will her fate be my fault? Can I live with that?*

She would need to go home, hide out, and take a long while to consider breaking the promises she had made to herself. Or, as her fears began taking over her thoughts, should she move to Anchorage and settle down instead? Anchorage might not be far enough.

Just then, the Google result on her phone popped up. *Papilio polyxenes*—Pap pillow poly jeans—that was the name of the parsley-eating caterpillar and its resultant butterfly. Of all things, *P.p.* happened to be the state butterfly of New Jersey.

Chapter 28

JULY 12, 2015 SUNDAY

While Afton had been spending the entire week struggling with how she wanted to live her life and not finding an answer, Joe Ivan had been struggling with his self-imposed deadline problem.

Joe rose early that Sunday morning, exactly one week after announcing the grim possible future of Katharine's cat. He didn't wake up exactly; he simply decided to get out of bed after not sleeping for the last six hours. He walked over to the room where Katharine was still sleeping.

He could not believe that he was capable of holding someone captive. Especially someone so beautiful and good as Katharine. He never intended it. He never once thought about what to do if Katharine refused to cooperate. Now the day had come to deal with his threat to kill her cat. He knew he could never do such a thing. So, he decided to make breakfast. He optimistically told Koshka, "A good meal can solve any problem!"

"What are you singing, Joe? Do I smell ham and eggs?" Katharine was awake.

"Yes, Katharine, I am going to bring you a surprise breakfast. Just like my father made for me. Fried eggs with bright yellow unbroken yolks, ham slices, and blini filled with lemon curd and dusted with powdered sugar, and strong coffee sipped through sugar cubes. And we will toast the black bread you made! You will love this just like I do!" Joe had never sounded happier.

Ten minutes later, he walked into her room with a pot of hot steaming coffee, two large mugs, and a blue-and-gold china bowl containing sugar cubes. While Joe left to get the rest of the breakfast ready, Katharine washed in the tiny bathroom and put on the clean clothes he had left for her. When she came out, she found not only two plates, platters really, filled with hot, fried, buttery food, but also flowers hand-picked from the surrounding forest.

While they ate, Joe told Katharine a little more about his life in Russia. "I lived in a small village with my parents and my older brother, Pavel. I studied English and mathematics and won prizes at my school. When we immigrated to Seattle, I was able to start the tenth grade. My Russian name is Ruslan Igorevich Ivanov, but now I use Joe Ivan.

"My brother, unfortunately, did not do well. Right away he started hanging out with gang members. Some of them were from Russia, too. I think that learning English was too hard for him, and he could not find work. Being in a gang was easier for him. Pavel did not want to leave Russia.

"I tried to help him, Katharine, but his heart was broken. He did not want to be happy. He was just angry all the time. He wanted to hurt himself and everything in the new place that my mother and father chose for him to live. I guess I am still trying to help him.

"He was arrested and sent to prison along with the other gang members for stealing the money. He was bitter because someone else stole the money from them, but they were the ones who suffered punishment. Whenever I visited him, he begged me to find the money and get vengeance. He blamed the 'thieves' who took his money for his imprisonment and for his sickness from his prison-acquired Hepatitis C.

"I know it doesn't make sense because he is dead now, but the money and revenge were all he wanted. He made me think that I wanted those things, too. So, Katharine, today is the day you will tell me where the money is, or I must kill Koshka the cat." Joe looked like he was ready to cry.

"Please don't kill Cat, Joe."

How could the little tiger's name be Cat? Joe almost smiled. Katharine was also called Kat by many of her friends. He thought he might like to call her Kat, too.

Pushing these tender musings aside, Joe adopted his sternest expression and shouted, "This is your last chance to tell me!" Katharine placed her elbows on the table and calmly rested her chin on her hands. She looked serious and a little sad but not frightened. She remained silent.

As soon as Joe realized that Katharine was not going to budge, he swept everything off the table into a large plastic dish pan and stormed out of the room. He tried to look like he was leaving to carry out his threat, but he suspected Katharine wasn't fooled. Now, what was he going to do? Katharine wasn't even crying or pleading with him not to hurt her cat. He simply didn't understand her. In truth, he really didn't understand himself, either.

Chapter 29

JULY 12, 2015 SUNDAY

Several hours passed before Joe had the courage to go back into Katharine's room. "Katharine, you are very fortunate. Koshka is missing. I have looked everywhere." In fact, Cat was in Joe's bedroom, sleeping on Joe's pillow.

Katharine looked delighted. "Ruslan, I knew that you would never hurt Cat." She wasn't sure why she used his birth name, but it just seemed right. After hearing him tell his story, he became a new person to her, Ruslan, not Joe Ivan. He became a real person she could love. However, Cat still came first.

"I knew that you would never hurt me or Cat. You have a good heart, and you are nothing like Pavel. He chose his life. He took a path that you would never take. You did all you could, but some people cannot be saved.

"Please, stop trying to frighten me, you're not any good at it, and I will tell you everything." Ruslan half-smiled in relief and nodded.

"You were right, Ruslan, Myra and I *did* work in the bakery in Seattle, and we *did* take the money. So, we are criminals, too. We brought it to Wildcreek, used some of it to open Greengrocers, and hid the rest of it in the mountains. A lot of the money still remains.

"I can't give you any of the details because I don't want anyone else to be involved, but I can tell you where the money is. All I ask is that you leave some of it for Myra and me to relocate somewhere else. The money was never ours, and you are welcome to it. We will never say anything. After all, we would be in as much trouble as you. Well, not quite as much trouble, maybe."

"Alright, Katharine. I will trust you. Draw me a map and I will bring the money back here. Then I will free you."

Joe packed a shovel and some plastic bags and left. Why did he trust her? Every minute that he was on the road he expected to hear a howling siren and see flashing red and blue lights lighting up the interior of his car. However, no such thing occurred, and he returned safely to the cabin. Unfortunately, he returned without the money.

"Katharine, there was no money! No money!"

The blood drained from Katharine's face. She looked frantically around the room until she found Cat. Then, she ran over to the corner, scooped the alarmed animal up off the floor, and sprinted into the bathroom. The sound of the bathroom door closing and locking was deafening in the quiet woodland cabin.

"I didn't know, Ruslan. You have to believe me, I didn't know!"

"Katharine, did you lie to me? I trusted you. You must tell me the truth! I found the place, but it was empty." Joe was really confused at this point. Katharine gained nothing by sending him on a wild goose chase. Why did she risk angering him? And why did she grab little Koshka? Did she really think that he would hurt her cat? That last idea nearly brought him to tears.

"Katharine," he shouted through the door, "Please tell me what this is about!"

Katharine heard the desperation in his voice and opened the bathroom door. She said, "Ruslan, let's sit down at the table. I know we can figure this out together."

After a few minutes, when they had all calmed down, including Koshka/Cat, the solution to the mystery of the missing money became obvious.

"Ruslan, Myra must have moved the money!" Katharine remembered the lunch conversation with Myra at the Magpie.

Joe remembered hearing Myra talking about moving "it". He did *not* mention to Katharine that he had been eavesdropping.

Over the next hour, they worked together to plan the retrieval of the money and the safety of all involved.

"Someone has to communicate with Myra, of course, and that person has to be you, Ruslan. I do not want to be found just yet. I think that maybe the sheriff might want to arrest me. There are some questions that I do not want to answer right now. I don't want to tell the sheriff where I've been since the night Julien died. And, also, I think there might be a traffic warrant out for me.

"But how should we contact her, Kat?"

"Well, communicating with Myra will be tricky. Maybe we should send a note to Myra tomorrow saying that I am fine, that I did not kill Julien Pidgeon, and that she should trust you. And that we love each other." Joe Ivan liked the idea so far, especially the last bit.

"The note would also say that we three should all share the money equally. You will show Myra the note but not give it to her. You will destroy it later or possibly give it to Efrain. He should then tell Myra that I was afraid to come home because I might be suspected of the murder and arrested for that or for my warrant. You will not reveal my current location until it is safe for me to go back to Wildcreek. Let's be hopeful that Myra will agree and tell you the new hiding place of the money. We can keep it safe if anything happens to her. The *Wildcreek Wing* made it clear that Myra is also under suspicion."

Joe and Katharine knew their plan was hardly brilliant, but they were optimistic. Unfortunately for all of them, however, the well-intentioned plan would never be tested. Myra would not be available to anyone the next day.

Chapter 30

JULY 13, 2015 MONDAY

The next day, Monday, was bright and a little cool for July. Greengrocers opened on time despite the difficulties arising from Katharine's absence. Mrs. Moser had already dropped off a few dozen apricot dumplings, *marillenknödel*, and Davina had supplied gluten-free black bean brownies.

"Well, that should be enough until the Krillo Bakery brings in reinforcements," Myra smiled at Mrs. Moser. "No one would drive all the way to Krillo or wait for the ferry just for coffee and pastry, so this new arrangement should suit Wildcreekers, Greengrocers, and the Krillo Bakery perfectly."

No customers had arrived yet, but it seemed to Myra that things at Greengrocers were turning around. Maybe she'd call Efrain and check if he could meet her for lunch.

Then she saw Deputy Miso drive up and park his car outside. She went out to meet him, and everything in her life changed.

A minute later, the entirety of central Wildcreek came to a stop for a moment in response to the loud rhythmic wailing coming from the sidewalk outside Greengrocers. Myra Briney had just been arrested for the murder of Julien Pidgeon, and she was frightened to death at the prospect of going to jail.

Chapter 31

July 14, 2015 Tuesday

The next morning, Tuesday, Davina used the law office intercom to tell Efrain that Sgt. Drucilla Skew was on the line. While keeping Sgt. Skew on hold, Davina offered him some unsolicited advice, "Morris insists that you *not* talk to that shrew, Skew. He says that she's a spy for the sheriff. And she lies."

Efrain rolled his eyes. Davina, or maybe Morris, had been at odds with Sgt. Skew since the day that Sgt. Skew cited Davina for creating a public nuisance.

"You *know* she lies, Efrain! How could anyone know that walking more than six ducks across the street in midday traffic was a public nuisance? The ducks were all on leashes, and the only person who complained was Barbara Rampart, that loony Wildlife Conservation Officer who everyone knows is a public nuisance herself—at least according to Morris."

Efrain was quick to respond. "Aside from the facts that Barbara Rampart is highly regarded in Wildcreek, that the ducks were not on leashes, and that Morris can be a terrible liar himself on occasion, I know that the good Sergeant Skew only calls when there is trouble. Trouble usually means possible bad press for the sheriff. Put her through!"

Communications Sergeant Drucilla Skew was responsible for all the sheriff's writing or drafting needs. Years ago, an anonymous attorney serving the Wildcreek Town Council once told Efrain that the sheriff's poor spelling skills and even worse legal judgment had resulted in a Town policy to bar the sheriff from using the internet, mail, or internal memoranda without prior review by a literate adult.

Sgt. Drucilla, to her dismay, was appointed to the position of WPD's Literate Adult. She also handled public relations matters and served as an on-call distractor for Brodie Buttars whenever the sheriff started to go off the rails. Hence, the button with her name on it in Brodie's drawer.

After Davina reluctantly transferred the call, Sergeant Skew began, "Efrain, did you know that Myra Briney was arrested yesterday for the murder of Julien Pidgeon?"

Efrain did *not* know and had been wondering why Myra hadn't returned any of his calls.

"Myra has been in our jail since the arrest. Do you represent her?"

"Yes, I *do* represent her and have been trying to reach her. There hasn't been anything in the *Wing,* and she hasn't called.

"Well, she's not going to be calling anybody, is she?"

"Why not?" Efrain asked, not really understanding the question.

"I'm sorry to tell you this, but Myra has not said a word since the moment of her arrest. And I don't mean she's exercising her right to silence! She just stares and doesn't talk. According to Dr. Topf, Myra is catatonic. The sheriff decided not to make the arrest public for medical privacy reasons—or so he told me.

"We're getting ready to transfer her to the Sunray Clinic custody room. She isn't responding to questions, and she isn't eating anything. No one has been able to question her. She hasn't been arraigned yet, so you, Efrain, need to hurry over to The Clinic right now. The sheriff doesn't want to release her, especially since her possible accomplice, Katharine Holmeier, has already fled. Deputy Marquart is waiting for you. Go! Now! Please!" And then, uncharacteristically, the usually polite Sergeant Skew abruptly disconnected.

Efrain, duly alarmed, grabbed his briefcase and headed off to The Clinic. He hoped Davina had not heard any part of the call. If she had, Myra's condition would become public knowledge within the hour. He had tried explaining confidentiality to Davina, but Wildcreek, after all, was a cozy small town.

At The Clinic, the formal arraignment on the charge of Murder in the First Degree was postponed until the accused, Myra Briney, was competent to proceed.

After the official order to continue was entered, Miso took Efrain aside to explain, "Sheriff Cannon insisted on Myra's arrest. My investigation revealed *some* evidence to support the charge, but a lot more investigation needs to be done.

"So far, Efrain, I've discovered that Myra packed the CSA bags and had enough knowledge of horticulture to substitute death camas for green garlic. She also could have known about the toxic properties of low larkspur. Turns out, it looks a lot like parsley. Then there's Julien Pidgeon's bank records. They showed a recent unexplained deposit of cash. And paperwork from the search of Julien's house indicated a "loan" from Greengrocers to Julien for five thousand dollars. I couldn't find any explanation for such a loan in Myra's records, and there was no evidence of repayment. Finally, other witnesses mentioned that Julien had harassed Katharine about dating him and hinted that Myra and Katharine owed him money. Several said that Julien never seemed to pay for anything. The evidence seems to suggest that extortion could be a motive. I hate to say this, Efrain, but it might be that Myra and Katharine are somehow involved in Julien's death."

Chapter 32

July 15, 2015 Wednesday

For the past nine days, Afton had been feeling worse and worse about her awkward conversation with Myra. She had avoided shopping in Wildcreek for fear of running into her. She had almost persuaded herself that she could do nothing to help Myra. Myra's emotional state still alarmed her.

She stopped answering her phone, even taking calls from Efrain, and left her laptop uncharged for days. She tossed the *Wing* into the trash and ignored her mail.

Increasingly restless, she started having trouble focusing on her daily routines. The day before, she forgot to place the pot in the coffee maker and had to clean up a large puddle of coffee on the counter. The day before that, she spent seven hours compulsively removing mustard seeds from their pods and saving them in old spice jars. No one she knew had ever agreed to take mustard seeds. Maybe she could pickle or cook with them? Did dogs eat them?

Ralph, noting his mistress' distress, stayed close by her—a dangerous, but valiant effort in light of her extremely disturbed state. Once, she nearly stepped on his rib cage while getting off her chair. How could she not see him? He weighed at least a hundred pounds and was excessively hairy.

"Ralph! I've made a decision." Not the life-changing decision she was hoping for, however. "I'm going to the Farmers' Market. And maybe I'll go to Greengrocer's, too, and ask Myra about my puffballs. I need to apologize to her." Oddly, Ralph looked almost happy when she walked out the door *with* her shopping bags and *without* him. He didn't even try to go with her.

The drive to Wildcreek worked its healing magic. Afton felt somewhat restored. Too soon, however, she came to the outskirts of Wildcreek and civilization. But, at least her parking karma was working properly.

She managed to find a parking space equidistant from the Farmers' Market to the north and Greengrocers to the south. Almost a miracle. In homage to the parking gods, she got out of her minivan and danced just a little—singing Tina Charles' "I Love to Love". Forgetting her troubles momentarily, she looked up at the sky and said, "What could possibly go wrong in this beautiful place!"

Her euphoria turned out to be short-lived. "Afton! Hey, Afton!" Afton recognized that voice. Was it too late to sprint back to the Odyssey? Yes, it was.

"Hey, Afton," puffed Greg Alatza, who was breathing heavily—most likely from his run over to her, but one could never tell. "It's a terrible thing about Myra. She might die!" Greg loved drama, both in his imaginary life and his real one.

"Wait—what did you say?" stammered Afton. "Did you say 'die'? Did someone try to kill her?" That, she hoped, might mean that someone else, not Myra, killed Julien. And, she thought selfishly, that might mean that Myra wouldn't need her help. "What happened to her?"

"Well, you know that Miso arrested Myra on Monday, right?" Afton looked a little dazed, so he added, "For killing Julien Pidgeon." Afton didn't know, but she nodded "yes" anyway. "So," he went on, "she hasn't spoken or eaten since. She's like a zombie. They're feeding her paternally, with an IV!"

"I think you mean parenterally, Greg."

"No, I think her parents are both dead. They can't take care of her now. Anyway, Myra's just lying in a bed in a locked room. And no one knows where Katharine is. Nurse Darling..."

Aha, thought Afton. Nurse Darling would love this kind of life-or-death situation. The good nurse hadn't had many positive things to say about Miso lately, and his arrest of the popular Myra Briney would provide her with even more opportunities to vilify him. Afton guessed that Miso most likely refused to do more than simply have dinner with Wildcreek's notoriously amorous nurse at some point in his investigation.

"Nurse Darling told me today that Wildcreek Animal Control was planning to euthanize Myra and Katharine's cat, but it seems to be missing. I hope somebody has found it and is taking good care of it." Greg harbored a soft spot for cats. Dogs were another matter. Greg and Ralph did not get along well.

"I hope so, too," Afton said.

"Nurse Darling thinks that Umberto killed Julien. He probably knows a lot of ways to kill people, and poisons have been used by the Corsican Mafia when knives weren't practical."

"Greg, that makes no sense. Helaine told me that she and Umberto left Corsica to get away from that part of his family."

"Maybe so, but jealousy has a way making people revert to their baser instincts. All of Helaine's talk about birdwatching…"

Afton interrupted Greg's ramble by pretending to see someone she knew in the distance. She waved to the nonexistent friend and said, "Gotta go, Greg. See you! Maybe at the Shortlist soon!" Then she hurried away before Greg could set a date for the Shortlist and enjoy his usual free drinks at her expense.

In fact, after hearing the sad news about Myra, Afton didn't feel like talking to Sarah, Rascal, or anyone. She just wanted to go home.

Chapter 33

July 15, 2015 Wednesday

When she got home, she put her phone and laptop on their chargers, tossed the mustard seeds in the trash, and fed Ralph a lamb sausage, his favorite treat. When she had completed all the preliminaries, including changing into comfortable pants and slippers, she opened a bottle of pinot noir and sat down in her most comfortable chair to think.

Afton now felt sure that some of Myra's troubles were Afton's fault. Partly, at least. Myra asked for her help, and Afton responded with platitudes. "Everything will be all right" she had told Myra. Now, as it turned out, things could not have been less "all right".

While Afton was engaging in her wine-fueled bout of self-pity and self-examination, Efrain called four times. She ignored his calls. She knew that he was calling on Myra's behalf, and Afton didn't want him to know how badly she had already failed on that front. Could she be trusted to find the answers that Myra needed?

All night long she battled with her thoughts and feelings of self-recrimination. On the one hand, she knew that Myra was innocent of Julien's murder and that she might have the skills to help discover the truth. Hadn't she done the same thing for Marcus, her mentor in Brewster County?

On the other hand, her success in Brewster County had come at a terrible cost: her job, her friends, her reputation, and even Marcus. He had committed suicide before she could prove he was blameless. She had waited too long; she had hoped that the judicial system would find its way. It had not.

She was not ready to tell anyone her story or to explain her initial reluctance to get involved in Myra's troubles, but maybe one day she would. Right now, she knew Myra needed her, and she would do all she could to help.

Afton began thinking that she should investigate just a little bit—to reassure herself that Miso was doing a thorough job. Perhaps she could point him in the right direction if necessary. But she recognized that those thoughts were only self-deception. She knew that once she started, she would not be able to stop—even if it meant leaving Wildcreek if she failed. She had moved a thousand miles away to start over. Might she need to do that all over again?

In the end, she called Efrain early the next morning. She knew that she would. And Efrain, her long-time friend, also knew that she would.

Efrain answered his phone immediately even though the sun had not yet risen—and in the Inland Northwest, the summer sun rises *very* early. He wasn't surprised that Afton seemed unconcerned about the time or that, without any of the usual greetings like "hello" or "how are you", she informed him she would be at his office at 2 p.m.

He thanked her and immediately went back to sleep. Myra, in her current state of catatonia, couldn't help him, and Afton wouldn't be available until afternoon. So, with the good feeling that came from knowing that Afton was finally willing to help him, he got some much-needed rest.

Chapter 34

July 16, 2015 Thursday

Afton didn't bother to get any rest. Relieving herself of her emotional conflict had created a new surge of energy. It was time to make a list of things she knew. She loved making lists. She had acquired the habit from her father.

He also taught her to pace around the room while working out a problem in her head. It worked! Her mother, however, hated the tracks he made in the carpets and always told her friends, "Don't marry an engineer—or, if you do, insist on tile floors!" Afton thought this was good advice. Tile floors were good for dog owners as well as engineers.

First on the list was something Afton believed must always be kept in mind. Perhaps the sheriff did make the right decision, and Myra did kill Julien. That was the easy way out, especially for Sheriff Cannon. But easy didn't seem likely in this case.

Second, who would want to kill Julien Pidgeon? This would be another list, a long one:

1. Myra—to stop Julien from some kind of blackmail over money?

2. Katharine—to help Myra, or stop Julien's aggressive sexual advances?

3. Thor—to defend Katharine? Or because of something in Thor's past?

4. Helaine—to protect people from Julien's cavalier attitude toward his XDR TB protocol? Or, in Helaine's mind—self-defense?

5. Umberto and/or Ben—to eliminate Helaine's possible lover or to avenge Julien's offensive behavior toward Helaine?

6. Rascal and/or Sarah—to help Thor?

7. Mrs. Moser—to stop Julien from his continued stealing?

8. Nurse Darling—to stop Julien from continuing to expose people to XDR TB?

9. Greg Alatza—Who knows!

10. Efrain—To help his clients, Myra or Katharine. Or to protect himself from something Julien might have found out?

11. The red-haired stranger ? Need to find out his name.

12. Everybody else in Wildcreek—to rid the community of a noxious thief and pest?

Third, what evidence existed? Afton decided to start by re-reading the articles in the Wing and asking Efrain what he had learned so far. At some point she would also need to talk to Miso. Nurse Darling also might have some information, but, on second thought, Efrain might be better at collecting it. He was the right gender for Nurse Darling.

Chapter 35

JULY 16, 2015 THURSDAY

"Hello, Davina. Is Efrain in his office?"

"Good to see you, Afton. Yes, Efrain is waiting for you, so just go on in... Wait! Stop! Don't touch those cookies! Biddie made them. Morris told me Sgt. Skew might visit."

"Yikes!" Afton pulled her hand away from the cookie platter. "Thanks for the warning!" She meant that wholeheartedly. Afton wasn't feeling like a cleanse that day.

Once safely inside Efrain's office, Afton plopped into the familiar chair and stared at her friend. She wasn't sure that she had forgiven him for referring Myra to her without warning her first.

"Afton, I know you were unsure about getting involved in Myra's case. I figured that out when you didn't answer my calls yesterday."

"You *knew* that when you told Myra to call me, Efrain. You should have let me know."

"I did know that. But I didn't know what else to do. Myra is in a catatonic state and doesn't seem to be recovering. I'm sorry. I really am. But you did call me back, and you did come. Here you are, right?" Efrain raised his brows and tried to look hopeful. He'd seen the eyebrow tactic work for Ralph; maybe a little canine charm would work for him, too. After all, Afton was a "love my dog, love me" kind of person.

Afton sighed. She was going to do what she could—whatever the consequences. "Okay, Efrain. Where do we start?"

Efrain started by repeating all the reasons Miso had cited for Myra's arrest: the CSA bags, Myra's knowledge of horticulture, Julien's bank records, Myra's accounts and bank records, Julien's harassment of Katharine, Julien's hints about money, and Julien's apparent stealing. Miso also suspected that Katharine might have been involved and was now in hiding.

"That doesn't seem like a strong case at all," commented Afton. She was making notes in a red diary as she talked. "And that's what I told Myra. I never thought Miso would arrest her without more proof. Now I feel terrible."

"You were right. The case *is* weak. And Deputy Miso is a good detective. But..." Efrain paused to consider a delicate way to explain his hanging "But..."

"But Sgt. Skew let me know a little more about how the arrest happened. It seems the sheriff is viewing the evidence through his own peculiar prism of media and politics. Miso had little choice in the matter.

"When Julien's body was first discovered, the good chief insisted that Julien committed suicide. When the forensic pathologist reported that plant alkaloids were found in Julien's blood and were likely the cause of death, Sheriff Cannon switched to a conclusion of accidental death. Finally, when confronted with the fact that death camas and low larkspur traces were found only in Julien's CSA bag—no one else reported symptoms from eating the contents of their bags—he was forced to agree to a murder investigation. And now that there's a murder investigation, he wants it wrapped up quickly. Myra's arrest was most certainly the sheriff's idea, not Miso's."

Based on her brief interview with Miso and her conversation with Myra, Afton thought that Efrain was right. Unlike the sheriff, Miso wasn't certain that Myra killed Julien. He would be open to new evidence and arguments should she or Efrain come up with something.

She also believed from her conversation with Myra, that Myra could not have planned and carried out such a crime. Myra would never murder someone with plants or use a CSA bag as a weapon. That would be too obvious. Those items would point directly to her.

Afton asked, "What did Miso tell you about Myra's financial records? Did Miso give you any details?"

Efrain looked down at his hands. Then he looked around the room. His splayed fingers obscured the middle part of July on the desk calendar in front of him. After a moment, he replied, "Uh, no... Miso didn't really say anything or give me any details. He mentioned extortion and a check from Greengrocers to Julien for five thousand dollars."

Of course, having handled many of Myra's and Katharine's financial affairs, Efrain could guess what else Miso might have found or suspected. Efrain felt badly about his answer to Afton, but he could not reveal all he knew about Myra, Katharine, or the source of some of their money. To some practitioners in the legal field, "lying by omission" was not really a thing. Efrain called it "being literally truthful".

Unfortunately for Efrain, Afton could recognize the signs of literal truthfulness in her legal ally and friend. She made a note to find out more about Myra's finances. They looked intently at each other. The silence between them was getting a little awkward. Time to go.

"Thanks, Efrain. I'll see what I can find out and let you know. I expect the same from you. I can't get to the truth if you hide things from me." She had a strong feeling that he was hiding something.

As she walked out of the office, she heard Davina offering a cookie to a reporter from the *Wildcreek Wing*.

Chapter 36

July 17, 2015 Friday

The next day, while Afton was revising her lists in accordance with Efrain's new information in the peace and quiet of her own home, Katharine was creating such a disturbance in the little cabin in the woods that nearby birds and deer were routed from their hiding places. Katharine had finally learned the truth about Myra's condition.

"Ruslan! You must go to Efrain and try to persuade him to rescue Myra! I don't trust the WPD to take care of her. She's in danger! If you don't do something, I will go myself! I don't care if I am arrested, too!"

"Katharine, going to see Efrain might be a serious mistake. Someone might recognize me and follow me back here. Then how could we help Myra?"

"Ruslan, I know Myra. She is always afraid. She still has nightmares about being arrested for taking the money. I'm sure that's why she moved it. Possibly she destroyed it!" Joe cringed at this idea. "We have to get her out of jail now! The *Wing* said that she is near death!"

Joe regretted bringing Katharine a copy of the *Wildcreek Wing*. But what else could he do? After all she had been through—all he had put her through—he just couldn't say no. How would he explain Katharine's disappearance to Efrain?

"Katharine, my love, WPD has issued a warrant for your arrest. What if Efrain tells them about me? I've heard that Deputy Marquart is looking for me. You know that I do not lie well." Katharine *did* know that. It was one of the things she liked best about him. He wasn't anything like his brother, Pavel.

But Katharine had devised a plan to keep them both safe. Finally, Joe gave up his objections and agreed to Katharine's scheme mainly because he loved her. Also, to be honest, he suspected that Myra was the only person who knew what had happened to the money. Joe prayed that Efrain was truly the friend that Katharine believed him to be. He made the call.

"Hello, Efrain McKinley's office." Davina, despite her Morris idiosyncrasy, was a knowledgeable and proficient executive assistant. "How can I help you?"

"I would like to meet with Mr. McKinley as soon as possible. I have information that might help Myra Briney."

Davina stopped arranging the Sharpies on her desk by color. "Could I have your name please? I think Mr. McKinley has an opening at 5 p.m. today. Is that too late?"

"No. Thank you. That is not too late. I will be there. But I prefer not to give my name." Davina thought that there was something familiar about the caller. Morris thought so, too. But neither of them could place him.

So, at precisely 5 p.m., a man of medium height, medium weight, and dressed in a too-large ball cap and a hooded windbreaker zipped up to his chin, walked into the lobby of Efrain's office.

"Hello. Mr. ah-ah-um... well, yes, Mr. McKinley is waiting for you." The man nodded and walked past Davina into Efrain's office. Morris started to tell her who the man was but then told her that it was best she didn't know. Morris could be frustratingly secretive sometimes.

Efrain watched silently as his mysterious visitor sat down and pulled a sealed envelope out of his jacket pocket. The man put the envelope on Efrain's desk and said, "Read it."

The outside of the envelope was addressed to Efrain. The letter inside was written by Katharine Holmeier, and it closed with Katharine's signature and that day's date. Efrain recognized the handwriting. He started reading:

Dear Efrain,

First, I am sorry about keeping so many secrets from you and Myra. My absence has caused her so much distress, I know. I feel that part of her illness is my fault. She was alone to face the suspicion of murder when I could have shared that with her. She may think that I killed Julien to protect her and myself from his threats. And I know that she moved the money because she was so afraid of being arrested.

I did not kill Julien Pidgeon, and I have proof. Unfortunately, I cannot come forward right now without causing even more harm to certain others. Perhaps, if you could let her know that I am alive and safe, her condition might improve. I don't care about the money, and I would give it all to you, if I had it, so that you would help her. I know that Myra couldn't have killed Julien, nor could she have put anything poisonous in a CSA bag. You know that, too. Please help her. Also, please do not try to find me or ask my messenger anything about me. I know there is a warrant out for my arrest.

Your friend and client,

Katharine

Efrain scribbled something on a piece of paper and put it back in the envelope along with Katharine's letter. He handed the envelope to the man sitting in front of him and said, "You had better go. Now." Joe did as he was told.

When Joe got back to the cabin, Katharine and Cat were at the door waiting for him. "What did Efrain say to do?"

Joe frowned. He did not want to involve anyone else in this mess if he could help it, especially because part of the mess was of his own making "He didn't really say anything that would seem to help Myra. He just gave us this note." Joe showed Katharine the note containing Afton's address. "I guess we should contact Afton Laurie. What do you think, my love?"

"I think Efrain is right. Myra and I trust him. We would all be in jail right now without his help. I'll figure out how we can contact her, and we'll do it tomorrow."

Chapter 37

While Katharine was working out her new plan of action, Miso was concluding that his investigation had come to a standstill. He felt the whole thing had gone from moving like a slow herd of turtles to fixed like hardened cement in just a few days. Catatonia might be the right word for the present condition of the investigation—just like its subject, Myra Briney. No one wanted to talk to him. They blamed him for Myra's illness and ostracized him from places like The Magpie and The Bed Pantry. Even Nurse Darling refused his calls. Miso needed a new direction. He needed action.

When Miso needed to work out an especially baffling problem, he turned to the Mountain. Depending on the level of the problem's difficulty, he would rent either a full day or just an afternoon Summer Scenic Lift Ticket at Schweitzer Mountain, a skiing and biking jewel in the Selkirk mountains overlooking Lake Pend Oreille.

From a dangling perch with a view of three states and the big lake, Miso could peel away the layers of emotion and confusion that distracted him from finding the answers he so desperately needed. This Saturday afternoon's ride was no exception. After several hours of riding up and back down in the swaying chairlift, the Mountain came to his rescue once again. As soon as he could, Miso jumped off and rushed to his car to call Afton Laurie. She immediately returned Miso's call and confirmed that she could meet with him at her house on Monday at 10 a.m.

Chapter 38

JULY 18, 2015 SATURDAY

While talking with Miso, Afton also received a message from Efrain. The message was strange and mysterious.

"Afton, stay home tonight. Someone is going to leave a letter for you or maybe even talk with you in person. Do this for Myra's sake. And don't call until tomorrow."

Afton felt like she had been asked to help with a puzzle without having all the pieces. Why couldn't Efrain have given her a little more information? She tried calling Efrain, but no one answered. Nevertheless, she would stay home that night and hope for more pieces.

The pieces, at least some of the pieces, arrived in the form of a letter, partially hidden under the mat on her doorstep. The delivery was announced by Ralph's furious barking and banging. He was leaping up to the top of the door frame as if to bar the intruder's entrance and devour them in the process. Only with extreme difficulty was Afton able to get past Ralph, open the door, look around, and finally retrieve the large-sized envelope addressed to her.

Once safely inside, she took the letter to her favorite chair, a leather recliner that rocked and swiveled so that she could see both the propane fire in the fireplace and a view of the moonlight on Littlecatch Creek. She called Ralph, who immediately settled down by the controls on her chair. She feared that someday he would figure out how to use them. Finally, she opened the letter, saw that it had been signed by Katharine Holmeier and another person, Joe Ivan/Ruslan Igoryevich Ivanov, and began to read:

Dear Afton,

My name is Joe Ivan. You may have seen me while I was visiting Wildcreek during the St. John's Wort Celebration. While there, I fell in love with your friend, Katharine Holmeier. She is fine but is hiding because she is afraid of being arrested. She is also terribly worried about Myra.

Katharine is living with me in a secret place. Please don't try to find us or tell anyone except Efrain that you have heard from us. Katharine trusts you and hopes you will be able to help Myra as soon as possible. She has asked me to tell you what I know.

On the night that Julien Pidgeon was killed, I saw Helaine Pia in the woods near Wright Lake, only twenty minutes from Julien's house. I was hiding behind a tree. She was arguing with a man. From what I could understand, the man was angry because she hadn't told him something.

Even during my few days in Wildcreek I had heard rumors that Helaine was having an affair. Julien was telling people that she was having one with him. That seems like a reason for Helaine to kill Julien, doesn't it? And Helaine believed that Julien was exposing everybody in Wildcreek to tuberculosis. That's a second very good reason to investigate Helaine. Finally, I saw Helaine driving toward Julien's house on the evening Julien was killed.

Neither Katharine nor Myra killed Julien. I know it, but I cannot talk to the police. Please, Ms. Laurie, find out who really killed him, so that Katharine and I can come back and take care of Myra.

Yours, Joe Ivan

Helaine Pia? Afton had not seriously considered the possibility that Helaine had killed Julien. Nothing about that seemed right, and Afton trusted her intuition. Could Helaine Pia be so bold as to go to Julien's house two days later and pretend to find him dead? Unlikely. Still, Afton added the information to her growing lists and resolved to call Efrain before she met with Miso on Monday.

Chapter 39

JULY 19, 2015 SUNDAY

The next day, Sunday, Afton rose early and walked as quietly as she could into the kitchen to avoid waking Ralph. She had left her laptop charging in the kitchen the night before, and she wanted to check the *Wildcreek Wing* online to find out whether there were any new revelations in the Julien Pidgeon investigation.

Apparently, she did not walk quietly enough. She heard the jangling of the tags on Ralph's collar seconds before something very large barreled into her from behind. From years of experience, Afton's muscle memory had already prepared for this. Her body barely wavered. "Okay, Ralph, I know, you think it's time to eat!" Afton had to postpone reading the *Wing*.

When she was finally able to sit down at the gray tile kitchen counter with her laptop and pull up the *Wing*, she was astounded to see a link to the Opinion section with the headline "Anonymous Letter to the Editor Advocates Poisoning Pidgeons in the Park". Afton's first thought was that the *Wing* had misspelt the word "pigeon". Her first thought was wrong, however. The Anonymous Opinion Writer had intentionally used Julien's last name, Pidgeon:

Dear Citizens of Wildcreek,

I have been a proud citizen of Wildcreek for more years than I would like to count. Until recently, I have felt safe and well-treated by the Wildcreek Police Department and its Chief, Sheriff Cannon.

But after the shocking arrest of Myra Briney, someone who has only served Wildcreek's best interests in providing wholesome and delicious food so that we don't have to drive all the way to Sandpoint to eat well, I have changed my mind, and I hope you all will, too.

First of all, Julien Pidgeon was a horrible human being. He walked into our stores and restaurants, knowing that he had an untreatable form of tuberculosis, without taking medications, keeping examination appointments, or wearing his required mask in public. He spread sickness and death.

Secondly, I and many others have observed him walking into stores and insulting the proprietors and customers. On top of that, he usually walked out taking merchandise without paying a penny! How is that okay with Sheriff Cannon? Lots of people have complained to no avail.

Myra Briney should never have been arrested. The evidence reported in the *Wildcreek Wing* does not seem at all conclusive. The poor woman might never recover her senses. And even if she did kill Julien Pidgeon, she has done Wildcreek a service. She should be thanked, not jailed.

I know that I may be giving away my age, but does anyone remember the Tom Lehrer song from 1959, "Poisoning Pigeons in the Park"? Forgive me if the spelling has been changed:

"...with each drop of strychnin'
we feed to a pidgeon,

it just takes a smidgen

to poison a pidgeon

in the park"

Well, Julien Pidgeon was like the people in the song who thought it was fun and easy to poison pigeons. Julien found it easy and even amusing to expose our community to life threatening illness, death and misery. Now the tables are turned. Whoever gave Mr. Pidgeon a smidgen was simply fighting back.

ANONYMOUS IN WILDCREEK

Afton found herself holding her breath as she read through the angry letter. She finally let it out when she got to the end. Were there others in Wildcreek who felt that way? Afton agreed that Myra should not have been arrested, and that the sheriff deserved to be criticized. Supporting a poisoning, even the poisoning of an evil person like Julien, however, was a different matter. Wasn't it? In any case, Afton added her thoughts about who might have written the letter, and why, to her list.

Chapter 40

JULY 20, 2015 MONDAY

Early the following morning, Afton and Ralph decided to walk north along the east bank of Littlecatch Creek in hopes of seeing the Belted Kingfisher. The familiar bird could usually be found perched on the branch of a certain dying pine hanging over the water. The creature was not at all afraid of Ralph and delighted in swooping down and flying over the water whenever Afton and Ralph came into view. Sometimes they would even see him catch a fish.

When they arrived home, Afton saw that Deputy Marquart had come early. It was only 9:30. She wished she had called Efrain before going on her walk.

"Hey, Ms. Laurie!" Miso called as he stood up from his seat on the front steps. He was waving with both hands. Before Afton could shout, "No! Stop the waving!", Ralph was bounding full bore toward the hapless visitor. Understandably, Ralph thought the greeting and waving hands might be for him.

Afton closed her eyes and expected to see a large pile of sheepdog and deputy when she next opened them. To her surprise, she saw her dog meekly eating treats from Miso's hand. Maybe Miso was smarter than she thought. Maybe... he would let her help him find Julien's killer.

A crisis averted, Afton invited Miso inside. Ralph, of course, went first, and they followed. Afton provided coffee, and, for the rest of the interview, Ralph sat alternatively on or at Miso's feet.

"Thank you for seeing me, Ms. Laurie. Efrain suggested that I talk with you again. I'm not sure what to ask you, but I'm out of ideas, and Efrain thought you might have some. He said you had helped him with some of his cases in the past. Were you in law enforcement?"

This was exactly the kind of question that Afton did not want to answer. "No, not exactly law enforcement, Deputy Marquart. I think Efrain just meant that he believes I have a talent for understanding human behavior and getting to the truth of things. *Some*thing like that, anyway. I make lists. That usually helps." Afton hoped her answer would keep Miso from asking anything more about her past.

Whether Deputy Missoula Marquart had superior powers of perception, or he was just lucky, he abandoned his curiosity about Afton's past life and concentrated on his current lack of direction. He said, "Please, call me Miso."

Afton relaxed, smiled, and said, "Call me Afton."

"The more I investigate, the more the evidence makes no sense," Miso sighed. "And I just don't think Myra Briney killed Julien Pidgeon. The evidence we have so far supports her guilt, but we must be missing something. After yesterday's "Letter to the Editor," the sheriff has ordered me to get to the bottom of this case 'like a snake on a slide down a well'. He doesn't care how I do it. So, Afton, I think that means he won't mind if I share all our facts and evidence with you. But only if you agree to let me know what you come up with, too."

"Okay, Miso, that sounds fair." Afton nodded. "Tell me what you have so far."

"So far, we know that only Myra prepared the CSA bags. She prepared the tags and placed the bags in the corner of the store. We know that the toxins that poisoned Julien Pidgeon came from plants that looked a lot like green garlic and parsley. Myra admitted to me that she was aware that death camas looked like green garlic and parsley looked like low larkspur.

"Traces of those plants were found in several places in Julien's kitchen—a Greengrocers CSA bag with Saturday morning's content label and Julien's nametag, Julien's blender, and the kitchen wastebasket containing stalks, leaves, and peels. Also, the bits of pesto still on the unwashed plates contained death camas and low larkspur traces.

"Then there are Julien Pidgeon's bank records. A cash deposit for five thousand dollars showed up around the same time as the date on an unsigned 'loan' document indicating Julien's receipt of five thousand dollars from Greengrocers. The document was in Julien's desk file drawer. Myra didn't mention anything like that to me, and now I can't ask her about it.

"Finally, several people told me they heard Julien making comments to Myra and Katharine about 'owing him money.' As far as I can tell, Greengrocers is a successful business, but it isn't making a fortune. What money would he be talking about?

"Just recently, we received the preliminary toxicology report from the Coroner's Office. It hasn't been made public yet because the investigation is not complete. I don't think the *Wing* knows about it, so please be careful about sharing this information. Efrain can know, of course, but Wildcreek doesn't need any more outlandish rumors floating around. Especially since this is only a preliminary report and there are still more tests to be done. Any leak, and the sheriff will blame me and fire me. Or worse, arrest me!

"In a nutshell, the report says that the opened Chianti bottles found in Julien's kitchen waste basket had only Julien's prints on them. One bottle contained wine mixed with a high level of low larkspur alkaloid—a lot more than could have been in the plants from the CSA bag. The other bottle contained no special additives.

"The pesto on the dinner plates contained both low larkspur and death camas. The toxin levels, again, were much higher than the plants used to make the pesto could have produced.

"Finally, I think I've figured out why Julien was in his car when he died. At first, I believed that his phone and car keys had just slipped into the cushions while he was sitting on the couch sometime that evening. But they were neatly bundled under the middle of a seat cushion. If Julien were extremely ill and trying to get to the Clinic, he would not have been able to call or drive there without his phone and keys. Also, we found no evidence of a spare key although most people have one. He could have been looking for the spare when he died."

Afton listened to Miso's summary of facts without interrupting. He had obviously given the evidence a lot of thought, and his words poured out of him in a torrent. When he came to a stop, he seemed at peace. Afton thought this might be a good time to ask a few questions.

"That's a lot to think about, Miso. Did you find any evidence that Myra possessed any concentrated versions of those plant extracts—like distilling equipment or internet searches? Did you find any evidence that someone might have been with Julien on the night he was killed? Or how the extra poison was added to the wine and pesto?"

Miso answered, "Not yet, yes, and not yet. The forensic pathologist fixed the time of death between 11 p.m. on Saturday and 3 a.m. on

Sunday. There were two table settings, and the amount of food served seemed to indicate someone was with Julien for part of the time.

"I've done my best to figure out where everyone was that evening, but no one so far has a perfect alibi. Myra told me that she was at home Saturday evening and all night waiting for Katharine, but Katharine never arrived. Then early on Monday, she drove to Greengrocers, found Katharine's car right where it was parked on Saturday, and moved it to the back of the store. After that, she went home and stayed there until Tuesday morning when she met with me at Greengrocers.

"Helaine was out birdwatching Saturday night and working at the restaurant on Sunday. Thor claimed he was at the Magpie on Saturday until closing at 1 a.m. and then went home. But Umberto and Ben told me that he left before 7 p.m.

"Wait a minute! I forgot to ask... Afton, where were you on Saturday and Sunday between the hours of 7 p.m. and 3 a.m.?" Miso wasn't smiling. Afton felt the zing of panic. She had been at home with no visitors. Ralph wouldn't be much help with an alibi. Was Miso going to arrest her, too? Then, a huge grin cracked the stern deputy's face. "Just kidding!"

"Anyway, it turned out that the Chianti bottle *did* come from the Magpie. Helaine always initials each bottle of their private label brand. Her initials were there, but her prints were not. We couldn't find any evidence that she was with Julien that night."

Afton felt a twinge of guilt. She had promised Miso to share what she discovered. Did that include Joe Ivan's letter about Helaine from two days before? Or did it mean sharing whatever she learned *after* today's promise? Well... she could spot a lame rationalization when she encountered one, and her thoughts about her promise were most definitely in the lame rationalization category.

However, rationalization or not, she knew she couldn't share any of Joe Ivan's information with Miso until she untangled her relationships with Efrain, Myra, Katharine, and Joe. Some or all of them were Efrain's clients, and she might be Efrain's agent of sorts. She had to talk with Efrain first.

"Miso, I'll do my best to help you with this. My thoughts right now are that you should try to find out more about Julien Pidgeon—especially about his life before he came to Wildcreek. I'm not sure why, but I have a strong feeling that we might find some answers in his past. Also, if you send me your preliminary reports, I might be able to come up with something."

Miso cocked his head and grinned. "Efrain was right. I feel better already. I'll get started today and let you know what I find. I'll send copies of the reports we have so far. No, no. Don't get up. I can let myself out. That is, if Ralph will get off my feet." Ralph licked Miso's hand and moved over to Afton's chair. Miso was allowed to go. Afton waved and hoped her hunch was at least in the ballpark.

After Miso left, Afton called Efrain's office and made an appointment for the next morning at nine. Davina told her that Myra's condition had not changed, and that Efrain was thinking about reopening Greengrocers with shortened hours until Myra recovered. Efrain a grocer? Afton seriously doubted whether he could tell a leek from a rutabaga.

Then, she spent the rest of the day on her lists. The results surprised her.

Chapter 49

July 21, 2015 Tuesday

Afton arrived at Efrain's office in a somewhat bedraggled state. Her long auburn hair was hidden from sight under an ivory Tilley hat, which she did not remove, and her eyes were completely lost in the shades of her sunglasses. Morris advised Davina not to say anything about Afton's appearance, and Davina wisely obeyed. Even more alarming was Ralph's absence. Davina did not comment on that either.

"Just go on in Afton, he's waiting for you." Davina pointed to Efrain's open door.

"Hi, Afton. You look tired. Long night? Did Miso give you a hard time?" Efrain lacked Davina's perceptive abilities.

Afton didn't know how to start. She just stared at Efrain. She'd spent most of Monday afternoon and night trying to create a believable picture from the facts she collected herself, Joe Ivan's letter, and the information from Miso. If she looked terrible, it was Efrain's fault. He kept telling people to go see her.

She decided to tackle the Joe Ivan matter first. She pulled Joe Ivan's letter from her bag and tossed it onto Efrain's desk.

"Read this!" Efrain read the letter. "Is this true? Did you know that Joe Ivan and Katharine Holmeier are somewhere in the area alive and well and living off the grid? What am I supposed to tell Miso? I'm supposed to hide information from a Wildcreek police officer... or deputy... or whatever he is? And another thing. Miso is asking me personal questions about my past. I don't like that!" Finally, she took a breath.

Efrain discerned that Afton was not at all happy with him. He thought a sheepish grin might help. It did not.

"Don't smile at me, Efrain McKinley! If you want me to help you, then you must respect my privacy. That has always been the way we've done things. Do not ever give out my name or address again without my consent... and it's your fault that I look like this!" Afton removed her sunglasses to reveal dark bruising under puffy, reddened eyes, ashy skin, and pronounced fine lines around her cheekbones and lips.

"I'm sorry, Afton. You're right."

Afton wondered why more people didn't use this tactic. "Sorry" and "you're right" worked wonders. Her angry feelings perished in a moment.

"Okay, Efrain, now what do we do?"

"Well," Efrain began, "I told Miso that you are working with me, so I think he understands that there are some things that you and I can't tell him. Katharine and Myra are my clients, and Joe Ivan might be one, too. Probably the best thing to do is to let me keep Joe's letter, and I will give Miso the information about Helaine. If he asks you about Katharine, refer him to me. I never meant to transfer my troubles to you. Again, I'm really sorry."

"Thanks, Efrain. Now, I guess it's time to get started on the problem of Julien Pigeon's death. It seems to me, after all my listing and thinking, that Thor, not Myra or Helaine, is a more likely suspect. Here are some of my reasons.

"We know that the death camas and the low larkspur were definitely in the CSA bag found at the scene. We know that Myra packed all of the bags, including one for Julian, and none of them contained parsley. Somehow, sometime, the poisonous plants were either substituted for the healthy ones or the entire bag was switched. It's more likely that the bag was switched because the low larkspur was meant to resemble parsley. Whoever switched Julien's bag with one containing the poisonous plants didn't know that the other bags didn't contain parsley. I'm sure I saw Julien check the name tag and list label on his bag. Then, he picked it up and eventually left the store—after stealing a few things, of course. Others saw him take his bag, too.

"Once I started thinking about the CSA bags, I remembered seeing Thor at his truck just before I went into Greengrocers that Saturday morning. He was shuffling around in the bags of St. John's Wort and didn't even say hello to me. I also noticed that the St. John's Wort bags were repurposed CSA bags and that they were placed haphazardly all around the bags containing the vegetables.

"Thor is at least as knowledgeable as Myra about plant toxicology. That's something Miso should look into, don't you think? The plant extracts indicate planning. You can't just go to the Wildcreek Drugstore and pluck them off a shelf.

"And Thor doesn't have much of an alibi. He told Miso he stayed at the Magpie until closing at 1 a.m. But, all the time I've lived in Wildcreek, Umberto has closed the Magpie at 9 p.m. on the day after the St. John's Wort Celebration to do a deep cleaning.

"Finally, one point in Myra's favor... she would not have added the low larkspur to Julien's CSA bag. Why? Because she knew that none of the other bags included parsley. She's really upset about the parsley issue. Don't even mention the word parsley when you get a chance to talk with her."

"I think you're right." Efrain now believed there was never too much of a good thing, like telling Afton she was right. "But why would Thor go to such lengths to kill Julien? We need a better motive than general dislike. Nearly everyone who met Julien generally disliked him. A lot of people hated him."

"Motive *does* seem to be a problem. I don't really understand the financial evidence that Miso mentioned. Did Myra or Greengrocers owe Julien money? Or did Julien owe Greengrocers money? That's hard to believe. It's my understanding that Julien was independently wealthy. I told Miso to dig into Julien's background. Hopefully, he'll find something and let us know." Afton looked into Efrain's eyes and waited.

"Yeah, let's hope." Efrain, however, was not at all hoping that Miso would find out something about the five thousand dollars that Myra gave to Julien. He wished Myra had listened to his advice. Also, he felt guilty about keeping that information from Afton and was worried that Afton had heard him talking to Myra about the matter when Afton visited his office a few weeks before the St. John's Wort Celebration. He had a feeling Afton knew something.

"And one more thing, Efrain. I'm going to call Miso and tell him the same things about Thor that I just told you. And if he calls you, please steer him away from questions about Brewster County. I really don't want to go back through all that. I really don't."

With that pronouncement, Afton replaced her sunglasses and walked out of the building with a wave to Davina but not to Efrain. She knew he was keeping something from her.

Chapter 42

JULY 21, 2015 TUESDAY

The interview with Efrain had left Afton unsettled. Her conviction that Thor had killed Julien was weakening. Perhaps blackmail over money *was* the real motive. She needed more fuel—fuel for her lists and fuel in the form of caffeine. Fortunately, both were available within walking distance at the Wildcreek General Store ~~and Café~~. Although not really a café any longer, Mrs. Moser's establishment would almost certainly provide a cup of tea and something sweet along with a useful exchange of information.

"Hello, Mrs. Moser. It's me, Afton!" The store appeared to be empty. "Mrs. Moser! Are you here?" Afton heard shuffling in the back.

"Oh, yes, dear. I'm here. Just let me get my knitting back in the bag." Mrs. Moser soon appeared in the arched doorway that led to her rooms at the back of the store. Her nimble fingers unsuccessfully tried to tuck a loose strand of silver behind her ear. "So nice to see you, Afton. May I help you? Maybe tea and a huckleberry scone? I'm experimenting. I've never used huckleberries before. Did you know they're a lot like blueberries, but they always have exactly ten seeds? I like that."

"Oh, Mrs. Moser! That sounds perfect." Mrs. Moser's warm welcome made Afton feel like she really was part of the Wildcreek community—no longer a stranger or tourist. Realizing that she was still wearing her black-lensed sunglasses, Afton pulled them off and gave Mrs. Moser her most gracious smile. Then she sat down at the small table near the pastry counter while Mrs. Moser prepared tea for them both.

"These scones are wonderful, Mrs. Moser!" Afton finished her first one in less than a minute. She resolved to take longer with the second one.

"Thank you, dear. I was thinking about sending some over to The Clinic for Myra when she comes to her senses. Poor child. She's not eating any real food. I can't imagine why Missoula Marquart would arrest her. He knows better."

"I've been thinking about that, too. Oh, I don't mean sending her food. My baking might make her worse. I was thinking about her arrest. I want to help her. Yesterday I talked with Miso, and he tried to explain. But I don't think he believes Myra killed Julien either. So, I'm checking on a few things myself.

"Do you remember the Saturday morning at Greengrocers right after the St. John's Wort Celebration? You were there, I think, when Julien came in to get his CSA bag, right?"

"Oh, yes. I remember it well. Wild pigs have better manners."

"Did you see him pick up his bag?"

"Yes, dear, he picked it up, looked at the label, and checked all the contents. He didn't say a thing about his bag. I was surprised, because he usually complains and tries to get free vegetables."

"He didn't say anything about not having parsley in his bag?"

"No, dear. Not a word."

Afton moved on from the subject of CSA bags. "Do you know Thor very well? I've talked with him a lot, but I don't even know his last name."

"Yes, I know him. He comes into my shop just to talk sometimes. Once he bought a silver cake basket from me and the credit card showed the name "Thoreau Jouett Browne Thomsen". He said Jouett Browne was an old family name. From Virginia. Just like that terrible Julien Pidgeon. My Johann and I always wanted to go to Virginia." Mrs. Moser looked slightly over the top of Afton's head and seemed to smile at someone.

Afton was elated. Mrs. Moser was a fount of information about the goings-on in Wildcreek. She tried another question. "Don't you think that Thor seems a little overqualified to be working as a farmhand for Sarah and Rascal? He seems to know a lot more about the science of farming. You know, like fertilizers, growing seasons, seed varieties... Why does he stay at Bullhead Farm? Everyone knows that he's infatuated with Katharine and that she hates the idea of farming. But he could find much better farming work near Wildcreek that might change her mind."

Mrs. Moser looked at Afton intently. She looked up and down and left and right. She sighed. Then she said, "Afton, you seem to be a good person, and I believe you are trying to help Myra. She *is* innocent, of course. So, I will tell you a secret."

Afton's blood pressure went up a notch. This was getting good.

"I know a secret about Thor, but I promised him I would not tell it. I'm not sure how it might help Myra, but it does answer your question about Thor. He stays with Bullhead Farm because he owns it. Not Sarah and Rascal. They sold the farm to him about six months ago."

Afton began to worry that Mrs. Moser might know her deepest secrets, too. And share them. The woman was uncanny. Was this what small-town life was like? For a minute, Afton thought about moving to Seattle.

"I can tell you something more," continued Mrs. Moser. "From Julien Pidgeon, I learned that Julien loaned Rascal ten thousand dollars. Rascal could not pay it back. Julien told me he planned to take the farm. Julien loved to talk about controlling other people with his money. He thought he could scare me, too, with his stories. He also told me he could take anything from Greengrocers that he wanted, including money.

"Of course, the next time Thor came to the store, I told him about Julien's plans. Thor knew nothing about the loan. He didn't think Sarah knew about it either. Rascal must have been too ashamed to ask for help.

"Thor was angry. He told me that he would put an end to Julien's reign of terror. Yes! He used those words. Later he told me that he bought the farm from Rascal and Sarah. With Thor's money, Rascal was able to repay the loan. Thor said he wanted to keep things just the way they had always been until Sarah and Rascal decided to retire. That decision would be completely up to them. If something happened to him in the meantime, the farm would belong to Rascal and Sarah again. Thor is very loyal to his friends, very kind and considerate."

"Just one more thing, Mrs. Moser." Afton was finishing her third cup of tea. "Some people are saying that Helaine Pia was having an affair with someone, and that Julien was threatening to tell Umberto. Could Helaine have killed Julien?"

Mrs. Moser shook her head vigorously. "Umberto does not like Helaine going out by herself for any reason. I have heard them arguing even from across the street in my store. But Helaine, she says she is always going out in the evening to look for owls. Yes, that is what she tells him. Some say she is seeing Julien, but I think that could never be true. How could anyone believe such a thing?

"Almost anyone could have killed Julien, but I doubt that Helaine would be able to make complex plant poisons without Umberto noticing. Also, I doubt if she would have planned to kill Julien at a dinner that we all heard her say she would attend. To me, it seems much more likely that someone who knew about the dinner took advantage of it. Julien's boastfulness about his prowess as a chef made him so obviously vulnerable.

"Helaine is no more a suspect than Myra. Just because she accused Julien of endangering people in Wildcreek with his cavalier attitude toward required tuberculosis precautions, it doesn't mean that she wanted him dead. She wanted him to start being responsible. Did you read Sunday's opinion letter in the *Wing*, Afton? I agree with that person. Julien's death was not such a tragedy. This investigation seems to be making everyone a suspect. The sheriff should stop this!"

Mrs. Moser, agitated now, rose and started clearing the table. Afton took the hint.

"Thank you, Mrs. Moser! I feel so much better. Your tea and encouraging words make me want to get back to work on Myra's case. Not officially, you know—just as a friend. May I stop in again if I have more questions? You might want to talk to Deputy Miso about some of this, too."

"Afton, you may come anytime. I think Johann is very fond of you. As for Miso, no, I will not be talking with him. He thinks I am a silly old woman who imagines things. Goodbye, dear, and take care!"

After driving home and taking Ralph outside for his usual business, Afton sat down at the counter to eat a leftover cheeseburger from the refrigerator. "Sorry, Ralph, there's only one." Ralph sat at her feet and watched her eat every bite. While she ate, she wrote down everything she could remember from her conversations with Efrain and Mrs. Moser so that she could add them to her lists and tell Miso later.

Chapter 43

JULY 22, 2015 WEDNESDAY

Miso woke up with a pang of anxiety. His dreams had been chaotic and incomplete. Myra was still in The Clinic, still catatonic, and still under arrest for the murder of Julien Pidgeon. On Monday, at Afton's suggestion, Miso had enlisted Deputy Buttars to investigate Julian's pre-Wildcreek past and to determine Greengrocers' business organization. Some witnesses believed that Myra and Katharine were partners, others remembered hearing Katharine say that she was only an employee.

Miso's worried thoughts must have alerted Buttars. Miso's phone started ringing with a call from the deputy. Buttars was excited.

"Miso, I learned a lot of really good stuff about Julien Pidgeon. His real name was Julien Ansfell-Dove. He changed his name to Pidgeon when he moved to Wildcreek. He wanted to hide his connection to news articles describing his similar reckless behavior in Charlottesville, Virginia.

"In Charlottesville, where he was first diagnosed with XDR TB, he was jailed for refusing to wear a mask or take any protective measures. Sound familiar? His arrival in Wildcreek was supposed to be a new start for him and a kind of 'medical probation'.

"He was born in Albemarle County, Virginia, and his parents were wealthy landowners. He attended the University of Virginia off and on and spent the rest of his time mismanaging his parents' tenant properties.

"After fifteen years of 'less-than-strenuous studying', he still hadn't finished a degree. At that point, he took a few years off to travel. His travels took him to Russia supposedly to work on a paper for a degree in history. Mostly, however, he studied Russian drinking habits. He'd already mastered the American version. Hah! When he returned to Virginia, he went back to his former life and so-called studies until he was diagnosed with tuberculosis—probably contracted in Russia.

"Most of my information comes from a retired history professor who agreed to talk with me only on the condition that his name not be made public. Apparently, the professor is worried about fielding calls from reporters—like the last time Julien was in the news. Other than the professor, however, no one wanted to talk about Julien. His parents are dead and everyone else hates him.

"As far as the business structure of Greengrocers goes, I'm still working on it. Greengrocers seems kind of mysterious. I called Efrain, but he's not returning my calls.

"I've got some news about what's going on at the office, too. The sheriff is trying to get Myra tried *in absentia*—while she's still unconscious. He argued that the trial would be shorter and less expensive that way. Wendell Turley, the prosecutor, told him the idea was crazy—and illegal. They got into a huge fight, and I had to use the drawer three times! If I were you, Miso, I wouldn't come back to the station just yet."

"Thanks, Buttars. I think I'll take your advice. Anyway, I just thought of something that I need to do. I'll call you later."

Miso had a sudden flash of inspiration. He'd go to The Clinic and visit Myra! He wouldn't be asking her any questions, so he didn't think Efrain would object. Seeing Myra again might spark some new ideas. He knew the visit was unorthodox, but he harbored a small hope that she would wake up and tell him something that absolutely proved her innocence. Had he been watching too many police crime dramas? Yes. But, against all odds, lead detectives on the small screen always had a lot of good luck rousing coma victims, and Miso was feeling lucky.

Unfortunately, after waiting more than two hours, Miso could detect only minimal signs of life in Myra. But, after eating a delicious huckleberry scone, or two, from a plate next to Myra's bed, he *did* get an idea. He and Buttars would be taking a little fact-finding trip over the weekend. Away from the sheriff and his cohorts. On the way, he would do his best to find out who made those amazing scones—without admitting, of course, that his first taste of one came from a coma victim's bedside plate. Not a good look.

Chapter 44

JULY 24, 2015 FRIDAY

B y Friday morning, Afton was worried. She hadn't heard from anyone about the investigation, and her lists were getting out of control. Myra's life was hanging by a thread mostly due to Afton's selfishness and her failure to recognize that Myra's fears of an arrest were well-founded. She thought, at least, that she could persuade Miso to help get Myra released and the charges withdrawn pending the continued investigation. Maybe, if Myra could somehow understand that she wasn't under arrest, she might begin to recover.

First, she called Davina and asked for Efrain. Apparently, he was too busy playing grocery store manager to take her calls. Technically, though, that did fall into the category of helping Myra and Katharine, but Afton thought that he just didn't want to answer her questions. She wanted to know more about Greengrocers' business organization.

Second, she called WPD and asked for Miso. Sgt. Skew answered and said, "Impossible. He and Deputy Buttars are out of town for the weekend. You won't be able to see either one until Monday. I'll make an appointment for you on Monday the 27th at 8 a.m. here at the station. Okay?"

"Where did they go? Can I call them?" Afton didn't want to wait.

"No, it's a secret. Sorry. You'll have to wait until Monday. Goodbye."

That was odd—even for Sgt. Skew. Having no other option, Afton decided to spend the rest of the weekend doing a little investigating on her own. First, she called Dr. Gadsberry. Then, she spent the next two days visiting shops in Sandpoint and Coeur d'Alene.

At 5 a.m. on the following Monday morning, Afton heard her ringtone, "Bat Out of Hell," playing in the kitchen. By the time she answered, a message was already showing from Miso. She called him right back.

"Miso, are we still meeting today?" Afton expected him to cancel. Her mood had not improved since her conversation with Sgt. Skew.

"Sure, of course, Afton. But I want to meet somewhere else. Not at the Sheriff's Office. Barbara Rampart is going to let us use the Panhandle Lakes Conservation Team's Sandpoint Field Office on Washington Avenue. Do you know it? I don't want anyone at WPD to get the sheriff all wound up before I have a chance to hear what you have to say and organize my thoughts. I'll explain more when I see you. Okay? At seven?"

Afton replied, "Okay." What could Miso have in mind?

She found out soon enough. Officer Rampart met her at the door and shepherded her into a meeting room in the back. Coffee was waiting on the smooth oak table along with what looked like huckleberry scones. Miso was smiling at her through a curtain of crumbs.

"Sit down, Afton, and don't say anything yet. I've got plenty to say. Have some coffee and one of these incredible scones. They're huckleberry. And you can have more than one."

Barbara Rampart cleared her throat. "Are those Melina Moser's scones? I hope she's not selling them, Miso. She told me she picked those huckleberries only for personal use. You know it's a crime to pick wild huckleberries with the intent to sell. It's a two hundred fifty dollar fine for a first offense. And I'm a little surprised that she gave them to you, Miso. I've heard she doesn't like you much."

"True, Barbara. But she gave them to Buttars. She likes him a lot. I asked him to go talk to her a couple of days ago, and he came away with three dozen! She says he reminds her of Johann. That's her late husband."

"Okay. Just checking. Text me when you are all done in here. I'll be out front." Barbara grabbed a scone and left, closing the door behind her.

"So, Afton, time to get down to business. Buttars and I have been doing some investigating into Julien's past... as you suggested. His reputation back in Charlottesville was just as bad as it was here. He'd been a terrible student, a terrible estate overseer, and a reckless tuberculosis patient. Those are all the same general motives that we have in Wildcreek.

"But, I went to visit Myra and while I was sitting with her, I realized that we knew very little about our prime suspect, Thor. I sent Buttars over to the Wildcreek General Store to see what Mrs. Moser might have to say about Julien and Thor. She told Buttars that Thor had come from Virginia originally and that Thor had purchased an expensive silver cake basket that he believed had belonged to his family. Unwisely, I think, she told Thor that she had purchased the basket from Julien.

"Buttars and I learned from Sarah and Rascal that Thor still has family in Seattle. We tried to find Thor, but he was never home and not answering calls. Sarah thought Thor was off drinking somewhere, but Umberto hasn't seen him either. Not since last Thursday. Anyway, Buttars and I decided to go to Seattle on our own on Friday. We got back late last night."

Miso picked up the last scone and started eating it very slowly, as if it were the last thing he would ever eat. He waited, smiling, until Afton could stand the silence no longer.

"Missoula Marquart! What did you find out?"

"We learned, Afton, that Thor and Julien knew each other back in Virginia. And what happened between them in Virginia provided Thor with a powerful motive to kill Julien Pidgeon—or Julien Ansfell-Dove—his real name.

"We were able to find Thor's adoptive family in Seattle—the Thomsens. They told us that Thor and his mother were evicted from their tenancy by a man named Julien Ansfell-Dove, the landowner's son. Julien took all the family's personal goods to pay for "expenses", including heirloom silver. Shortly afterward, Thor's mother killed herself, and the Thomsens, also tenants at the time, adopted Thor. Later they moved to Seattle.

"The Thomsens also told us that Thor received a degree in Organic and Sustainable Agriculture with a minor in Chemistry from Washington State University. That fits with our profile of Julien's poisoner.

"I guess I was just so focused on Myra's mysterious finances and Katharine's disappearance that I overlooked a few things. I'm still concerned that Myra and Katharine might be Thor's accomplices, or that they killed Julien because they were being blackmailed. But, I think I have enough evidence to get a search warrant for Thor's cabin. It might take some time. The sheriff isn't going to like people thinking that WPD arrested somebody by mistake. He's *really* not going to like it."

By the time Miso was done talking, Afton was energized with anticipation and relief. "Miso, I knew you could do it. I *knew* it! Now we are getting somewhere. Go save Myra—go get her out of that clinic and back on her feet!"

Afton didn't mind that a lot of the same information also appeared in the lists she brought to the meeting. She, too, was more than ever sure that Thor had a part in Julien's murder.

"Miso, here is a copy of my list of possible reasons why Thor might have murdered Julien. You've covered most of them, but I noticed from your reports that Thor's estimation of the time he left the Magpie on Saturday night had to be a lie and not just the faulty memory of a drunken witness. He told you that he left at 1 a.m., closing time, and that he always leaves at closing time on Saturday nights. But the Magpie closed at 9 p.m. for a special cleaning on that particular Saturday. In one of the reports you sent over, you noted that Umberto remembered Thor leaving before 7 p.m. That would give Thor plenty of time to go to Julien's for the pesto dinner. He was probably the unidentified guest.

"Great, Afton. I can't believe I forgot about that. Thor *doesn't* have a passable alibi for Saturday night. I'll add that to my warrant affidavit. Thanks!"

Chapter 45

JULY 27, 2015 MONDAY

Miso had to wait until late afternoon to get both the sheriff and the Town Prosecutor in the same room to discuss the warrant for Thor's cabin. They had been the guests of honor at the Wildcreek Osprey Club's monthly luncheon meeting. Both men were still glowing from the warm congratulatory remarks made by prestigious members concerning the speedy conclusion of the Julien Pidgeon murder investigation.

"So, Deputy Marquart, what's so important?" The sheriff glared at Miso. "Mr. Turley and I have a lot of work to get done today!" Wendell Turley cocked a caterpillar-like eyebrow. As far as Wendell knew, the only plan for the day was to continue on to the Magpie for more congratulatory drinking.

"Sheriff, Buttars and I have been working on the Julien Pidgeon case, and we now think that there's a good chance that Thoreau Jouett Browne Thomsen killed Julien Pidgeon, not Myra Briney. We want to get a warrant to search his house. We also think..." Miso had never been good at easing into potentially inflammatory subject matter.

"Thoreau Joe Brown Who?" The sheriff was shouting now. "What are you rambling about? We've got that woman in custody who put poisonous plants in Pidgeon's grocery bag. Today you want to waste Town resources on some stranger no one's ever heard of? What do you think the *Wing* will say if it turns out that *you* arrested the wrong person?"

Miso decided not to remind the sheriff that it was the sheriff himself who insisted on arresting Myra. Miso had wanted to wait. "Look Sheriff—and Prosecutor Turley—since then we've learned a lot about Julien Pidgeon..." Miso outlined the latest information about the relationship between Julien and Thor. He added Thor's lie about his alibi, Thor's knowledge of plant chemistry, and everything else he, Buttars, and Afton had discovered. Just to be safe, however, Miso didn't mention talking with Efrain McKinley or Afton Laurie.

After a while, Wendell Turley seemed to be coming around to the idea of a warrant. "Well, Miso. I still think that Myra Briney may be guilty, but, like you say, we need to be as sure as we can be. Go ahead and write your affidavit. Bring it over to my office tomorrow, and I'll look at it. There doesn't seem to be any real urgency, so let's plan on serving it... maybe Wednesday afternoon. What do you think, Sheriff?"

Sheriff Cannon glared at his turncoat colleague. "With any luck, the *Wing Ding* won't get wind of it until Friday's news cycle." Fewer people read the *Wildcreek Wing* on Fridays and Saturdays.

"And let's see if we can speed up that Briney woman's transfer. Efrain McKinley has been calling me about some private hospital for her. Miso, call McKinley and tell him we'll expedite the transfer if he keeps quiet about it."

Believing that he had done all he could, Miso hurried away before the sheriff could find a reason to change his mind. Myra would be in a safer place, and he needed to warn Buttars to stay out of the office for a while. The sheriff wasn't happy.

Chapter 46

July 28, 2015 Tuesday

The next morning, Miso dropped off his warrant affidavit and then treated himself to a late breakfast at Cedar House. He was confident that Wendell Turley would have the warrant ready for him Wednesday morning. Feeling that things were now well in hand, except for the growing number of missing people, he decided to spend the rest of the day trying to find Thor.

Before driving all the way out to Bullhead Farm, Miso called Thor several times from Cedar House. No answer. Then he called Rascal Woods.

"Sarah and I haven't seen him, Miso. We're starting to worry. I'm going over to his cabin now, and I'll let you know if he's there. He hasn't been eating with us for days and that's not like him." Ordinarily, Rascal would add a joke about Sarah's cooking keeping Thor away, but even Rascal realized the time wasn't right for levity.

"Okay, Rascal. Please call me if you see or hear from him. Thanks."

Rascal's walk from the Big House to Thor's cabin took approximately ten minutes. As he approached, Rascal noted the presence of Thor's truck in the drive. Rascal was relieved. He and Sarah depended on Thor's truck to take produce into town. If Thor agreed that the carrots were ready, they would need to complete the picking, washing and loading no later than ten o'clock the next morning. The Wednesday Farmers' Market started at noon, and people were asking about carrots. Rascal didn't want to miss another sale day because Thor had gone AWOL.

Rascal knocked on Thor's door, but he had the feeling no one was home. He knocked a second time and yelled out Thor's name. After a few minutes with no response, Rascal went around the house looking in windows. No sign of Thor. Normally, Rascal and Sarah were extremely careful to respect Thor's privacy, but Thor had not been around lately. Such a long absence was unheard of. Thor's whole life was wrapped up in the farm or drinking at the Magpie. Something seemed wrong. So, a concerned Rascal used his copy of the cabin key to open the front door.

"Thor, are you home?" Rascal tried calling out a few more times. Nothing. He walked around the house. Except for the lack of Thor, everything looked like it always did. The usual piles of agricultural magazines and history books were scattered around in all the rooms, and the kitchen table was covered with more papers and some glassware and tubing that Thor used for soil testing. A small television took up a full third of the tiny kitchen counter.

One thing, however, did seem out of place and out of character for Thor. Rascal's attention was drawn to an open photograph album next to several beakers on the table. Rascal looked closer. He couldn't help himself. A boy in one of the pictures looked like Thor. Another depicted a family sitting around a table with a large birthday cake perched on top of a beautiful silver cake basket. Rascal continued turning the pages. He found pictures of a farm, handwritten recipes on yellowed paper, and several letters from people named Jouett Browne. Most surprisingly, he found the same silver cake basket materialized on the table next to the album. He turned back to the photograph of the birthday party just to make sure. Yes, the basket was the same one.

Rascal knew he shouldn't touch any of Thor's things, but he'd already looked through the album, why not check out the cake basket? After all, he was present when Thor bought it from Mrs. Moser. It was lovely... and valuable. He picked it up.

When Rascal lifted the basket, he noticed that it had been resting on a pile of papers. The papers looked like lab notes. Upon closer inspection, the notes seemed to be records of experiments with death camas and low larkspur. Rascal's first instincts had been right—something was wrong here. He quickly used his phone to photograph the notes and all the items on the table. Then, he hurried out of the cabin and headed for the Big House to find Sarah. In fact, he was in such a hurry that he failed to notice Thor in the wooded area between the cabin and the house.

Thor, however, *had* gone AWOL. He had borrowed an old off-road enhanced Ford Bronco from a friend in Krillo and had spent the last couple of days tracking Katharine Holmeier. Finally, giving up, he turned around with the intention of heading home by way of the Hanging Ear Bar in Krillo. As it turned out, he made it to the Hanging Ear, but after a few too many beers, the friend who owned the Bronco had to pick him up and do the rest of the driving back to Bullhead Farm. Thor arrived just in time to see Rascal leave his cabin and go back to the Big House. He followed Rascal to the Big House porch and concealed himself where he could see and hear everything.

Rascal found Sarah sitting on the front porch in their so-named "swing that no longer swung." A few years ago, it had fallen to the porch floor and stayed. Sarah was browsing intently through a well-thumbed copy of *Small Town Living* by Erin Austin Abbott, and humming "Stairway to Heaven." She was completely absorbed.

"Sarah, I've got something... something to show you! You won't believe it!" Nearly out of breath, Rascal plopped down beside her. "Look at these photos! Thor wasn't answering the door... but his truck was there... I went inside to check on him... he wasn't home... these were on the table! What should we do?"

Sarah looked up from her book and stared at her husband. He was waving his phone, sputtering out unintelligible words, and growing increasingly purple. Did she need to call 911?

"Rascal! Take a breath. What's wrong?"

"Everything's wrong, Sarah! I think Thor killed Julien Pidgeon. Look!"

Sarah looked. On Rascal's phone were pictures of the notes for extracting alkaloids from death camas and low larkspur. There were also pictures of the open album, the distillery equipment, a silver cake basket, and the entirety of Thor's kitchen table.

"What the...? Rascal! Thor's not a killer. He can't even kill squash bugs without a couple of beers first! That can't be right. Is there even such a thing as organic death camas? Thor would only use organic." Sarah realized she was just rambling on from shock at that point and stopped talking.

"Should we call the police?" Rascal had calmed down and was starting to regain his senses. "Maybe this isn't what it looks like. Maybe we should talk to Thor first." Then Rascal had an idea.

"Sarah, what do you think? Maybe we can talk to Thor and promise not to tell anyone about this—*if* he sells the farm back to us at a *very reasonable price.*" Rascal used air quotes to frame his finale and nodded furiously.

Sarah's heart sank. Rascal was talking about the destruction of her dreams. She wanted to stop farming and live in a nice house in town with a small country garden in the back. She and Rascal were both getting too old for the intense physical work and the uncertainty brought on by weather and insects. Skiing was the only exercise that held any interest for her. Besides, she had already figured out a way to live on their pensions alone. The Hackensack Fire Department had been good to them.

"Rascal, what are you thinking? Let's go inside and talk about this!" Sara was using her spoon voice. Rascal meekly followed her into the house.

Once inside, she continued. "No way, Rascal! We've already made our decision. We're winding down our part of the farming operation, and Thor is going to take over all of it. He's young, and he loves Bullhead Farm. He's our friend, and he helped us keep the farm when Julien Pidgeon tried to take it. What is wrong with you? Let's get some beer and talk more about the good life without plantings and harvests! Just types of snow."

Sarah, the former fire lieutenant from Hackensack, New Jersey, knew how to manage people. She was good at managing Bullhead Farm, and she was an expert at Rascal management. Before the evening was over, Rascal was full of venison chili, ale, and expectations of other delights soon to come. He even admitted that he only wanted the farm out of guilt for losing it in the first place.

Sarah told Rascal to delete the photos and proposed a toast to a better, farm-free life. Rascal raised a Cold Smoke can in whole-hearted agreement. But, in all the festivities, he completely forgot to delete the photos or call the Wildcreek P.D.

From his hiding place near the porch, Thor had heard Rascal outline the plan to get the farm. He had heard every word of the conversation on the porch. When Sarah and Rascal went back inside the house, he walked back home to eat his dinner alone and wonder why his life seemed to be one disappointment after another. First his mother's suicide, then Katharine's disappearance, and finally, Sarah and Rascal's plan to retake the farm.

Then, as if all that were not enough, another disappointment suddenly knocked on his door. Sadly, Thor was not to learn of Rascal's later change of heart and would never know that his friends, Sarah and Rascal, had chosen *not* to betray him.

Chapter 47

JULY 29, 2015 WEDNESDAY

S arah and Rascal awoke on Wednesday morning feeling pretty good about themselves. Their only worry, or so they thought, was getting the carrots ready.

"Let's just pick half a load today," Sarah suggested. "We can do the whole thing ourselves if we can't find Thor." Neither wanted to say it, but they had mixed feelings about picking carrots with Julien's killer. They had decided not to say anything, but they weren't sure they could hide their feelings from Thor just yet.

"Sounds good, but let's finish our coffee first. Wednesday afternoons aren't usually busy anyway." They got to work and were ready to load the truck by eleven. The carrots looked great, and the weather was fine. But Thor had not yet appeared.

Sarah's phone rang. "Nope, Miso. We still haven't seen him. He's supposed to be helping us get the carrots ready for market, but he hasn't shown. Sarah paused, listening to Miso. "Sure. Sure. We'll call the minute we know something... About where he is, I mean. Okay?

Anyway, right now we've got carrots to sell. We'll call Thor again. Maybe he can drive the truck over here—if he's there, of course!"

Rascal called Thor. Thor didn't answer. "Okay, Sarah. Let's go over and see what's going on. I've got truck keys, so we can drive it back here to the Big House if we need to. I don't want to go by myself, though. After what we saw yesterday, I have a bad feeling." Sarah had a bad feeling, too.

When they arrived at Thor's cabin, they found the truck parked in the same place that it was parked the afternoon before. Once more Rascal knocked on the door and shouted for Thor. This time, however, when Rascal started looking through the windows, he saw something new. Thor was lying on the floor near the kitchen sink. Dead drunk or... dead?

"Sarah! We've got to get in there now!" Rascal ran back to the cabin's front door. With Sarah by his side, Rascal pulled the key out of his pocket and pushed it into the lock. He found that the door was unlocked already.

"Strange. Thor always locks his door. Even when his Blood Alcohol Content is well over twice the legal limit, he still manages to make sure his door is locked. And that's fairly often." Rascal rushed over to Thor. He sighed, turned around and said, "Sarah... uh... call 911. There's nothing more we can do for him. He's dead."

"Are you sure, Rascal? Are you *sure*?"

"Of course, I'm sure. You and I have seen lots of dead people. Thor is definitely dead. I don't want him to be dead, honey, but he *is* dead. He's got a little hole right by his heart. You're gonna have to call 911."

"Okay," Sarah said. "Aren't you worried that someone might think we killed him? To get the farm back? It goes back to us, you know. Let's just look around a little bit first. Don't touch anything."

So, very quickly, they looked through the cabin, removed some documents related to the sale of the farm, and then went back to their house to call 911. Finally, there was nothing else to do. The carrots weren't going to market, and there was no help for Thor. They both sat down on the "swing that no longer swung", embraced, and cried for their lost friend.

Chapter 48

July 29, 2015 Wednesday

While Sarah and Rascal were grieving the loss of Thor, Miso was driving to Thor's cabin with a search warrant and an arrest warrant for Thor—happy that Myra was on her way to a safe place. As he drove, he was singing what he could remember of the *South Pacific* song, "A Cockeyed Optimist." Sheriff Cannon was doing the raving and bellowing, Julien was the one who was dead, and Miso, himself, was the cockeyed optimist who was hoping for the best but secretly dreading what he might find.

Even though Miso had so far been unable to find Thor, the sun was shining, the day was only half over, and Miso believed that Myra would get better. He also hoped that WPD would get some additional definite proof about the identity of Julien's killer. His one worry was that the arrest warrant might be premature. Who knew what would be found in Thor's cabin? Maybe nothing. But... the sheriff had insisted on an arrest warrant believing it would divert the torrent of criticism that would come after his flawed decision to arrest Myra. So, whether Miso liked it or not, he was going to serve an arrest warrant.

At the same time, Miso was also listening to an on-scene KPND Radio report of the sheriff's press conference. The sheriff, apparently, was standing on the steps of The Clinic along with Wendell Turley and Efrain McKinley. Sheriff Cannon was complementing himself on his compassionate decision to release Myra Briney to Efrain for transfer to a private psychiatric hospital in Coeur d'Alene.

Someone in the crowd asked, "What about your compassionate decision to arrest Myra in the first place, Sheriff? Who's the next person to receive your boundless generosity? Whoever wrote the 'Pidgeons in the Park' letter better look out, too! We heard that you issued an arrest warrant for 'Anonymous in Wildcreek' this morning. Hah!"

Miso didn't get to see the dark look that Sheriff Cannon bestowed upon the Wildcreek Town Prosecutor. He didn't get to see Wendell turn a mottled red color and say under his breath, "Nobody did that, Sheriff. The warrant was only for Thor, just like you wanted. And we kept that quiet. Just don't say anything right now. *Please* don't say anything. It's only a made-up provocation!"

Miso did, however, get to hear what the sheriff said to the crowd and to his listeners, "Prevarication! I can make up a prevarication just as well as the next guy. And better! As it turns out I did issue an arrest warrant this morning!" Wendell Turley nudged Sheriff Cannon and put his finger to his lips. The sheriff ignored the gesture.

"I issued and served an arrest warrant for Thor Joe... ah... umm..." Wendell quickly whispered something else in the sheriff's ear. "That's right! For Thor Thomsen. He's been arrested."

The broadcast ended just as Miso received a call on his police radio. The dispatcher told him that a 911 call had just reported a dead body at the cabin on Bullhead Farm. The caller disconnected before any other information could be obtained, so the dispatcher could not tell Miso who the body was supposed to be. Miso activated his emergency lights and ignored the speed limit.

After he made the turn into the long driveway to Thor's cabin, he saw Thor's truck parked out in front. No one seemed to be around. Miso got out and carefully approached the house. Rather than knock on the door, he went around to the kitchen window and looked in. From that vantage point, Miso could see most of the upper body of Thoreau Jouett Browne Thomsen.

Miso immediately made the appropriate calls on his radio and then decided to wait for the forensic team to arrive before entering the house. Thor was beyond help. Miso was hopeful that Dr. Gadsberry would come with the team. WPD needed all the help it could get. In a rapid reversal, the Julien Pidgeon matter seemed to be getting worse, not better.

"Sarah? This is Miso. I'm calling from Thor's cabin..."

Sarah cut him off and said, "Just a minute, Miso. Here's Rascal."

Rascal took Sarah's phone and began talking. "Miso! Did you find Thor yet?"

"Have *you* found him yet, Rascal?" Miso waited for the answer.

"Uh... Sarah and I will be right over." Rascal hung up. Rascal wondered whether you could hang up on someone if you didn't have a hand-held receiver. He decided that you could.

Miso's afternoon was not nearly as happy as his morning. By the time the forensic team was done, he knew who had killed Julien Pidgeon, and Myra Briney was on her way to a probable recovery. But now, he had a new murder to solve.

Dr. Gadsberry told Miso all that he could. "The lab notes appear to be recipes for extracting death camas and low larkspur alkaloids. The distilling equipment was probably used to do that work. More testing will be needed. My unofficial—stress, *unofficial*, not-to-be-repeated-outside-the-investigation opinion is that Thor was stabbed with a long, narrow, pointed, sharp instrument, not a blade, more like a skewer.

"I hope I don't need to remind you that the final forensic pathology report has not been completed in the Julien Pidgeon case. I'm waiting for additional testing. If you want to know more about the medical aspect of either case, call me personally or check with the Coroner's Office—not the *Wildcreek Wing*."

Miso noted that the photo album supported the information about motive that he had gained from Thor's adoptive parents. Regretfully, Miso would have to give them the terrible news that their son had been murdered.

Miso had other things to do, too. He called Wendell Turley and told him to get the arrest warrant quashed right away. Serving an arrest warrant on a dead person would not be a good news story. He also asked the prosecutor to dismiss the preliminary charges against Myra. There was no evidence that she and Katharine were Thor's accomplices. Nor could Myra have killed Thor. She was still in a state of hypokinetic catatonia, right? Wendell agreed.

The *Wildcreek Wing*, on the other hand, thought that arresting a dead person *was* a good story. Hadn't the sheriff announced that the arrest warrant had been served? The article that appeared in print two days later repeated details of the sheriff's earlier mistaken arrest of Myra Briney and the unfortunate effects on her health. The rest of the article focused on the sheriff's motives for making arrests in anticipation of actual evidence. No one was safe in Wildcreek—not even in death! The *Wing* promised follow-up articles on the murders of Julien Pidgeon and Thoreau Jouett Browne Thomsen. "Murderers Among Us" would be the title of the new series.

Chapter 49

August 7, 2015 Friday

F or days, eight days to be exact, Afton had been at home, restlessly adding items to her lists of chores to do in the house and garden. Occasionally, she crossed one off. Mostly, she waited for Miso to call. Why hadn't he called after the article in the *Wing* that reported Thor's guilt and murder? Why hadn't Efrain called? And finally, why did she have a strong feeling that the matter of Julien Pidgeon was not settled? The evidence against Thor seemed overwhelming. Maybe she would be able to talk to Miso tomorrow at Helaine's "Welcome Back from Jail" party for Myra. Everybody would be at the Magpie for the happy event—except perhaps Sheriff Cannon.

The next evening at the Magpie was a wonderful success, at least until it wasn't. Wildcreek was ready for some good news, and Myra's improved health was a great reason to celebrate. She looked good, but she wasn't really her old self yet. The great outpouring of love from all her friends, however, turned out to be just the thing to speed her healing.

Afton arrived soon after the party began. Miso was already there. Helaine, her long, wavy blond hair streaming behind her, was fluttering around like a beautiful butterfly and handing out small cups of Pica Pica. Umberto and Ben were working furiously at the Bar trying to keep up with the orders. Miso, on purpose, failed to notice that a fifteen-year-old was serving Bunny Marys—vodka drinks made with carrots generously donated by Sarah and Rascal.

Miso did notice Afton. He made his way straight for her when he saw her walk through the door. "Afton, I know you must have questions. I should have called, but the sheriff has been keeping me at the office. He's looking for someone to blame for the negative *Wing* articles, and I didn't want him to know about you at all. He's definitely looking for a scapegoat."

"That's okay, Miso. I thought it might be something like that." Afton forgot about her earlier frustration. She was flattered that he had been waiting for her. "Can we talk here?"

"Sure," Miso said. He drew her into the back corner furthest from the crowd around Myra. "Afton, I want to get your thoughts on Thor's murder. I can't believe that someone around here would kill Thor because he killed Julien. My impression was that most people believed Thor was justified."

"Hmm," Afton mumbled, thinking aloud. "Thor's murder and the evidence in his cabin led to Myra's release. Could that have been a motive? But who would have known about all the evidence in the cabin?" Afton wasn't sure why she said that, and she wished she hadn't.

She hoped she hadn't unintentionally steered Miso toward Sarah and Rascal. All her instincts told her that Thor's killer was someone else. In fact, she was certain the two murders were committed by the same person. But before she could explain her ideas to Miso or turn the conversation in a different direction, a tipsy Helaine walked up to Miso, grabbed his arm, and pulled him to the center of the restaurant.

"Ladies and Gentlemen!" Helaine shouted as she raised Miso's arm in the air—or tried anyway. "This sad example of Wildcreek PD's finest is the reason that our guest of honor, Myra Briney, is here with us in body, but not really in spirit. He is the one who arrested her. She begged him not to, but he did it anyway. Shame on you, Deputy Missoula Marquart..."

After a couple more minutes of accusations in a similar vein, Miso extracted his arm from Helaine's grasp as gently as he could and walked out of the Magpie. Needless to say, his temper was more than lost. He *really* wanted to arrest Helaine for something. The weeks of work to get the right result while managing the sheriff had gone unnoticed and unappreciated. Why care about these people? They elected Duh Frank. They could live with him from now on.

Chapter 50

August 9, 2015 Sunday

Predictably, Sunday's *Wildcreek Wing* was not kind to Miso or to the Wildcreek Police Department. The *Wing's* scathing editorial, peppered with inflammatory quotes from Helaine, rekindled the town's anger over the Julien Pidgeon investigation. There was talk about a recall election for the sheriff and a rehash of the usual derogatory remarks about law enforcement mismanagement.

Then, exactly one week after the *Wildcreek Wing's* brutal editorial, the *Wing* published an article announcing that the coroner had received a final toxicology report—another leak from an unknown source according to the coroner. The report included the results of testing by a privately retained forensic laboratory and the results of Dr. Gadsberry's second autopsy. The report was a bit of a bombshell—a good example of the negative consequences of publishing leaks of preliminary results.

According to the *Wing*, Julien Pidgeon did not die directly as a result of toxins from death camas, low larkspur, or a combination of the two. The report revealed that the levels of toxins in the wine, pesto and Julien Pidgeon's body would have made him seriously ill over the course of several hours, but, after extensive testing, were not high enough to kill him. Dr. Gadsberry determined, instead, that Julien had been suffocated while in an extremely weakened state, most likely where he was found, inside his car.

In the *Wildcreek Wing's* "expert" opinion, the new report left open the possibility that Julien's killer might also have killed Thor. "Perhaps," the *Wing* proposed, "Thor intended only to make Julien sick. If so, the real killer might still be roaming the unprotected streets of Wildcreek. Anyone could be the next victim! No one was safe! The killing must stop!" But never one to follow its own advice, the next big killing in the town was the one made by the *Wildcreek Wing*. It sold more newspapers that Sunday than ever before.

Unfortunately for Deputy Miso, Sheriff Cannon and Prosecutor Turley were both avid, if not admiring, readers of the *Wildcreek Wing*. After reading the article with his morning coffee, Miso knew he would get a call. However, he was surprised to get it as early as 9:30 a.m. A harried Sgt. Skew asked him to report to the Sheriff's Office immediately. Then, leaving no time for Miso to reply, she disconnected.

So, at 9:40 a.m. Miso walked into the Sheriff's Office. He was not sure if he would be walking out again still carrying his badge and gun. He tried calling Buttars from the lobby to get some idea about the sheriff's intentions, but Buttars wasn't answering. Hopefully this didn't mean that the drawer distractions were unavailable.

Miso took the stairs to the fourth floor, in part, to delay his meeting with the sheriff. Maybe Buttars would be in the stairwell—Buttars used the stairwell for frequent breaks. The sheriff, who thought sitting and shouting were strenuous exercises, never thought to look down past the fourth-floor stairs to find anybody.

Fortunately, Miso did find Buttars. Buttars was waiting for him. "Miso, it's so crazy up there. I don't know what's going to happen, but it's not good. They made Sgt. Skew and me leave. She's in bad shape. Is catatonia catching?"

"Not funny, Buttars. Who is 'they'? Who is up there with him?"

"Chief Deputy Fonda Dan is up there! And Prosecutor Turley. Here, take this. That's all I can do for you now." Buttars handed Miso the key to the special desk drawer. "If you get a chance, press the red button. It activates all the other buttons simultaneously."

"Thanks, Buttars," Miso sighed. He continued up to the sheriff's office on the fourth floor. The echoes of Buttars' quickly retreating footsteps on the stairs sounded like a movie machine gun. The future was not looking bright.

Before Miso could knock, the door to the sheriff's office opened. Miso had a moment of panic. Were there cameras in the stairwell? No. They must have heard his heartbeat.

"Good morning, Sheriff," Miso tried to smile. "Fonda, Wendell... how can I help?"

"You can start by doing your job instead of drinking at that damn Woodpecker bar for one thing! What made you go to Myra Briney's party anyway? You *arrested* her, Miso! You are the one who arrested Myra Briney!" Fonda Dan and Wendell nodded in agreement.

Miso wanted to say, "I followed orders, sir. I thought everybody knew that!" Instead, he said, "I'm really happy that Myra has been released and that she's recovering. I know you are, too. WPD should show its support. I had no idea that Helaine Pia would react that way."

"Well, she did. And so did the *Wing Ding*. And so did half the town. Now you've got to fix this mess you've made!" Fonda Dan and

Wendell again nodded in agreement. "You are going to go out there, find a new suspect, and make an arrest by 3p.m. this afternoon."

"I... I don't think I can do that, Sheriff," Miso stammered. The 3 p.m. deadline baffled Miso.

"We don't care what you think, Miso. Your job is to find and arrest the person or persons who killed Julien Pidgeon and Thor Thomsen. You've had plenty of time, and you have plenty of choices. Pick one.

"You could arrest Helaine Pia, for example. She discovered the body and her alibi is wobbly. Don't you watch TV? The one who discovers the body is usually guilty.

"Or... you could rearrest Myra Briney. After all, she and Katharine Holmeier hated Julien Pidgeon. Thor could have made the poison for them and then threatened to go to the police. Katharine could have killed him and then gone back into hiding. We're keeping that warrant active. And the best part—the *Wing* would have to apologize to me for pressuring this office into releasing a killer." The sheriff really seemed to like this idea.

"Or..."

"Okay, okay, and okay!" Miso shouted an "okay" to each angry official. He had to stop the sheriff's tirade before the whole town went to jail. Arresting Myra Briney again was a horrifying suggestion. For a short minute, Miso enjoyed the idea of arresting Helaine Pia. Then, he thought about Afton and what she might say. Her opinions had become important to him.

"Just give me a few days, sir, to re-interview Helaine Pia and delve into Thor's possible relationships with Myra and Katharine. I promise I'll have something for you by Friday." Miso had no idea what that "something" would be. Right then, he desperately needed time.

The sheriff, Fonda Dan, and Wendell Turley went into a three-person huddle. When they came out, the sheriff spoke for all of them.

"Fine, Miso, you have until Friday. If you aren't ready to make an arrest, you are suspended. Maybe fired. Got that?"

"Yes, sir."

"Wendell, go find Sgt. Skew." Fonda Dan seemed to be taking over. "We need her to change the wording in the sheriff's speech for the press conference this afternoon. She needs to change 'arrest today' to 'arrest imminent, no later than Friday'. And make sure he says 'Magpie' instead of 'Woodpecker'. And don't let him say 'effing'. Oh, and Deputy Marquart will *not* be attending the press conference." Fonda Dan liked to dictate orders even more than her husband—a well-known fact evident at home as well as at the office.

Miso was happy that he'd managed to get through the meeting without having to use the special drawer key. However, the first thing he did after leaving the Sheriff's Office was to make a copy of the key before returning it to Buttars. The second thing he did was to call Afton with more than a few questions. She wasn't answering, so he left a message. Hopefully, he didn't sound too desperate.

Chapter 51

AUGUST 17, 2015 MONDAY

Afton returned Miso's call early Monday morning. Very early. She hadn't heard the news broadcast of the press conference the day before and only learned about it from the article in the *Wing's* Monday morning edition. Miso started talking first, right out of the gate.

"Morning, Afton. Tell me why I shouldn't go and arrest Helaine right now. She found the body, her alibi was birdwatching with no witnesses, and she hated Julien Pidgeon for possibly contaminating the town with XDR TB. She told me on the morning she found his body that she just wanted to talk with him. But we've all seen her hide from him whenever he walked into the Magpie. She had Ben give him free beer to make him pass out. She's made fools of us! And I'm going to lose my job!"

"Miso, calm down. We've already talked about this. You've—*we've*—done a great job in discovering Thor to be the poisoner. I suggested that you investigate Julien's past, and you did. You found Thor's history and motive. And you found overwhelming evidence of the poisoning in Thor's cabin. As for the suffocation, that could have been Thor as well, although I doubt it. I can't see Thor waiting around for Julien to sicken to the point of near death in the front seat of his car.

"I doubt if Helaine would wait either. Helaine doesn't seem to have much patience or be much of a planner. She may be a master mixologist, but she could never have produced the death camas and low larkspur extracts. Also, there's never been anything to indicate Helaine and Thor could have been working together. I *know* you, Miso. You won't let your temper or the sheriff cause you to arrest someone without any plausible evidence at all. You should at least reinterview Helaine before you arrest her.

"Something is missing here, Miso. We need to keep looking." Afton felt certain that Helaine did not kill Julien or Thor. "I want to help you. We work well together. If you get me the rest of your reports and photos of the physical evidence, I'll do my best to find out what happened and let you know what I think. After that, if you still want to arrest Helaine—well, that's your call."

Miso realized that Afton was right. His anger at Helaine and the sheriff was getting in the way of a professional investigation. He might not be able to meet the sheriff's deadline, and he might lose his job. But he never wanted to doubt that he had done his best.

"Okay, Afton. I'll have Buttars deliver copies of the reports and photos as soon as possible. After all, what can the sheriff do now? Fire me? He's already planning to do that, anyway. Tell Ralph to stay calm if he hears a knock on the door late tonight. I need Buttars in one piece for at least a week.

"And one other thing. Remember what you said at Myra's party? You know, about who else might know about the equipment in Thor's cabin? Were you thinking about Sarah and Rascal?"

Afton *had* been thinking about Sarah and Rascal when she spoke to Miso at Myra's party. She had been thinking that she didn't want to tell Miso all that she knew because some things, like the farm sale, might possibly lead him in the wrong direction. She felt strongly that the items in the cabin were important, but they were not evidence against Sarah and Rascal.

"No, Miso, I didn't mean to suggest that either Sarah or Rascal killed Thor or Julien. I'm not really sure what I meant..."

"Okay," Miso said. "Call me as soon as you find something. Thanks. Goodbye, then."

Was Miso beginning to doubt her? Afton worried that she might be doing more harm than good. She wouldn't be surprised if Miso were losing confidence in her. She was losing confidence in herself, too.

Just as Afton suspected, Miso *had* noticed the change in Afton's voice when she answered his question about Sarah and Rascal the day before. What was she not telling him? After stewing about it most of the night, he came to a decision. He would send Buttars to re-interview Mrs. Moser. That strategy worked out well the last time. And maybe, just maybe, Buttars would come back with apricot dumplings—a sure-fire antidote to WPD politics.

Miso waited until dawn to call Buttars at home. "Hey, Buttars! This is Miso. Thanks a lot for taking that package over to Afton last night. Any trouble with her dog? No? That's great!" Miso was also at home. He had no desire to see the sheriff or his minions, Fonda Dan and Wendell Turley.

"I need you to go over to the Wildcreek General Store and talk with Mrs. Moser. Something is going on with Sarah and Rascal Woods.

Could you find out more about their relationship with Thor? Thor seemed to confide in Mrs. Moser, so maybe she might have insight into any problems that might provide a motive for his murder. I'm going to track down Sarah and Rascal and try to interview them today. Call me when you're done."

"No problem, Miso. I've been spending most of the day in the stairwell. The sheriff is on a rampage and keeps mumbling your name. I really need some sunlight and fresh air. I'll just drop off a quick note for Sgt. Skew, leave by way of the basement exit, and walk over to Mrs. Moser's. Wish me luck!"

Buttars was truly an optimist—like Winston Churchill who didn't think there was much use in being anything else. Miso loved Buttars for that and wished him the *very* best of luck. Miso hoped for luck, too. He called and left a message for Sarah and Rascal Woods. They never returned his call.

Chapter 52

AUGUST 19, 2015 WEDNESDAY

Very early Wednesday morning, Miso was awakened by a knock at his door. Looking out the small middle window at the top of his Craftsman front door, he saw a smiling Buttars holding a paper bag with handles. Miso opened his door hopefully. Today could be a good day.

Buttars said, "I brought coffee, too!" The day *was* looking good.

After they consumed a dozen apricot dumplings between them and drained a pot of extra dark roast coffee, Buttars ruined the rest of Miso's day by recounting his interview with Mrs. Moser.

"You were right. Mrs. Moser did know something interesting. Sarah and Rascal do not own Bullhead Farm. They sold it to Thor this spring and have kept the whole thing secret. I'm still looking for the paperwork. The Assessor must have *some* record of the sale.

"Put simply, the sale came about because Rascal borrowed money from Julien Pidgeon, at a high rate of interest, to pay for farm expenses. When Rascal couldn't pay it back, Julien threatened to take the farm.

When Thor found out about the situation, he offered to buy the farm from Rascal, and then Rascal could use part of the proceeds to pay Julien.

"The interesting part is that Thor wanted to keep the transaction a secret and allow Sarah and Rascal to manage the farm for as long as they wanted. Thor agreed that if he died before both Sarah and Rascal, Bullhead Farm would revert back to them.

"I got all of this from Mrs. Moser. She was surprised that we didn't know about the farm sale. She said that she told Afton Laurie all about it and thought that Afton would have told us."

For the second time in a month, Miso lost his temper. He almost never did that. On the betrayal scale, Afton's omission, in his opinion, had far surpassed Helaine's angry public accusations. Thor was murdered, and because he was dead, Rascal and Sarah got their farm back. That seemed like an excellent reason to kill Thor.

"Sorry, Miso," Buttars understood immediately. "You should call her and sort this out. Afton is one of the few people who still believes in us." Buttars really was an optimist.

Miso thanked Buttars and walked to the door with him. He asked Buttars to look into the farm sale in more depth and to find out where Thor got the money for it. When Buttars was safely out the door and into his patrol car, Miso called Afton.

"Afton, why didn't you tell me that Sarah and Rascal sold their farm to Thor? They could have learned about Thor's attempt to poison Julien and were blackmailing him. They could have killed Thor to get the farm back. They could have killed Julien, too, for threatening to take the farm. They could have..."

"Miso, just wait a minute. I'm sorry I didn't tell you about Bullhead Farm. The whole thing seemed to be settled and not relevant anymore. There are some good reasons why Sarah and Rascal shouldn't be suspects, and I worried that the sheriff might order you to arrest them. Let's meet and talk about this on Friday. I'll even go to the sheriff with you—and maybe get Efrain involved. I think the sheriff might be a little afraid of him.

"Anyway, I have a strong feeling that the farm transaction is not part of any crime. In fact, I believe that I might find something in the paperwork you sent over. Just give me a chance. There are some facts in the reports that you didn't mention to me before. Go interview Sarah and Rascal again and let me know what they say. We can figure this out. I know we can.

"Oh, and there's one other thing I didn't tell you because I thought it might be privileged and possibly not credible anyway. I got an anonymous note under my door a few weeks ago. I can't tell you who sent it, but the writer said that Helaine Pia had been seen at Wright Lake on the night of Julien Pidgeon's death. The note also said that she was with a man who was arguing with her. The implication was that Helaine was arguing with Julien at Wright Lake and killed him. But, Miso, I don't think that happened."

Miso was in no mood to be placated. "I thought we were supposed to be *sharing* information, Afton. Now I'm not sure I can trust you. Perhaps our 'partnership' isn't working. I want all the copies of my reports back by Friday... if I still have a job!" Miso ended the call.

How could a day that started out with apricot dumplings turn into such a disaster? After his call to Afton, Miso, ironically, followed her advice and attempted to interview the Woods duo. When he saw that neither Sarah nor Rascal had returned his call, he drove to the Wednesday afternoon Farmers' Market to try and find them there. But no one seemed to know why Sarah and Rascal's booth was vacant.

Then, while he was buying a bar of lavender soap from Alma Wuthers, she mentioned to him that Sarah and Rascal had left for

Hackensack, New Jersey, to take care of Sarah's mother who was recovering from hip surgery. They should be back in a few weeks.

"Why did they both have to go? Doesn't somebody have to manage the farm here?" Miso worried that Sarah and Rascal had fled.

"If you knew Sarah's mother, you would understand. It takes a village for that old lady. Honestly, Miso, we don't want Sarah and Rascal to bring her back to Wildcreek. We have too much craziness here already, right?"

Miso said, "Right."

Giving up on Sarah and Rascal for the day, Miso left to call Helaine Pia at the Magpie. Miso told Ben, who answered the call, that he would be at the Magpie at four in the afternoon the next day to ask Helaine a few more questions.

Chapter 53

AUGUST 20, 2015 THURSDAY

The next day, Thursday, had come—only one day before Miso's deadline to find a new person to arrest. Reluctant, *extremely reluctant*, to make an appearance at the office, Miso tried calling Buttars.

"I'm sorry, Deputy Buttars is unavailable," answered a harried Sgt. Skew.

"Drucilla, this is Miso. How are things going over there?"

"Oh, just fine, Miso. We've missed you. But don't tell me where you are. If the sheriff asks, I want to claim ignorance."

"Got it!" Miso replied. "I need to know if there are any messages for me. Like, Sarah or Rascal Woods, Helaine Pia, Afton Laurie... anybody?"

"Well, we *did* get a call this morning, as a matter of fact. Do you know a Melvin Billings? He told me that he wanted to talk with you about Helaine Pia. He wouldn't say more and just left his number. Do you want it?"

"Sure, thanks, Drucilla. You can tell the sheriff that I am diligently following up on promising leads and may be out of cell phone range for a while. I'll call back later today."

"Okay, Miso. Good hunting. But don't take too long!"

Miso immediately dialed the number for Melvin Billings. He was working from home and still in his pajamas. It was hard to feel "official" in pajamas. After a few seconds, someone answered.

"Hello? This is Deputy Missoula Marquart. I'm returning a call from Melvin Billings. Is he there?"

"Great! Thanks for getting back to me, Deputy Marquart. I'm Melvin Billings. I've been listening to the news for the last couple of months, and I think I need to tell you a few things. I might be able to clear up some of the confusion about Helaine."

"I'm all ears, Mr. Billings. Do you mind if I record the call? I don't have my notebook."

"Sure, no problem. You can call me Mel."

"And you can call me Miso, Mel. What do you have to say?"

"First of all, I know Helaine Pia because she and I go birdwatching together. And that's all we do. I realize there's been some talk about Helaine having an affair, but if she is, it's not with me. Helaine and I don't want her husband to know about our meetings because he won't believe the truth—that we are just watching birds. Helaine told me about Umberto's family in Corsica. I don't want Umberto or any of his family to be angry with me. She told me I would be vulture food if he found out she was seeing me."

From what Miso had heard, Mr. Billings was probably not exaggerating about Umberto's family. Umberto had told Miso, on more than one occasion, that he had moved all the way from Corsica to Wildcreek, Idaho, just to get away from his family's generational violence. Helaine, too, had made jokes about sending Umberto's brothers to

Julien's house for a "friendly" visit. However, it didn't sound likely that the Corsicans would be bringing along a concoction of death camas and low larkspur on such visits.

Melvin continued, "On the Saturday that Julien Pidgeon died, Helaine was with me looking for a Boreal Owl nest that we suspected was in the wooded area bordering the south edge of Wright Lake. We were in the woods from about six in the evening to four-thirty the next morning. And if Helaine told you that she was at Bongo Lake on the night of the murder, it was only to protect the nest so the owls could raise their babies in peace. She wasn't really lying. You understand, right?

"Anyway, I remember this clearly because Helaine found the nest first and didn't tell me. I guess she thought we were both watching the same owl. I ended up wasting most of my time trying to track a male owl who was hunting for food. When I learned that she had been watching the female and babies all that time, I was not happy. Uh... but not unhappy enough to *kill* anybody. So please Deputy Marquart, don't arrest me!" Melvin offered a weak chuckle.

Miso was not amused by Mel's attempt at humor. He also wasn't happy that Helaine seemed to have a believable alibi. She had always claimed that she was birdwatching during the time of Julien's murder. Umberto said that he saw Helaine come in at 5:00 a.m. Sunday morning. So, if Billings was accurate about their time in the woods together, Helaine would not have had time to commit the somewhat complicated murder of Julien Pidgeon—even if she were at Wright Lake and not Bongo Lake.

The information from Billings also explained the anonymous note pushed under Afton's door. The note's author must have seen Helaine and Melvin arguing at Wright Lake and assumed that the argument was with Julien.

Miso had been looking forward to confronting Helaine that afternoon about the argument at Wright Lake. He didn't want to admit it, but he had hoped just a little that the interview would lead to enough evidence for an arrest. He was still angry about Helaine's performance at the Magpie. Could he at least arrest her for wasting his time by failing to mention Melvin Billings and lying about her whereabouts? Probably not a good idea.

"Thank you, Mel. Would you mind giving me your address?" Miso took down Mel's personal information and thought he might have Buttars check out the story. He thought about calling Afton, too, to tell her about Billings, but he was still angry with her for not sharing information. In addition, he suspected that Afton would tell him not to arrest Helaine. He was almost sure that he wouldn't do it, but he didn't want to give up the image of Helaine behind bars just yet.

Chapter 54

AUGUST 20, 2015 THURSDAY

While Melvin Billings was kindly providing an alibi for Helaine Pia, Helaine was reading and re-reading the *Wing* articles that quoted her comments about Miso. When Ben told her that Miso was coming in to talk with her at four that afternoon, Helaine became alarmed. One of the articles mentioned that the sheriff would arrest someone by Friday. Was Miso coming to arrest her? She was sorry that she had treated him so poorly. Even Myra had chastised her for the scene she'd made at the Magpie.

Helaine had chosen the window table by the front door to do her reading. The restaurant would be closed until eleven, so she had plenty of time to think about the upcoming interview. Occasionally, she looked up from her reading and, while drinking unlimited cups of Umberto's Corsican Saint Jean coffee, rested her eyes on Mrs. Moser's store across the street and the traffic going by.

The news articles made her think about the night of Julien's murder. Should she tell Miso about Melvin Billings? That would allay

Miso's suspicions, but Umberto would be sure to find out. Something else was worrying her as well. It was something about the drive past Julien's house on the night of his murder. She just couldn't figure it out. Maybe Mrs. Moser could help her remember. Mrs. Moser would know what to say to Miso, too.

Helaine had seen Mrs. Moser drive out of her driveway earlier, so she knew she would have to wait. The waiting was torture. Helaine hoped that if she could just give Miso some new information about Julien's killer, then maybe he might forgive her. She would have to check with Mrs. Moser soon and then investigate a few other things, too, before Miso showed up for the interview.

Helaine continued watching and reading until she saw Mrs. Moser return and turn into the side drive. Mrs. Moser had a private yard and parking area behind the store. She had a beautiful little kitchen garden there, too.

"Ben!" Helaine called for her son who was in the kitchen slicing onions. "Ben! I'm going out for a while, but I'll be back in time for lunch service. Don't forget to put more white wine in the refrigerator. The Cuvee Faustine Blanc, please. Thanks!"

"Okay, Mom!" Ben called from the kitchen. Later, he would wish he'd left his onions to go talk with her.

Chapter 55

AUGUST 20, 2015 THURSDAY

A t 3:45 in the afternoon, Deputy Miso walked through the front door of the Magpie, strode over to the bar, and asked Ben to let Helaine know that he was ready for the interview. Ben said nothing. He turned around and went into the kitchen. After a few minutes, Umberto came out with a grim expression on his face.

"Miso, hello! How can I help you?"

"Hello, Umberto. I called yesterday and arranged a meeting with your wife for four this afternoon. Do you have a private place we can talk?"

"I'm sorry to tell you Miso, but Ben and I haven't seen her since this morning. She was reading in the dining area and then yelled that she had to go out for a while."

"Do you know where she went?"

"No. We have no idea. She left her purse and phone here. And she didn't take the car. We couldn't even call her. She was supposed to help with lunch service, but she never showed up. We were hoping that you knew something. We thought maybe you arrested her!" Umberto glowered at Miso.

"No, no, no, Umberto. I was actually coming with good news. I just need to confirm a few details, but it looks like we have good evidence now that Helaine really was bird watching on the night of Julien's murder."

"I wish you had told her that, Miso. She was worried, especially after the party for Myra, that you might decide to arrest her. Who knows what that sheriff would try to make you do? This morning, she was reading all the *Wing* articles about the murder. Especially the one that announced an arrest on Friday. That's tomorrow, right?"

"Right. I'm sorry, Umberto. I didn't find out about her alibi until this morning. I wish I'd called earlier with the news."

Miso's energy had dropped to zero. He felt dizzy and slightly nauseous. How could he investigate when the sheriff's threats intimidated potential witnesses? He decided to ask the sheriff tomorrow for another week to find Helaine, Sarah, and Rascal. He doubted Sheriff Cannon would extend the deadline, but Miso was out of ideas.

Fortunately, Umberto had a good idea. He called to Ben for the "good" American whiskey and then, much later, managed to get Miso home safely and in fairly good shape. Umberto was a good and loyal friend. Loyalty was important in the Pia family.

Chapter 56

AUGUST 21, 2015 FRIDAY

Miso's phone alarm went off at 5 a.m. the next morning. He wanted to get up early in hopes that he could talk to his missing witnesses before meeting with the sheriff. Perhaps one of them could point him in the right direction.

First, he called Umberto. "Has Helaine returned?"

"No," Umberto told him. "Helaine has not come back or called. All of us, the whole Magpie family—me, Ben, and our three kitchen staff are planning to close the restaurant and do a building-to-building search within walking distance of the Magpie."

"I'm not telling you not to do it, Umberto, but be careful. Some people will probably be calling WPD to complain. Do not in any way give the impression that the search was sanctioned by law enforcement. Be courteous and give your reasons. Most people in Wildcreek will probably join in the search. Wildcreekers are good neighbors and are more than willing to help each other in a crisis.

Just as he finished talking with Umberto, Miso saw that Sarah Woods was calling. "Hi, Sarah, I was going to call you today as soon as I could find a number for you in New Jersey."

"I heard that. Greg Alatza told us. What do you need?"

Miso, wondering how Greg Alatza had learned Miso's intentions, asked, "Well, first of all, I need to ask you more about what you and Rascal were doing on the night of Julien's murder and what Thor might have been doing."

"On the night of Julien's death, Rascal and I were on the phone all evening and night with various doctors and caregivers trying to find a place for my mother. We found one, but it didn't last long.

"Then, when the situation became impossible, we had to go back to New Jersey and care for her ourselves. We can provide phone records and witnesses to the conversations if you want them."

"Sarah, we've learned that you sold the farm to Thor, is that right?"

"Yes, Thor promised to let us stay on the farm for the rest of our lives if we wanted—as if we were owners. But we didn't want to stay. We were tired of farming. We had no reason to kill Thor. We are planning to put the farm up for sale as soon as we get back to Wildcreek."

"Did you have any idea that Thor was extracting alkaloids from poisonous plants?"

"No! Thor was a very private person. He always came to the Big House to eat, so we rarely went over to his cabin." Sarah hoped Miso was done with this line of questioning. She'd stretched the truth a little. She and Rascal had learned about the poisons the evening before Thor's body was found.

Miso felt deflated and empty. Not only were Helaine, Sarah, and Rascal unlikely killers, Miso had nowhere to look for a likely one. Mechanically, with the muscle memory of many years, he put on his uniform—badge, gun and hat—maybe for the last time and headed over to the Sheriff's Office.

On the way, he called Deputy Buttars to get some idea about what he might be facing. Buttars got right to the point.

"Who's going to be arrested today? Helaine? Sarah? Rascal? Somebody else?"

"Nope, nope, nope, and nope." Miso wasn't feeling very talkative.

"Okay, Miso, I'll get the buttons ready. But I don't think they're going to help this time." And, in fact, they didn't.

Before Miso got to the office, Buttars tried to draw the sting by suggesting that more investigation was needed before an arrest could be made. The suggestion was not well taken.

When Miso walked through the door of the fourth-floor office, the sheriff, Prosecutor Turley, and Chief Deputy Fonda Dan were waiting for him. Buttars was at his desk trying to remain invisible, and Sgt. Skew was in Hawaii for a sudden four-week vacation. Miso received no greeting from the sheriff—just a question.

"So, Missed the Mark Miso, why haven't you arrested Helaine Pia yet? We've already written the press release. After what she did to you, I'd think you'd want her in jail as soon as possible!"

"Well, Sheriff, it looks like she has an alibi for the Julien Pidgeon murder, and I haven't been able to question her about the Thor Thomsen murder. I called and made an appointment to interview her, but she was gone before I got over there. We can't seem to find her—she disappeared yesterday morning. Her family is worried that something may have happened to her." Miso prepared himself for the explosion of recriminations about to erupt from a now shaking Sheriff.

"I'll tell you what happened to her, Miso! Your incompetence allowed a double murderer to get away! You warned her that you were coming, and she took off! Lucky for all of us, I figured this would happen and prepared accordingly. You're not going to force me to apologize to the *Wing Ding* for something that is entirely your fault! Wendell, hand Buttars the warrant for Helaine Pia's arrest and hand Miso his suspension papers. Now!"

Buttars, who was too intimidated to use the buttons, meekly took the warrant from Wendell Turley. He noticed that there were two warrants in the stack. One for the arrest of Helaine Pia, and one to search the Magpie. The search warrant mentioned, among other things, skewers.

After leaving his badge and gun with Buttars, Miso went home, donned his pajamas, and went to sleep. When he woke up, he began a five-day-long binge-watching odyssey, watching any sport he could find—baseball, tennis, golf, NFL pre-season, Premier League soccer... Who knew that snail races were televised? Fortunately, and intentionally, he avoided that evening's local news broadcast of the sheriff's press conference.

But Afton was not so fortunate. She watched the sheriff belittle his deputy, call Helaine a mass murderer, and congratulate himself on making Wildcreek safe again. Fonda Dan, the Chief Deputy, waved a kebab skewer around in the air and told the crowd that a skewer from the Magpie had been the weapon that killed Thor Thomsen. The *Wing* reporter at the scene finished by asking if Deputy Miso was now sitting around in his underwear watching TV. Typical of the *Wing*, the reporter got it wrong. Miso was in his pajamas.

Afton called Miso right after the newscast. Miso did not answer. He did not answer *any* of her four calls that night.

Chapter 57

AUGUST 22, 2015 SATURDAY

On Saturday morning, Afton tried calling Miso again. This time
he answered. She told him she was sorry for not telling him
everything, but she got no further than that.

"Afton, don't call me anymore. Every time I take your advice,
something bad happens. I got a warrant for Thor, and he was dead.
I delayed arresting Helaine, and now she's gone. I listened to you, and
now I'm suspended. Please... just leave me alone." Miso knew that he
was being unfair, that Helaine should not be arrested, but he didn't
care. He didn't care about anything, and he didn't want to talk to
anybody.

Miso's abrupt ending to their conversation left Afton feeling abandoned. For years she had lived in Wildcreek with only Efrain and
Ralph as close friends. People knew *of* her, but they didn't *know* her.
She had been happy with that. Why did she let Efrain talk her into
trying to help Myra? She can't help people. Not anymore. Even by
helping find the truth, she had made everything worse. Just like she did

in Brewster County. Her instinct or her intuition, or whatever those feelings were, seemed to be going haywire. She had depended on them all her life to make sense of the world, and now they were seemingly gone. Weren't they? Wildcreek would be better off if she kept to herself in her cabin on Littlecatch Creek.

So that's what she did. Except for occasional outings to the Short List with Greg Alatza or shopping in Sandpoint, she stayed at home. Greg was perfect company for Afton because he preferred to do all the talking—about himself, of course. And he never turned down a free meal.

By Tuesday, Miso's self-pity had reached rock bottom. After listening to a report describing physicist Stephen Hawking's new theory on black holes, Miso decided to fall into one. His mind exhausted itself with thoughts about the mistakes he had made. His attention span became miniscule—it had always been short. He added baking shows to his day-long binges. Sleep was difficult, and his shower hadn't seen action in days. In fact, he didn't even know the day was Tuesday and had to look it up.

Without consulting anyone, he express-mailed a letter of resignation to the sheriff with copies to Fonda Dan and Wendell. The letter was short and to the point. "I quit. As of today, Tuesday, August 25, 2015. Sincerely, Missoula Griswald Marquart." The letter made him feel better. Almost happy. Whatever had happened or would happen to Helaine Pia, he would not be part of it—or responsible for it.

Chapter 58

AUGUST 26, 2015 WEDNESDAY

Miso woke up on Wednesday morning and took a shower. He found that he no longer had any interest in who would win *Cake Wars*. That surprised him. He lingered over his coffee and watched all three hours of *The Dan Patrick Show*—without falling into unfocused reveries or picking up old sports magazines.

Unbidden, thoughts about his last week as a WPD officer began to surface. Now a regular citizen, he tried to push them aside. A mere inkling of an idea, however, kept returning to him. He thought he might know how to find Katharine Holmeier. But, even if he could find her, why would he want to?

Miso continued to worry about Katharine. Someone at the WPD might come up with the same idea about her location. It occurred to him, that because he was no longer an employee of WPD, he had no duty to reveal her whereabouts even if he knew. He decided to call Efrain and do whatever he could to keep Katharine from suffering the same fate as Myra—from being arrested for something she didn't do.

"Hello, Davina," Miso tried not to sound like a deputy. "I was wondering if I could talk to Efrain for a few minutes. I just need to tell him something about one of his clients. Nothing bad."

"Deputy Miso! So good to hear from you. Morris was just telling me that I should go over to your place and check on you. Do you want company? That Sheriff has gone completely overboard. He's insane!"

"No. Not necessary, Davina. But thanks! I only need to talk with Efrain for a few minutes." Miso could not believe his bad luck. His first effort to make contact after becoming a regular citizen had resulted in a near visit from Davina and Morris. He would have to be more careful in the future.

"Okay, Miso, no problem. He's in his office. I'll put you through. Take care!"

"Miso! Is that you?" Efrain tried to be solicitous. "What do you need me to do? I can't believe sheriff suspended you. You and Buttars were the only competent officers in the department. Wildcreek is in big trouble. *Big* trouble."

"Did something happen to Buttars?" Miso had heard nothing in his isolation.

"Yes. He was suspended shortly after the search of the Magpie. Apparently, the sheriff was angry that Buttars had not brought back everything on the warrant 'shopping list'. Sheriff Cannon wanted a skewer with Thor's blood on it and copies of airline tickets issued to Helaine. Buttars refused to go back to the Magpie and 'look again'".

"Efrain, that's terrible news about Buttars. Maybe I'll call him. I should let you know that I'm not suspended any more. I resigned yesterday. And don't worry, I feel better than I've felt in months.

"I just called you to tell you that I think I know how to find Katharine Holmeier. And if I can figure that out, then maybe someone else might be able to. If you know where she is, you should tell her to move away from the Wright Lake area. A couple of witnesses have provided information that led me in that direction. One of the witnesses was Afton Laurie. She told me about a note she received from a witness who saw Helaine Pia at Wright Lake. I'm guessing you know the identity of that witness. You don't have to say anything. I just wanted you to know. And you might want to talk with Afton."

"Thanks, Miso. I've been trying to get in touch with Afton, but she doesn't answer. Have you heard from her? What do you think? Maybe, we should all meet at Greengrocers tomorrow. You, Afton, and me."

"No thanks, Efrain. I just wanted to let you know about Katharine. No meetings for me. I'm not sure what I'm going to do next, but it won't be meetings." Was there a whisper of a smile hiding in Miso's answer? Maybe. A small one. Meetings were the worst.

Chapter 59

AUGUST 27, 2015 THURSDAY

The next day brought alarming news. A waste management operator found a leg stuck to the bottom of a dumpster at the Trapper Road Station. Dr. Gadsberry was one of the first to arrive and, after a brief examination, opined that the leg belonged to a woman of middle age and blonde complexion. The leg had been severed from the hip with an extremely sharp blade and then completely drained of blood.

Dr. Gadsberry refused to speculate as to whom the leg belonged, but rumors of Helaine Pia's dismemberment abounded. A severed leg was not the kind of news that could remain secret in a town like Wildcreek. Soon, stories were spreading everywhere that a vampire killer was now terrorizing Wildcreek. A sizeable crowd of citizens began picketing the Sheriff's Office, throwing garlic cloves at the door, and painting crosses on the windows.

Another news story that day, overshadowed by the news of the severed leg, was the discovery of a bouquet of death camas and low larkspur placed on top of Julien Pidgeon's grave mound along with a necklace. A *Wing* reporter, who had been thinking about ways to make the vampire story last a few more days, had gone to Julien's grave to "check" whether anyone, dead or alive, had "escaped" from it. Finding the bouquet and necklace seemed good enough, however, so he put his shovel back in his car and called for a photographer.

On Friday, Umberto Pia identified his wife's leg. He agreed to remain on call in case other parts of her could be found. The Magpie closed, and due to a shortage of WPD officers, the Fire Department loaned a few firefighters to keep guard over it.

Ben stayed at home playing video games. He couldn't help wondering what could have happened to his mom. Should he have asked her more questions when she said she was going out? He'd thought that she was just going birdwatching again, and he didn't want his dad to know.

The sheriff held another disastrous press conference. "We, the good people of Wildcreek, need a new suspect! And fast! Helaine Pia obviously didn't die fleeing arrest. What was wrong with that woman? She seemed to seek out trouble and danger. And worse, the search for the rest of her threatens to use up the balance of the WPD yearly budget!" Sergeant Skew was still in Hawaii and later swore under oath that she had nothing to do with the script.

The constant pressure from the *Wildcreek Wing* continued to infuriate the unrestrained sheriff. The *Wing* wanted to know why WPD was always issuing warrants for dead people. Reporters managed to get a list of currently outstanding arrest warrants and prominently published it as the "Death List." Katharine Holmeier, unfortunately, was on the list.

Desperate and out of rational ideas, the sheriff called a meeting where no minutes were to be taken. The attendees, Fonda Dan, Sheriff Cannon, and Wendell Turley needed to decide what to do next.

"Dear, I think our only option is to re-arrest Myra Briney. She's ambulatory now, and she has no real alibi. She and Katharine Holmeier could have planned the murder together, right?" Fonda Dan was full of ideas, but not good ones.

"That's going to be a little hard to sell, Fonda Dan. Myra was in jail when Thor Thomsen was killed. And she hadn't been able to communicate with anyone for quite a while."

Wendell suggested, "Why don't we just leave the warrant out for Katharine Holmeier and tell the *Wing* that she is now our suspect?"

Fonda Dan chimed in, "We should also issue warrants for Sarah and Rascal Woods. Miso never had a chance to write his reports, so technically we don't know that Helaine and the Woods probably had passable alibis."

"Um, I don't think that's going to work, Fonda Dan." Wendell rarely opposed the Chief Deputy. "Judge George told me there is now a moratorium on warrants until this whole 'Death List' thing gets cleared up. So, no more warrants."

"Well, what are we going to do?" The sheriff waited. Apparently, he couldn't come up with even one outlandish suggestion.

"I think," whispered Wendell, "that we should get Miso and Buttars back in here." Wendell ducked, just in case Fonda Dan started throwing things.

"You handle it, Wendell. Meeting dismissed!" The sheriff got up and walked out.

Wendell Turley correctly concluded that neither Miso nor Buttars would listen to his pleas. So, he called Efrain McKinley. Efrain decided that getting Miso and Buttars back into the WPD would definitely be the best option for his clients. After a bit of negotiating, Miso and Butters were offered their jobs back with a thirty percent raise and veto power over press conferences. For Buttars, it was that last part that clinched the deal.

For Miso, the matter was more complicated. Since his departure, he had been feeling better than he had in months. With his experience, he could easily get work with a larger, more stable law enforcement agency. Also, he wasn't confident that he could solve the Julien/Thor/Helaine murders, and he might end up a scapegoat once again.

On the other hand, Buttars and Efrain were urging him to go back. They were his friends, and they needed his help. He, too, was invested in finding out what really happened to Julien, Thor, and Helaine. Finally, without any clear direction, he decided to let fate make the decision for him. He would wait for a sign. Miraculously, and fortunately for Wildcreek, fate sent him a sign the next day.

In between bouts of worry over going back to WPD, Miso continued his habit of watching hours of miscellaneous sports. Saturday's choice was the Montana Grizzlies against the North Dakota State Bison at Washington-Grizzly Stadium in Missoula, Montana. He knew that the Grizzlies were greatly outmatched, but his father named him Missoula Griswald Marquart for a reason, and Miso was a loyal son. Also, in his present frame of mind, watching a slaughter might cheer him. He felt a sort of comradeship with the beleaguered team.

Amazingly, astoundingly, and with only seconds to go, the Grizzlies won on a fourth-and-goal score from the one-yard line. No other team had beaten the Bison in a regular-season, non-conference game that year. That had to be a sign. All of a sudden, Miso had a strong desire to call Afton. But he held off until Sunday just to be sure.

Chapter 60

AUGUST 30, 2015 SUNDAY

On Sunday, his decision made, Miso felt a heavy burden fall from his shoulders. He should have called Wendell first, but instead he called Afton. Looking back, he realized he had treated her unjustly, and he wanted to repair the damage. He was elated when she answered his call.

"Afton, it's me, Miso. Look, I haven't been myself lately and... well... I was wrong to blame you for the way the investigation was going and... um... I'm going back to the Sheriff's Office on Monday, and I want your help." Miso waited, hoping Afton would forgive him and help him solve the murders.

"Let me get this straight, Miso. You want me to help you with an investigation that is spiraling out of control, that has grown to three murders and counting, that has produced very little evidence against a living person sufficient to support a conviction or even a warrant, and that seems to be in the hands of a group of people who strongly dislike each other. Do I have that right?"

"Not exactly, Afton. I don't *strongly* dislike you." Miso smiled, but he wasn't sure that Afton got the joke. Phones weren't the best vehicle for this kind of humor. "Maybe I could come over and fill you in on what's happened lately. At least as much as I know. Ralph probably misses me, right?"

That much, at least, was true. Ralph hadn't seen anyone other than Afton for ages. He felt socially—and treat—deprived. He could tell that Afton was tired of his baleful stares and moans.

"Okay, Miso. You can come over. But I want you to know that I don't think I can help you. My truth compass seems to be pointing in all the wrong directions. I don't want to hurt anybody or make your life worse." The last point was a hint that Afton was still a little upset about his earlier remarks. But he could fix that.

Miso said, "Fine. I'll be there in forty." It was only a thirty-minute drive to Afton's cabin, but Miso thought he should stop for coffee and chocolate croissants on the way. The croissants from the Mean Bean were pretty good, and he could get dog treats there, too. Better safe than sorry.

Miso's meeting with Afton and Ralph went well. The croissants helped. At one point, Efrain called to join in on the effort to win her back and immediately made a proposal.

"Afton, I have an idea. You know that when we were working together before—well, sort of working together before—we were making real progress. The problem was that we didn't have a way of easily sharing information. Sometimes I told Miso something but not you, or sometimes you told me something but not Miso. That caused a lot of friction, and things fell apart.

"What if we form a team or a group? We could meet regularly and make sure everybody is up to date. There could be emergency meetings, too, if one of us needs help. Of course, this would be informal and not part of any official law enforcement action. We can work out the confidentiality issues and invite experts, like Dr. Gadsberry, when we need an education about some aspect of a case. No one person would be responsible for the successes or failures. We could support each other when things get stalled or political.

"At the very least, we should include me, you, and Miso. Buttars would be good, too, if he's interested, and if the sheriff will let him out of the station. What do you think?"

Afton gave Ralph a big hug and said, "I love the idea of a team, Efrain! That's what we all need. How soon can we get started? There's so much work to do to untangle three murders. When is the first meeting?"

Miso smiled at Afton and said, "I agree wholeheartedly! Dr. Gadsberry was asking me if there was some way to share his information without seeing it in the *Wing* the next day. He and the coroner will love this plan. And I'm sure that Barbara Rampart can make the Conservation Office meeting room available when we need it. In fact, it wouldn't be a bad idea to have a Wildlife Conservation Officer on the team as well."

Efrain spoke up again. "You all know that I'm a part-time grocer now, right? I don't have a lot of time to organize something like this, and I know that none of you want Davina and Morris involved." Efrain couldn't see them, but they were all shaking their heads 'no!'

"So, I nominate Afton Laurie as chairperson, or captain, or whatever title she chooses. Everybody agree? Afton, you don't get a vote." Of course, they all agreed.

That issue settled, Afton made her first request of the new group. "I think we need a name for ourselves. If no one objects, I want to call us the Wildcreek Whodunits. The name reminds us of our purpose and helps us not to take ourselves too seriously. We're not the FBI after all."

Miso was fine with that idea. He had been considering the names of his favorite sports teams, but Afton's idea was better. Efrain liked it, too.

"Okay, everyone. Miso will let me know the soonest time we can get into the Conservation Office for a meeting, and I'll set it up."

Efrain ended his call. Afton fed Ralph. And Miso went home to watch Jason Day win on the final day of golf at the Barclays. He hadn't watched a cooking show in five days. Things were really looking up.

Chapter 61

AUGUST 30, 2015 SUNDAY

L ater that evening, Afton got another surprising phone call. Sarah and Rascal had heard about the troubles in Wildcreek and were calling to check on her and get some reliable news. Afton told them about the new team effort to solve the murders and about her agreement to help.

Sarah, in turn, told a couple alarming stories about life with her mother in New Jersey. Afton, like Alma Wuthers at the Farmers' Market, agreed that Mrs. Funk should stay in New Jersey. Then Rascal took over.

"Afton, we called for another reason, too. We heard that the sheriff was thinking about issuing a warrant for us. You have to believe me, Afton. Sarah and I did nothing wrong." Afton heard a scuffle in the background. "Well... Sarah did nothing wrong. I did something a little bit wrong, but I didn't kill anybody."

"It was Tuesday, the day before we found Thor's body. Miso called us asking if we had seen Thor. We hadn't, but I told Miso I would go to the cabin and look. I knocked and then looked in all the windows. Thor wasn't there, but weird things were on the kitchen table. I knew I shouldn't have gone inside, but I did anyway. I saw the notes about distilling plant toxins and the silver cake basket that matched the one in some pictures of Thor's family. To make a long story longer, I took pictures of everything, locked up, and went back home.

"The next day, when we found Thor's body, we looked around and took away some paperwork concerning the farm sale. We were scared that someone might think we killed Thor to get the farm back. We don't want it back."

Sarah interrupted, "I told him to delete the pictures, but he says he forgot. We still have them if you want them. And the farm paperwork."

"Don't worry, Sarah. I'm sure our team is on the right track now, and it doesn't lead to you. Take pictures of the farm paperwork and send them to me along with all of Rascal's photos as soon as possible. I'll let you know if they are of any use. Thanks. And, Sarah, I hope your mother recovers soon. We miss you!"

"We miss you, too! We miss Wildcreek, and Thor, and the Magpie, and clean air... Please figure this out so we don't have to worry about getting arrested! And before my mom gets us arrested here!"

As good as her word, Sarah sent the photos within the hour. Well into the early hours of Monday morning, Afton pored over Sarah's attachments, her notes, her lists, Miso's evidence files and the case reports. By breakfast time she thought she had found something. But it needed checking. Finally, she thought she might know who killed Julien Pidgeon and Thor Thomsen. The reason for the murders, however, still eluded her.

Chapter 62

AUGUST 31, 2015 MONDAY

Too early on Monday morning, Afton called Miso and left a message for him to call her. She didn't know if he'd officially rejoined WPD yet, but there was no time to waste. An hour later, she called him again. Luckily, he answered.

"Miso, how are you? Can you talk?"

Miso attempted to tell Afton he was fine, but he wasn't quick enough.

"Good. Listen, after I looked at your evidence again, I got an idea. Do you have any more information about the fibers found on Julien Pidgeon? Would you be able to compare them to other fibers if I provided some to you?"

Miso tried to ask why she wanted fibers analyzed, but Afton began talking again before he could utter a word.

"Thanks. I'm checking on a few things, but I'll be ready to present something to the team by tomorrow afternoon. Sorry about all the mystery, but I want to make sure I'm right before I accuse someone."

Once again, Miso tried to break into the conversation. But all he heard was...

"Of course, I'll be careful. Thanks again. Bye!"

After her mostly one-sided conversation with Miso, Afton quickly fed Ralph, made a quick call to Davina Binns, and then headed off to Wildcreek for eating, shopping, and a little investigation. Her first stop, at 8:55 a.m., was the Wildcreek General Store and Café. Mrs. Moser was just opening the shop's front doors.

"Hello, Afton. I'm so happy to see you. It's been so long! You will bring good luck after all these days of sorrow."

Afton blushed. She didn't think she would bring good luck.

"No Mrs. Moser. I haven't been lucky lately. I'm just here to look around and possibly find something for Aunt Biddie's birthday."

"Well, dear. You're welcome to look at anything. Would you mind if I quickly take this basket of cookies and muffins over to Greengrocers? I'll be back very soon."

"No problem, Mrs. Moser. I can take them if you want."

"No, no, dear. I must admit that I am also going to chat with Davina for a few minutes, too. I like to hear what Morris has to say. Will you be alright?"

"Oh, yes, Mrs. Moser. Take your time." Mrs. Moser took about thirty minutes. Afton didn't mind the wait at all.

Afton's next stop was Efrain's office and was happy to catch him there. Lately, he had become "Mr. Greengrocers" wearing a green apron adorned with eggplants and squash blossoms when greeting customers during his frequent shifts at the store. However, Afton needed a favor that did not involve organic produce.

"Efrain, thank you for unruffling everyone's feathers yesterday. I feel like we're really going to get some answers soon."

Efrain had been hoping to hear something conciliatory like that from Afton. He was elated that she seemed back to her old self again. "So, Afton, how can I help you?"

"Well, I guessed from reading the letter under my door, that you know where Katharine Holmeier is staying. Right? And if you do know, I would like to meet with Joe Ivan and Katharine soon. If you could arrange for them to come to the Magpie on Friday afternoon at 5 p.m., I think we might be able to bring an end to all of this. They should go in through the back door and stay in the kitchen. You and Myra must be there, too." Afton noticed Efrain's furrowed brow and frown. "Please, Efrain, you'll just have to trust me."

"Hmm... uh... okay, Afton. If I *do* know where they are, I'll do my best to help you. If I *don't* know where they are, I guess they won't be there at 5 p.m. on Friday.

"Sure. Remember, Friday at five. We'll talk more about this at our Whodunits meeting in a couple of days." Afton was about seventy-five percent sure that Efrain had just told her that he would talk with Joe and Katharine, and if they agreed, he would bring them to the meeting on Friday.

Finally, as her last stop of the day, Afton arranged to meet Miso in the third-floor stairwell of the sheriff's building. The stairwell was acquiring a distinctive "lived in" look.

"Miso, I need to drop off a few things with you, especially this list of people for you to contact. Please do all you can to persuade them to attend a meeting at 5 p.m. on Friday at the Magpie. Food and drink will be served. The Whodunits, hopefully, will meet before then to discuss a plan that I think you'll like.

"Afton, this is too many meetings! I promised myself when I quit the WPD that I would never go to a meeting again. Except for the Whodunits, I'm not going to meetings anymore—on principle."

"Stop being such a baby, Miso. After Friday you'll be able to keep your promise. And please call me on Thursday if you are unable to get everything we need, including the invited guests."

Then, she clattered down the steps and went home after a quick stop at Safeway. Ralph was happy that his mistress was happy and that she brought him salmon bites. Afton bought wine and smoked oysters for herself.

The next day, at lunchtime, the Whodunits held their first meeting. Dr. Gadsberry showed up with carne asada and fish tacos as a gesture of goodwill. As they ate, they worked out the details of a plan to resolve all three murders. Each member of the team provided key information that finally solved the mystery. If all went as planned, the murderer of Julien, Thor, and Helaine would be revealed and arrested on Friday.

Chapter 63

SEPTEMBER 4, 2015 FRIDAY

On Friday, the 4th of September, at 4:30 p.m. in the afternoon, Afton and Miso arrived at the Magpie to meet Umberto and Ben. They arranged a long table across the room from the bar with small tables and chairs arranged in a rough semi-circle facing the front—one end of the semi-circle by the bar and the other end by the long table. Another table, at the front of the restaurant, was set up facing the semi-circle for Afton, Miso, and Buttars. Umberto and Ben had stools immediately in front of the bar so that they could keep the food and drinks replenished.

Next to arrive, through the back entrance, were Efrain, Myra, Katharine, and Joe Ivan. Their reunion had been a happy one. Myra had lost her moribund manner and was smiling and talking as Joe and Katharine eagerly told Afton and Miso how they met and fell in love. The two may have left out a few things, of course, like Katharine's early kidnapping and imprisonment, and the large amount of stolen money, still undisclosed to all but a few, but no one asked for details.

Miso assured Katharine that he would not be arresting her on the traffic warrant that day and asked her to wait in the kitchen with Joe.

Finally, the other guests arrived, making thirteen in all: Buttars, who came with Dr. Gadsberry and Melvin Billings, Mrs. Moser, who came with an extraordinary *Sachertorte* , and finally Davina Binns. Davina acknowledged that Morris wasn't on the guest list, but he insisted on coming anyway. Apparently, he also told Biddie that she was not allowed to come, "We're trying to solve a murder, not cause one!"

As soon as everyone was settled, Afton started. "Welcome everyone. I hope no one minds, but our purpose today is not actually to discuss a community watch program or any of the other things you might have been told." Afton looked over at Miso. "Some of you may have guessed that. Instead, we're here to find out who killed Julien Pidgeon, Thor Thomsen, and Helaine Pia." No one spoke up, and no one tried to run out of the room. Afton was certain they would stay at least until the food was gone—including the cake.

"In order to do that," Afton continued, "we have included two people who have not been seen in Wildcreek for a while—Katharine Holmeier and Joe Ivan." This announcement caused murmurs of surprise and smiles. Everybody turned to look as Katharine and Joe emerged from the kitchen and took seats at the table next to Efrain and Myra.

Umberto, always the charming and attentive host, brought out Swiss Chard and Cheese Dumplings, *Strozzapreti*, slices of Chestnut Flour Tart, *Torta Pisticcina*, and an array of meats, cheeses, and olives. Mrs. Moser sliced her cake into sixteen pieces and served a slice to each guest on a blue china dessert plate with a silver fork. Ben served drinks to order. The whole room seemed more like a party than a meeting with a serious purpose. But that was the Wildcreek way. Good food first.

Afton rose from her seat at the front table and began, "Now that everyone has food and drink, it's time to start putting our heads together to figure out what's happening in Wildcreek before it becomes the city with the highest murder rate *per capita* in the United States—or a ghost town." No one laughed at that.

"To start with," she continued, "everyone in this room has something to share. Most of us know each other. Two people, Sarah and Rascal Woods, cannot be here, but they have agreed to let me speak for them."

"Let's start with the St. John's Wort Celebration at the Magpie on Friday, June 26th. Except for Deputy Buttars, Dr. Gadsberry, and Mr. Billings, all of us were there and probably watched Julien Pidgeon making a scene about serving green garlic pesto to Helaine the next evening at his house. To our collective surprise, Helaine agreed."

Ben interrupted, "She didn't want to go to his house, she just wanted to get him out of the kitchen. She was terrified of his XDR TB. And I know she didn't go to his house because Julien called the Magpie on Saturday afternoon and canceled the dinner."

"Are you sure that it was Julien Pidgeon who called?" Afton asked.

"Pretty sure. The connection wasn't great, but the caller had a long, drawn-out Southern accent just like Julien had. His voice sounded a little scratchy, though. My mom was *really* happy that she didn't have to go.

"Then she told me and my dad that she was going birdwatching." Ben looked over at his dad. "Umm... I don't think my dad believed her. So... maybe she could have done something to Julien Pidgeon that night." This thought had been weighing on young Ben's mind for months.

"Well, Ben, I think Mr. Melvin Billings might have some answers for you—for all of us. Mr. Billings?"

Melvin nodded and waved his hand weakly. He desperately wished that he had chosen a seat farther away from Umberto. "Okay. I retired from the East Bonner County Library District in 2014 and became an almost full-time birder. I met Helaine in Wallace where she was attending a Friends of Miners support group. I was telling her about all of my interesting birding experiences, and she said she would like to go with me sometime. Over the following months, she became an avid birder.

"Anyway, together we discovered a Boreal Owl pair, and later the nest, at Wright Lake and spent lots of time watching the owls. We decided to keep it a secret, so the family could raise their owlets in peace. Apologies to anyone we directed to Bongo Lake.

"Helaine joined me at Wright Lake at about 6 p.m. on the night Julien Pidgeon was killed, and we left each other at about 4:30 a.m. the next morning. And I just want everyone to know... ah... Helaine and I never had an affair of any kind. It was me who called her on July 3rd. I'd just located a Hudsonian Godwit." Melvin looked over at Umberto. "Really, Mr. Pia, we only cared about the birds... only the birds!" Melvin crossed his heart with his right forefinger. Umberto nodded but his frown never left his face.

Miso spoke up and looked at Dr. Gadsberry. "We were able to determine that it takes forty minutes to drive from Wright Lake to the Pia household at the designated speed limit. Dr. Gadsberry calculated the time of Julien's death to be between 9 p.m. Saturday night and 3 a.m. Sunday morning. Correct, Doctor?"

"Correct. It might have been a little earlier, but not later than 3 a.m. on Sunday."

"So," Miso said, "it seems that Helaine hardly would have had time to poison Julien or suffocate him later.

"In fact, the person who poisoned Julien Pidgeon seemed almost certainly to be Thor Thomsen. When we arrived at the scene of Thor's murder, his cabin, we discovered equipment for extracting the deadly alkaloids from death camas and low larkspur and some notes about how to process and store the poisons. And, as you all know from reading the *Wildcreek Wing*, death camas resembles green garlic, and low larkspur looks a lot like parsley.

"Julien was poisoned with both the plant material and the extracts. The plant material was found in the pesto and in the CSA bag. The added extracts were found only in remnants of the finished pesto and in a wine bottle that appeared to be from the Magpie." At this point, several people gasped audibly, uttered sharp profanities, and dropped their glasses onto the nearest table. Umberto's mouth was hanging open in silent anguish.

"Wait a minute, everyone! The wine is fine! Umberto was able to prove that the label on the wine bottle at Julien's house was a forgery. There's no need to worry!" Miso knew that he would be hearing from Umberto later.

"Now, to continue." Miso resumed his outline of the investigation. "Because the extracts were not part of the contents of the blender, we assume that they were added to the pesto and wine sometime just before consumption.

"And, although we cannot be sure, it's possible that Thor was the person who, pretending to be Julien, called Helaine to cancel the dinner and then appeared in her place at Julien's house. He likely brought the extracts and the wine with him and may have intended to implicate Helaine in Julien's death by leaving a Magpie brand wine bottle. We also have a theory about the way the plant material made its way into Julien's dinner on that fatal Saturday.

"Myra, do you know who packed the CSA bags for the Saturday before Julien's death?"

Myra looked at Efrain and then at Afton. They both nodded encouragingly. "I did, Miso. Just me. I told you that."

"Good. Tell us about the parsley and the CSA bags."

"Okay. So, when I made up the list of ingredients for the bags, I included parsley. I posted the list outside on the bulletin board at Greengrocers, too. Later, I found out that there was a shortage of parsley and couldn't get enough to fill the bags. I meant to cross out parsley on the labels, but I just didn't have time. A lot of people called asking about the parsley, and I had to explain over and over."

Miso asked, "Did Julien or Thor call about the parsley?"

"No, not that I know. I was expecting Julien to be really angry and demand his money back or something. He was like that. Always trying to get things for free or just stealing them. Also, Thor always gave his bag to Sarah, so I doubt that he even noticed that there was no parsley."

Afton chimed in, "I was talking with Thor later at the Farmers' Market, and he mentioned that he had parsley in his bag. I thought maybe Myra found some for him."

Myra shook her head "no".

"One more question, Myra. Did Thor bring anything into the store that morning?"

"Of course. It was the St. John's Wort harvest. He brought in bags and bags of St. John's Wort in CSA bags and made several trips, I think. We were running out of room! Right, Katharine?"

Katharine nodded and said, "That's right. He used CSA bags to pack the flowers and brought them into the store from his truck. That's what he does every year. Thankfully, he finished just before Julien Pidgeon arrived. Those two hated each other." Katharine blushed, thinking that she had probably been the cause.

Afton added, "I saw Thor at his truck fiddling around with the things in his bags. I didn't think anything about it until recently. Then he came back into Greengrocers right after me with his arms full of bags."

Miso followed up. "Davina Binns. How are you today?"

"Fine, sir. And Morris says 'hello', too."

"If I understand correctly, you watch the counter at Greengrocers on Saturdays while Myra and Katharine go to lunch."

"That's right, Deputy. When they come back, I take all of the leftover CSA bags and go home. That's sort of my compensation."

"Were there any leftover bags that day?" Miso was keeping his questions short and hoped that Morris wouldn't have anything to say.

"Yes. There was one bag, but I don't know who it belonged to. It didn't have a name tag. And... by the way, Morris thinks you look better today than you have in the last two months." Miso sighed.

Afton took over from Miso at that point. "We know that Julien Pidgeon walked out of Greengrocers that Saturday morning with a bag containing death camas and low larkspur. The bag must have contained the other listed ingredients, too, or Julien would have called to complain.

"We believe that when Thor brought his first load of St. John's Wort into Greengrocers and put it down near the other bags, he removed Julien's name tag as he was picking up his own CSA bag. He then took the bag and label to his truck and attached Julien's name tag to a bag that he had prepared according to the list that Myra posted earlier in the week. Thor's newly prepared bag, however, contained death camas and low larkspur.

"Thor wasn't aware that no one else received parsley in their bags, so he didn't realize that adding low larkspur for parsley would make him a suspect. In fact, he must never have known because he talked to me about the parsley in his CSA bag at the Farmers' Market later that week. No one else, including him, had anything like low larkspur or parsley in their bags.

"Finally, the name tag switch explains the one remaining CSA bag, unidentified, and left for Davina to take home. That bag was the original bag—

the one packed for Julien by Myra.

"But," Afton continued, "Why would Thor go to such lengths to murder Julien Pidgeon? What could his motive have been? He couldn't seriously believe that Julien was his rival for Katharine's attention. No one, not even Thor would believe that."

Umberto spoke up. "I am sorry to say that I had many angry conversations with Thor about Helaine's birdwatching. I believed that she was not a faithful wife and may have caused Thor to believe that I wanted to be rid of her. Perhaps he thought he would do me a favor to get rid of Helaine and her possible lover, Julien Pidgeon. I am so ashamed of myself, so ashamed!"

This time, Ben turned to comfort his father. "Dad, Afton is right. No one would believe that Mom was having an affair with Julien. She knew he was sick and didn't want to go anywhere near him. It would be more likely that *she* killed him. Uh... I mean... I didn't mean that she did kill him! She didn't! She..."

Afton came to his rescue. "Don't worry, Ben. We don't think Helaine murdered anyone. In fact, later in the investigation, we were able to learn the real reason. Mrs. Moser, would you share with us your conversations with Thor?"

"Yes, dear." Mrs. Moser smiled. "I'm so happy to be helping. Thor was such a nice young man. He came to my store many times. He had a sadness the same as I have from missing my poor Johann, and we could understand each other. He told me that he used to live in Virginia and that his family was forced to leave their home. After that, his mother committed suicide. He believed that Julien Pidgeon was the one who forced his family from their tenant farm and stole all of their family possessions.

"I hated Julien Pidgeon, too, and I am not at all sorry he is dead. He stole hats from my store and took things from other people, always. Some people may not like to speak ill of the dead, but I have no problem saying that he was a very bad person.

"Oh, and Thor also told me that Julien Pidgeon tried to steal the farm away from my dear friends Rascal and Sarah. But Thor saved them by buying the farm. Then Rascal could pay off Julien's lien against the farm. That made Thor happy, and it also made Sarah and Rascal happy. They were getting tired of farming."

"Thank you, Melina," Miso said. "We were able to corroborate those facts by interviewing Thor's adoptive parents in Seattle and later from photo albums found in his cabin after he died. Did Thor ever mention that he was afraid or that someone might want to harm him?"

"No, Deputy. Everyone liked Thor. Except maybe that devil, Julien Pidgeon."

Miso shook his head. "Yes, you're right. Everyone liked Thor, but someone did kill him."

"Yes," Mrs. Moser said. "Someone did do that."

Afton then turned to the subject of Helaine Pia's murder. "Please forgive me, Umberto and Ben. I know this will be difficult for you, but the harsh circumstances of Helaine's death may finally point us in the direction of the killer we seek."

"Ben, would you tell us about the last time you saw your mom? Take as much time as you need."

Ben looked down at his hands, gripped white-knuckled on his knees. "My mom was at one of the window tables at the Magpie on Thursday morning, the 20th, reading old newspapers and making notes. I know she was worried about Deputy Miso coming to interview her at four that afternoon. At one point, all of a sudden, she jumped up and told me that she was going out for a while, and that she would be back in time to help serve lunch."

"But there's more, isn't there?" Afton did her best to sound reassuring.

"Yeah." Ben looked at his dad and said, "I'm sorry."

"When Mom didn't show up for a couple of days, I didn't know what to do. I thought Mom had rushed out to look at some bird, and I knew that would make Dad mad. The deputies were asking my dad questions about where he had been. I... I thought maybe my dad killed her because he thought she was having an affair. I forgot completely what she had told me about her birdwatching on the night Julien died because, at the time, I didn't think it was true, anyway.

"She told me that on the night Julien was killed, when she was on her way home and driving past Julien's house, she saw a car parked in a construction cut out in the wooded area next to his driveway. She said that she saw the driver's profile and thought it looked familiar. But she wasn't sure who it was.

"I don't really see how this helps, though." Ben kept his eyes glued to his hands on his knees. But Umberto, who was well known for his temper, gently put his arm around his son and touched his forehead to the top of Ben's bowed head. Ben visibly calmed in response.

Afton asked the group, "Did anyone see Helaine around noon or afterward on the Thursday she disappeared? She would not have had her car, so we presume she was walking somewhere. Mr. Billings?"

"No, I'm sorry, I didn't see her or hear from her anytime that Thursday or afterward."

"Mrs. Moser, did you see her come out of the restaurant?"

"Oh, no, dear. I did go out to Safeway at one point that morning. I might have missed her."

Miso elected to handle the technical details. "Once again, thanks to the *Wildcreek Wing*, most of you know that Helaine's left leg was severed at the hip, drained of blood, and discovered stuck onto the bottom of a waste station dumpster. Unfortunately, we don't yet have cameras at those stations, so we don't know where, when, or how it got there. Also, we haven't found any other body parts. And, knowing that all of you are rational, intelligent human beings, I'm sure you all are well aware that there are no vampires in Wildcreek. Any questions about that?"

"What was Helaine's blood type? Davina asked. "Morris wants to know." Miso rolled his eyes, ignored the question, and turned back to Afton.

Just then, Miso's phone rang. He listened for three or four minutes, said things like "Are you sure it's not there?" and "Look again" and "Call me if you find anything", and then ended the call. He gave Afton a dark look.

Miso continued. "I've just received news that an important piece of evidence has disappeared. I need to step back for a few minutes and make some phone calls. In the meantime, maybe Afton can relay what she learned from Sarah and Rascal Woods."

"Thanks, Miso. As you know, Sarah and Rascal Woods discovered Thor's body on Wednesday morning, July 29th. That's when Deputy

Miso found the distillery equipment, plant remnants, and pho-
tographic evidence of Thor's relationship to Julien Pidgeon.

"Recently, Sarah and Rascal called me with a confession of
sorts." The group started a low rumble of whispering. "No, no,
I'm sorry everybody. They did not confess to any of the murders.
But apparently, on the day before Thor's murder, Rascal entered
Thor's cabin and discovered the distillery items on the kitchen
table and a few other things. He took photos of everything he
saw and went back home without calling any law enforcement
agency. He told me that—for just a little while—he considered
using the photos to force Thor to deed the farm back to him
and Sarah. Sarah told him to delete the photos and stop thinking
about farming. He finally came to his senses and resolved to call
the police the next day—after talking with Thor. But he forgot to
delete the photos.

"The next morning he went back to Thor's cabin to see if Thor
had come home. That's when he saw Thor's body and called 911.
Then, he and Sarah—and they are not proud of this—looked
around for paperwork that might show they had a motive to kill
Thor, found the farm sale agreement, and took it back to the Big
House. They had heard rumors that the sheriff was willing to
arrest anybody on little or no evidence just to be done with the
investigations." Miso and Buttars both nodded in confirmation.

"Anyway," Afton continued, "Sarah and Rascal sent the photos
Rascal took, as well as photos of the farm sale documents to me. By
that time, a small group, including myself and Deputy Miso, had
formed to share information and work on the cases. Everyone in the
group shared information, and, after study and discussion, we formed
a plan. Last Monday, I spent time talking with people and collecting
items. By the end of the day, I had physical evidence to support the

group's theory. Dr. Gadsberry was amazing. The necessary forensic examinations were all completed yesterday.

"In fact, we thought we had everything we needed until just now when Deputy Miso got a call. It seems that a key item is missing. The other items that we *do have* are: a necklace with a cement pendant, a bouquet of death camas and low larkspur, some craft supplies, photos of the interior of Thor's car, and photos of the contents of Thor's cabin before and after Thor was found.

"In fact, you might say that Rascal Woods is the real hero here. He put the team on the right track. An item from Rascal's photos was missing from the photos later taken by the forensic team at the scene of Thor's murder. That item could only have been taken by Thor's killer. And last Monday I found it in the killer's possession—the same person who actually killed Julien Pidgeon as well as Thor Thomsen, and Helaine Pia.

At this point, Deputy Miso and Deputy Buttars moved to the end of the food table farthest away from the front windows. Heads turned, wondering what was going on. Davina cried, "No! No! Morris! It can't be true!"

But it was. Deputy Buttars apologized and handcuffed Mrs. Melina Moser. He said, "Don't worry, Melina, you can be sure that we'll find the silver cake basket... and the rest of Helaine, too."

Umberto, who had been jealously eyeing Mrs. Moser's *Sachertorte*, jumped up, knocked over his chair, and yelled, "*Stragna*! Witch!" Her cake is probably poisoned! It's sitting on a silver cake basket!"

Mrs. Moser, who had been sweetly smiling at Miso just a minute before, pulled a knitting needle from her waistband and lunged toward the screaming Corsican shouting, "You imbecile, my cakes are the works of an artist! They are divine! It's your red sauce that is killing us!"

Miso and Buttars managed to tackle her seconds before she could impale the hysterical Mr. Pia. Then, Miso called the forensic team across the street and told them he had found the cake basket. Incredibly, Mrs. Moser had brought it with her to the meeting.

"But what was the rest of the evidence you found?" This question came from Efrain. He wondered who would be defending Mrs. Moser. Not him. He had been part of the plan to catch her.

Afton wrapped up the case for the rest of the guests. "In Rascal's photograph, taken the evening before Thor's body was found, the silver cake basket was sitting on the table next to the family photo album open to a picture of a birthday party for young Thor. The cake basket on the table matched the cake basket in the photograph. The forensic photographs, however, taken the morning after, don't show the cake basket anywhere in the cabin on the day of Thor's murder.

"This last Monday," Afton continued, "I visited Mrs. Moser's store. I saw the cake basket in plain view in a display case. I also noted the sharp Swiss carving knives in another case. We've all seen them countless times.

"Mrs. Moser asked to leave for a few minutes, so I used that opportunity to take a knitting needle and some yarn samples from a few of the shawls she knitted and wore herself. And don't worry, anyone, Judge George had already issued a search warrant. It has been under seal until an arrest could be made." Afton flashed Efrain a wolfish smile. He smiled back

"I checked her small garden in the back and found both death camas and low larkspur. And after that, I found Helaine's necklace on top of Melina's compost pile. I'll need Umberto or Ben to identify it later."

Umberto asked, "You mean that ugly rock that my Helaine always wore? She wore it to show her compassion for Melina and Johann and their ordeal at the hands of the East German police. Now we learn that Melina killed her? How could that be true?"

Dr. Gadsberry explained the results of the latest forensic analyses. "The knives from the display case could easily have dismembered a body. The knitting needle was the right size to inflict the wound in Thor's chest. The pendant was interesting. It was a piece of the Berlin wall. We were able to compare it with known samples on display in Las Vegas.

"The yarn from the shawls matched the fibers found in Julien's nose and lungs. There weren't many but they were unique—Qiviut—and not found in Wildcreek. The yarn is extremely costly. Finally, we confirmed that some of the plants in Mrs. Moser's garden were indeed both death camas and low larkspur. The bouquet on Julien's grave most likely came from there."

Some loud scuffling came from Mrs. Moser's direction. "Please, please, I am not a bad person! You are wrong. Let me explain!" Mrs. Moser was frantic.

Efrain told her to stop talking, and Miso recited her Miranda rights.

"I understand, but I must tell my story. You must listen to me. I have been thinking about what I would say for a long while now." So, at her insistence, they let her talk.

Chapter 64

September 4, 2015 Friday

Mrs. Melina Moser adjusted the skirt of her Edelweiss-print shirtdress and proceeded to tell her story as if it were something that happened in the distant past.

"Two weeks before the St. John's Wort Celebration, I sold an antique silver cake basket to Mr. Thor. He did not know that I had purchased it from Julien Pidgeon. Sarah and Rascal were with him, and they, like me, were *greatly* surprised that Thor was willing to pay so much for an old cake basket—usually the tourists were the only ones who bought such things.

"Almost immediately after Thor walked out of my shop with the basket, Julien Pidgeon arrived at the store. He made many insulting comments, as usual, and commented on the absence of the cake basket. I did not tell him who bought it. I think he did not like that. When he left, he took another hat—but he left twenty dollars on the counter! Why did he do that? I do not know, but it frightened me more than his habit of stealing hats! Of course, I later noticed that a Wüs spatula was missing from the cutlery cabinet.

"After that time, Thor came often to my store to visit me and to share with me his story. It was just as I told Deputy Miso and all of you. Julien Pidgeon destroyed Thor's family, took all their family heirlooms, and ultimately caused the death of Thor's mother. That's what I think.

"I learned other things about Julien Pidgeon, also. At the Magpie during the St. John's Wort Celebration, I learned from Greg Alatza who heard from Nurse Darling that Julien had active XDR TB. I know about that sickness—Extensively Drug-Resistant tuberculosis. Not a small number of Russians in the Soviet Union suffered because of it. It was very alarmingly contagious.

"In the Magpie, I could see that Julien was not careful about his disease. He was reckless around food and drink. To stop him from harming the customers, Helaine Pia agreed to have dinner with him. I knew she did not want to. Who would willingly have dinner with Julien Pidgeon—even if he was well? No one!

"He was dangerous. He was a bully. And he was a thief. His insults were cruel and demeaning. Myra and Katharine at Greengrocers were his victims, too. He stole from them without consequences. They were afraid of him, and no one seemed to be able to stop him. Now you see why I decided to do it. Yes, Deputy Miso, I did kill him, Julien Pidgeon, and I am not sorry."

At this point, Efrain interjected, "Thank you, Melina! You don't need to tell us anything else. You've explained enough. You're probably tired now and need some rest, right? Time to go..." Miso gave Efrain a dark look.

"Oh, no, Mr. Efrain. I must continue. I am so ashamed that I remained silent when Miss Myra was arrested. In a way, I am just as bad as that demon Julien. I allowed a good friend to nearly lose her life from fear. My belief that her troubles would go away in a short time was foolish. In trying to protect my friend Thor and rid Wildcreek of a terrible pest, I caused even more harm. I will tell you what happened.

"On Saturday night, late, I drove to Julien Pidgeon's house intending to tell him all that I knew and then stab him with my needle. He would not suspect an old woman like me to be a threat. But when I got to his house, I saw that Thor's truck was there. So, I drove into a small side road nearby and waited. Thor was in the house for a long time. I was worried that Thor might do something foolish.

"When Thor finally left, I drove up the driveway to the house and entered by way of the front door. It was not locked. No one seemed to be there. I walked all around and called for Julien. No answer. Then I checked the garage and saw that devil slumped over in the driver's seat of his car. He was completely still, and his mouth looked as if he had been vomiting. But he was still alive. I realized that Thor must have tried to poison Julien and failed.

"I didn't want Thor to once again be harmed by Julien Pidgeon even in death, so I tried to think of something to prevent that. I opened the front passenger side door wearing gloves, of course—the gloves I knitted with qiviut yarn that match the shawl I am wearing now—and, of all things, I saw my hats in the back seat! I became furious remembering Julien's pride in getting away with stealing things from people.

I held the soft musk ox yarn of my gloves to Julien's nose. He was breathing, but just barely. He was still alive! Then the idea of killing him with the spoils of his own crime overtook me. I could not resist. I grabbed two of the hats from the back seat and pressed them against his face. I could not press hard, but I pressed for a long while until my arms could no longer work, and Julien, I believed, was no longer living. Then I went home.

"I went home with all three hats and burned them. I am still very sad about those hats because I liked them very much. Johann liked them, too. But what could I do? They might have been infected with tuberculosis.

"The stories in the *Wing* confirmed my thinking that Thor was trying to kill Julien. When I saw Thor taking Julien's name tag from a CSA bag on the Saturday before Julien's death, I should have known that Thor was planning something foolish.

Anyway, I thought Thor would be happy to hear that I had finished the job for him. I began to have an idea that might keep him from worrying about being arrested. I tried to call him to tell him about it, but he didn't answer his phone. I called several times, but no answer. Then I visited his cabin late at night several times. He was never home. Finally, on my fourth visit, he answered the door. I handed him a large bag of freshly baked dumplings and told him I had good news for him. I explained how I had helped him and how we could celebrate together and work out a way to help Myra.

"But Thor was not happy at all. He became angry like a crazed bull. I don't know why. Did he think I would say something to the police? He accused me of killing Katharine and demanded that I tell him where she was. Clearly, I am not a madwoman! No one would want to kill Katharine! But instead of thanking me, he tried to kill me with his hands! Sadly, I was forced to stab him with my needle to get away. Johann was terribly upset about that!

"Immediately, I ran to my car and locked the doors. After a little while, Thor did not come out. So... I went back to the cabin and saw that Thor was indeed dead. I thought it might be a good idea for the sheriff to think that Thor killed Julien and that Myra had to be innocent. I could no longer save Thor.

"I very carefully removed any trace of my visit to Thor and left. By then, I had the feeling of a good day's work being done. Oh, yes, and I took the cake basket and the dumplings, too. I decided to keep the basket for myself as a reminder. I thought only Thor and Julien would know it was *the* cake basket. I wish I had taken the time to look at the old photograph album on Thor's table.

"Anyway, after that, things seemed to be getting better. Myra was improving and seemed to be safe from re-arrest. But something very bad happened. Just after I returned from Safeway on Thursday morning, Helaine Pia came into the store and told me that we needed to talk.

"Helaine said that she had seen me waiting in a lay-by near Julien's house very early in the morning on the day of Julien's murder. Helaine wanted to take me to the Sheriff's Office to explain why I was there. Helaine was insistent. I asked her if I could go in the back room to water my plants before leaving. Then I would go and tell Miso all that I knew.

"Oh no! I could not do that, of course. And Helaine would not be persuaded. So, again I had to stab someone. So, so dreadfully regrettable. But, as you all have seen, I had excellent and extremely sharp knives in my shop, and I was able to... you know... take care of the body."

Miso, who was completely absorbed in Mrs. Moser's story, should have been more alert. Umberto, a master chef and proud Corsican, also had excellent and extremely sharp knives. He leapt out of his chair and charged at the woman who was calmly talking about disposing of his wife's body. Fortunately, however, others in the audience were more vigilant. Buttars and Efrain managed to prevent the enraged husband and father from making an early end to Mrs. Moser with his personal Vendetta knife, his *Sperone*.

"Certainly, Mr. Pia," Mrs. Moser continued, "I will need to show you where to find Helaine. Maybe tomorrow. I am truly sorry about her death. She was a good person who wanted to help... even when her help would only have made things worse. I tried to make her understand that.

"I think everything would have been fine if people had just minded their own business. Why did people try so hard to find Julien's killer? Thor and I did a valuable service in ridding Wildcreek of Julien Pidgeon. I tried to make that clear in my letter to the *Wildcreek Wing*. He was a monster. He tried to make us believe that we were helpless, and that he could do anything or take anything he wanted. He was happy to take the lives of our loved ones by exposing us to a deadly disease. He laughed about it. And worst of all—he called my beloved Johann so many terrible names!

"So... I took something from him that *he* loved. His *life!*"

Epilogue

Four days later, on September 8th, Mrs. Melina Moser hanged herself in jail while Sheriff Cannon was holding a press conference to congratulate himself on finding the culprit of the recent murders. He'd ordered the entire staff of WPD to stand behind him on the outdoor stage, so no one had been watching the inmates. Mrs. Moser left a note saying that it was time to go and be with her beloved Johann and that she was so very sorrowful, but she could not remember where she had put the rest of Helaine.

Two weeks later, on September 22nd, Rascal and Sarah took over Mrs. Moser's store. It turned out that Mrs. Moser had left it to them in her will. Even before the ink was dry on the transfer of title, Rascal had painted over the "and Café". They decided to rename the store but spent the next several years trying to agree on a new sign. They never managed it.

On Thursday, October 8th, Katharine and Joe got married. It was Octopus Day. Their wedding song, "When You've Got Trouble" by Liz Longley, accurately described their future joys and troubles, tangled all together in the sixteen arms of a magnificent loving, fighting, sharing, color-changing "octosphere."

On Thursday, October 15th, Rascal and Sarah sold their farm to Katharine and Joe. Joe promised Katharine that she would never have to do any farming—only baking. Katharine promised Joe that he would always have her support for his uncertain success in the realm of organic farming. No one asked where the money came from.

On Friday, October 16th, Myra and Efrain officially took over Greengrocers with a law office fitted out in the back. Efrain called the office "GreenAttorney". Efrain's first task as a grocer-lawyer, or lawyer-grocer, was to help Myra and Katharine use the rest of their "re-purposed" money to create a foundation for tuberculosis patient care and research in Helaine's name. Fortunately, Myra had finally remembered where she'd relocated the stash. Again, no one asked about the money.

On Saturday, October 31st, Afton met Miso for drinks at the Magpie's annual Halloween Party. On a whim, she dressed as Michelle Maxwell. She was astounded to find that Miso came dressed as Sean King. How did that happen! Afton tried to remember where she got the costume idea. Greg Alatza? Miso swore that he came up with the Sean King idea all by himself. The two brilliant detectives promised each other that they would get to the bottom of the mystery.

In fact, along with the other Wildcreek Whodunits, they did proceed to solve many more mysteries in their lives. But never that one.

Finally, on November 26th, Thanksgiving, the *Wildcreek Wing* published Umberto's belated announcement of the results of the contest to guess the secret ingredient in his red sauce. No one guessed correctly, but at the next year's St. John's Wort Celebration, the citizens of Wildcreek would get another chance.

The murders may be solved, but one mystery remains... click here to discover the secret ingredient in Umberto's red sauce.

site.sallywolfgangauthor.com/umbertos-red-sauce

If you had fun following the mystery, I'd be so grateful if you'd take a minute to leave a quick review. Reader reviews are one of the best ways to help authors like me reach more readers—it tells bookstores, online platforms, and algorithms that people are enjoying the story!
mysticvalleypress.com/products/chaos-in-a-cake-basket-pb

Acknowledgments

So much of the writing in this introduction to the cozy town of Wildcreek comes from my first impressions of Lake Pend Oreille—the beauty of the lake and mountains and the lovely people who live there. I want to thank all of those friends who shared their passion for it with me.

Of course, the book would never have left my laptop had my husband of nearly thirty years not given me grounded critical advice as well as the encouragement and confidence to share it with readers outside the safe family circle. Thank you, Wes, for being kind—but not too kind.

To those first outside readers of the manuscript—my good friends Teresa and Mike—my gratitude is as deeply felt as the deepest part of Lake Pend Oreille itself. More than 1158 feet of gratitude.

Finally, thank you to Mary Barbee and her talented staff at Mystic Valley Press for helping me and many other authors to present beautiful, professional, and entertaining books to our readers. Serendipity played an important role in our collaboration, and I hope that it continues to make its way through our lives for years to come.

If anyone decides to search for Wildcreek, Krillo, or Brewster County, they will embark upon an impossible quest. Those places are entirely a creation of my own—as are all the characters. However, Lake Pend Oreille, Sandpoint, Wallace, and Coeur d'Alene are all real places and are worth seeing. I've tried my best to present some of North Idaho's fascinating natural history and even a little actual history, for example, silver mining and submarine testing. And it really is true that picking wild huckleberries for commercial use can result in a $250 fine. Just a reminder...

About the Author

Sally Wolfgang, a felony prosecutor for over 25 years, has always been an avid student of human behavior—both good and bad. Her years of experience provide her with endless material for creating complex characters and tangled webs of intrigue and hapless adventures. Her most memorable experience was the privilege of testifying before a United States Senate Committee on the importance of the Violence Against Women Act.

Along with her husband and their Old English Sheepdog, George, she lives part-time near the Superstition Mountains in Arizona and part-time on the shores of Lake Pend Oreille in the Idaho Panhandle.

Find out more about Sally and her books at https://sallywolfgan gauthor.com

Lake Pend Oreille

Lake Pend Oreille's name is taken from the French verb meaning "to hang" and the word for "ear". Over the years, people have speculated that the lake's name referred to the ear-shaped hanging earrings worn by the indigenous peoples who lived in the area. Others believed that the name came from the distinctive shape of the lake itself. It looks like the outer edge of a human left ear. The fur trader David Thompson, one of the first non-indigenous people to explore the lake, named it Kullyspel Lake in honor of the Kalispel Tribe that lived on its shores.

However the Lake got its name, it boasts many notable features. It's size, 148 square miles, and its depth, 1158 feet, allowed the United States Navy to conduct submarine training there during World War II. As late as the year 2001, the U.S Navy was using the world's largest unmanned autonomous submarine, the *Cutthroat LSV 2* (Large Scale Vehicle 2) to conduct research in Lake Pend Oreille. If you happen to be in the area of Athol, Idaho, you should visit Farragut State Park and its museum which commemorates the sacrifices Idaho sailors made in the war.

Lake Pend Oreille is nearly twice as deep as Loch Ness in Scotland, so it is not surprising to learn that Idaho's deepest lake has its own monster of sorts—the Pend Oreille Paddler. At various times, the creature has been described as a 60 foot long sturgeon-like creature, or an undulating giant with humps and eyes as large a basket balls. So far, no one, not even the U.S. Navy is willing to say there is proof that the Paddler *does not* exist.

The awe-inspiring size and beauty of the lake made it immeasurably significant to the many early peoples who lived on or visited its shores, including the Kalispel, Kootenai, and Coeur d'Alene peoples. They lived harmoniously with nature, relying on the lake's abundant resources for sustenance and spiritual experience.

For the Kalispel, in particular, the lake played, and still plays, a critical role in their creation stories and cultural identity. According to their oral traditions, the Great Spirit created the lake as a place for them to gather food and seek wisdom. The Kalispel were sometimes called the Camas People due to their reliance on the *blue-flowered* camas bulb that grew along the Pend Oreille River. The waters were also believed to hold healing powers, and various ceremonies were conducted at the lake to honor the spirits and to recieve guidance.

For a more detailed account of Lake Pend Oreille and its history, I recommend reading the Keokee Guide Book *Legendary Lake Pend Oreille: Idaho's Wilderness of Water.*

Tunnel 57

In *Chaos in a Cake Basket*, Melina Moser tells her customers, Sarah and Rascal Woods, Thor Thomsen, and Afton Laurie, about her escape from East Berlin into West Berlin with her husband Johann through a tunnel underneath the Berlin Wall. The tunnel was later named Tunnel 57 because 57 people were able to escape over a period of two days before its discovery—making Tunnel 57 the most successful escape plan in the history of the infamous Berlin Wall.

How did the Berlin Wall come about? After World War II, the defeated Germany was divided into four Allied occupation zones – the United States, Great Britain, France, and the Soviet Union. The city, Berlin, was also divided among the four allies even though it was located entirely within the Soviet Zone.

After a while, mainly due to Cold War issues, the four occupation zones were reorganized into two separate nations—the democratic West Germany and the communist East Germany. West Germany included the three zones controlled by the United States, France, and

Great Britain while East Germany included only the Soviet zone, the largest zone by far.

In 1961, to stop East Germans from fleeing to the West by way of West Berlin, East German soldiers started laying out miles of barbed wire that would later be called the Berlin Wall. The Wall sealed the border between East Germany and West Germany for 28 years.

Needless to say, the abrupt sealing of the East German border left many German families, friends, and work colleagues with no way of seeing each other. Persons caught in the act of crossing illegally into or out of East Germany faced incarceration as political prisoners. Some were shot in the act of crossing. Despite the enormous risk, however, as many as 300 people escaped through tunnels over the course of 30 years.

Tunnel 57 was one of those tunnels. It was one of many attempted during that time by an East German civil engineering student, Joachim Neumann and his friends. Using a Swiss passport, Joachim left his family and his girlfriend, Christa, and escaped into West Berlin. Once there, he and a group of friends began planning and digging tunnels.

When one of Joachim's early tunnels was discovered, his girlfriend, Christa, was arrested and imprisoned. Even more determined to succeed, he and his friends began digging again—this time starting in the cellar of an abandoned bakery and, 476 feet later, ending in the outhouse of an apartment building on Strelitzer Strasse 55 in East Berlin.

On October 3, 1964, the tunnel was opened for its secret business. Unexpectedly, on the day of opening, Joachim received a letter from Christa. She had been released from prison early. With quick action and a lot of help, Christa was able to get to the outhouse entrance on the second night and escape to the West.

Unfortunately, an informant alerted East German soldiers. An officer was shot, and the escapees were blamed. The tunnel was closed after 57 East Germans escaped to the West. Much later, forensics proved that the East German officer had been shot by one of his own comrades.

www.ingramcontent.com/pod-product-compliance
Lightning Source LLC
Chambersburg PA
CBHW031121210626
46816CB00016B/1749